D0122194

The Cherokee Rose

Also by Tiya Miles

The House on Diamond Hill: A Cherokee Plantation Story
Ties That Bind: The Story of an Afro-Cherokee Family in Slavery and Freedom

The Cherokee Rose
A Novel of Gardens and Ghosts

Tiya Miles

JOHN F. BLAIR, PUBLISHER
WINSTON-SALEM, NORTH CAROLINA

JOHN F. BLAIR,
PUBLISHER

1406 Plaza Drive
Winston-Salem, North Carolina 27103
www.blairpub.com

Library of Congress Cataloging-in-Publication Data

Miles, Tiya, 1970-
    The Cherokee rose : a novel of gardens and ghosts / by Tiya Miles.
        pages   ; cm
    ISBN 978-0-89587-635-5 (hardcover : acid-free paper) — ISBN 978-0-89587-636-2 (ebook) 1. Cherokee Indians—Georgia—History—19th century—Fiction. 2. Plantations—Georgia—Spring Place—History—19th century—Fiction. 3. Plantation life—Georgia—Spring Place—History—19th century—Fiction. 4. Chief Vann House (Spring Place, Ga.)—Fiction. I. Title.
    PS3613.I532243C48 2015
    813'.6—dc23
                            2014040639

10 9 8 7 6 5 4 3 2 1

In memory of
Peggy Pascoe, Josie Fowler, and Helen Hill:
"dewdrops from the sky"

For my sisters and our daughters:
Erin Miles, Stephanie Iron Shooter, Maryanna Rose
Gone, Nali Azure Gone, Noa Alice Gone, Baylee
Rain Iron Shooter, and those yet to come

Contents

"*The Cherokee were driven from their homelands in North Carolina and Georgia over 100 years ago when gold was discovered in their lands. The journey [was] known as the 'Trail of Tears.' It was a terrible time for the people—many died from the hardships and the women wept. The old men knew the women must be strong to help the children survive so they called upon the Great One to help their people and to give the mothers strength. The Great One caused a plant to spring up everywhere a Mother's tears had fallen upon the ground.*"

"The Legend of the Cherokee Rose,"
Cherokee Nation Cultural Resource Center,
Tahlequah, Oklahoma

"*We don't just live in a house, but with it. The houses and rooms in which we live and lived stay with us. Hopes and dreams are buried in them, as are cries of love and the bruises of violence.*"

Joy Harjo, "The Song of the House in the House,"
A Map to the Next World

Prologue

Dust to Dust

SHE FAILED TO HEED THE WARNING when the men began to dig in the Strangers' Graveyard on the outskirts of town. Negroes were buried there, and Indians, too, and Indians who were mistaken for Negroes. The man with hard, iron eyes and hair the color of river sand was the first to break ground. Wielding his blunt-edged shovel like a knife, he tore into the tender earth, displacing soil and sediment heap by heap. He was the leader, the master, the maker. The others simply followed, plunging into the people's bones with lock-jawed excavation machines.

The Strangers' Graveyard had rested in peace for more than a century, floating out of place and time. It had been forgotten, an island of brambles and spindly trees, except by those who cared for it and those who cared nothing for it. Once, many years ago, the graveyard trees were sentries with bottles of colorful spun glass suspended from their branches. But now their powers of protection were lost, and the burial ground lay naked. It was open land, good land, valuable land in the sand man's eyes.

Trucks dumped mounds of dirt into adjacent refuse piles, the faded bones of human remains churning beneath the wheels. A collarbone, bleached and brittle. A skull with sunken sockets for eyes. The far-flung skeleton of a small slave child. The sand man, unperturbed, instructed his crew to lay a foundation. While workmen mixed thick cement and cut the flesh of trees to size, the man began to prowl and prod the vast perimeter of his property. His daily walks spread farther and wider until he reached the line. He eyed the river and the cane beyond his acreage, the hill and sun-kissed fields. On the day his crewmen poured cement on the site of the gutted burial ground, the sand man crossed the border and entered the dwelling place. He strode the Cherokee Rose Plantation, land not his own, grasping a shovel and brittle map, stomping white roses to force a pathway.

She had crossed a border, too. She had crossed the bridge. Watching him closely from beside the attic dormer, she peered down the slope of the overgrown hillside. Beyond the graceful brick façade and covered rear veranda, beyond the yard where slaves had toiled and medicinal plants had grown, lay buried the dreams of her foremothers. The sand man consulted his map, shifted his shovel, and plunged it into the ground. She feared the worst. *Matricide.* A way must be found to gather descendants—bone of her mothers' bone, flesh of her mothers' spirit. To call upon them—the ones who came later and had no memory—to know and protect the past.

Dust motes floated like cottonwood spores in the dappled sunlight around her. She breathed softly against the house and felt the attic walls expand. Reaching for the brass latch that sealed the half-moon window shut, she turned its rigid thumb and pushed. Warm, sky-born air sprang into the garret. The dust of two hundred years flew into a shifting wind.

Part I
Our Mothers' Gardens

"I began to look about me and saw instead the most beautiful roses I ever beheld, another of these exquisite southern flowers—the Cherokee rose. The blossom is very large, composed of four or five pure white petals, as white and as large as those of the finest Camellia, with a bright golden eye for a focus."

Frances Anne Kemble,
Journal of a Residence on a
Georgian Plantation 1838–1839

1

Jinx Micco walked the path to her Craftsman cottage, breathing a sigh of false relief. After work, when she could be alone with her thoughts, used to be her favorite time of day. But that had changed with the column. She fumbled in her messenger bag for her keys, ignoring the ugly garden beds beside the doorway. If her Great-Aunt Angie had still been tending them, the beds would have brimmed this time of year with long-lashed black-eyed Susans and heavy-headed sunflowers. Nothing grew in those old plots now except for the odd clump of scrub grass, which Jinx knew her great-aunt would have plucked the moment she saw it.

She stepped into the husk of a house, breathing in the musty smell of 1920s plaster. The place was hers now, its walls covered with a faded floral wallpaper, its furniture curve-backed and overstuffed, its rayon Kmart curtains edged in scratchy lace. Photographs of family members, framed and mounted, crowded the walls like scrapbook pages. Jinx was not a lace-and-flowers kind of girl, but she had kept it all anyway.

She hadn't changed a thing in this house since the inheritance—not the throw pillows, not the dishes, not the harvest-gold appliances. The cottage looked exactly as Aunt Angie had left it.

Jinx changed out of her khaki pants and slipped into comfy cut-off sweats. She unwound her hair from its braid to let it fall loosely around her face, toasted now after countless walks in the Oklahoma summer sun. Jinx settled into her aunt's easy chair and dove into one of Deb's charbroiled burgers, watching a rerun of *Charlie's Angels* on the old rabbit-ear TV set. She wished she had some strawberry rhubarb pie for dessert; she was sure she had ordered a slice. Instead, she settled for a handful of Now & Laters, annoyed at having to unwrap each candy square. Jinx washed her dinner plate, switched off the television, and raised the windows. A moist breeze ruffled the curtains as she settled into her great-aunt's study to start her evening's work.

Angie Micco had been a pack rat, collecting any and every book on Muscogee history, saving each Sunday issue of the *Muskogee Phoenix*, and scouting out past editions of old Creek-area newspapers. She had century-old back issues of the *Phoenix*, the *Eufaula Indian Journal*, the *Muskogee Comet*, and the *Muskogee Cimeter* stacked to the roofline of the terra-cotta bungalow. Leaning over an open book at her great-aunt's desk, Jinx tried to focus on her research. But she couldn't shake the nagging sense that something was wrong. Ever since her last column, she had felt out of sorts. The source of her discomfort was not internal, like a stomachache or guilt pang; it was external, like a free-floating irritant in the air. And now she was up against a deadline for her next installment of the "Indian Country Yesterday" column she had created. Her editor, a third cousin through a second marriage, was getting antsy. *Read*, she told herself. *Focus*.

She was supposed to be researching the Green Peach War of 1882, a major event in late-nineteenth-century Creek history. "Traditional" Creeks led by Chief Isparhecher, the ousted judge who wanted to maintain a tribal government, had waged a flash battle with "progressive"

Creeks led by Principal Chief Checote, who wanted to run the Creek government like the United States. The traditionalists were the heroes of the story, the progressives glorified sellouts. When it came to the black-and-white of Creek history, Jinx took a hard line. Gray was just not a color she believed in. She had never been one of those hesitant students who had trouble making up or speaking her mind back when she was taking graduate-school seminars. One professor who she knew didn't think she belonged there had even called her work "potentially polemical." She had shot back that he was "potentially racist" and asked why no Native American historians were on his syllabus. He gave her a C in the class, tantamount to an F in graduate school, and wrote in the margin of her final paper that her analysis "lacked sufficient nuance."

Jinx leaned sideways and plucked the folder on Chief Isparhecher from the "People" drawer of her great-aunt's filing cabinet. She loved that Aunt Angie had kept paper files on historical figures in the Creek Nation. She skimmed an old clipping on Isparhecher and his motley crew of anti-assimilationist activists, squinting at the tiny print and pushing back a loose skein of hair. She jotted down interesting points on her legal pad. Later, she would turn those points into an explanatory argument and send in her column for the *Muscogee Nation News*.

Jinx's hand itched. Her legs felt cramped. Something was wrong in her great-aunt's house. Something was out of balance, like a dish off a shelf, a door off its hinge, a weed in the garden.

"Morning, Deb," Jinx said from her perch on a stool at the *L*-shaped diner counter.

Deb Tom was a big-boned woman with bay-brown skin and silver hair that rolled down her back in waves. Some tribal members considered it a flaw that she had such prominent black ancestry, but they didn't dare show their feelings out in the open. Deb's words could be sharper than her homemade hot sauce, and the helpings just as generous. And Deb didn't hesitate to throw offending customers out of her café and on to the street corner. Everybody loved Deb's home-style cooking too much to cross her. That's why Jinx was there.

"Well, well, well, if it ain't Jinx Micco. Didn't think I'd see you around 'til dinnertime." Deb held a coffeepot in one hand, made the rounds refilling mugs, took her own sweet time circling back to Jinx. "Coffee?" Deb said. She knew Jinx didn't drink it.

"No thanks. I'm saving myself for Coke. I've been thinking about what you said the other day, about my column on Mary Ann Battis. What didn't you like about it? Why were you so pissed off?"

Deb was a regular reader of "Indian Country Yesterday" and usually had positive feedback. But she had given Jinx flack for that piece on black Creek Christians, the one that mentioned a mission-school student named Mary Ann Battis back in the East. As a descendant of Cow Tom, a famous black Creek interpreter from the nineteenth century, Deb had taken offense—unwarranted offense—at the nature of the subject matter.

"Maybe you should leave poor Mary Ann alone. She was just a girl."

"Maybe I should, and maybe I shouldn't. I can't tell yet. You were mad enough at me to forget the dessert in my carry-out last night. Don't you think I have a right to know why, Deb?"

"How come you had to be so hard on Mary? Telling the story like she betrayed her own mama? The way I read it, you made that girl responsible for the entire downfall of Creek traditional religion."

Sam Sells, a retired breakfast regular who always took Deb's side, turned his eyes away from his eggs to glare at Jinx.

"Come on, Deb." Jinx lowered her voice. "The story wasn't even mostly about that student. It was about the Methodist missionaries' failed attempts at converting Southern Creeks in the early 1800s. I had to write that Creek traditionalists rejected Christianity, and that the

Creeks' black slaves were the first to accept the faith, because that's the way it happened. Those first slave converts were the ones who laid the groundwork for Creek conversion to Christianity down the line. Battis was just an example. Who would have thought that a part-Creek child of an Indian mother and black father would want to stay behind with white missionaries while her mother was removed to Indian Territory? It made an interesting ending for the column. Is it really that big a deal? Can't you forgive me? And could I have some Coke, please, and some pancakes with bacon?"

Deb was staring, apparently unimpressed with Jinx's argument and command of the facts. "That's exactly what I'm talking about. *You* see her life as no big deal, but she was big to somebody. Didn't your auntie, the great tribal historian, teach you that words can be swords, that words can be scalpels—and saving graces, too? What you wrote is the last impression anybody has, the last thing anybody might remember, about that girl. They'll say she was a sellout who rejected her own mama in a nation that reckoned kin along the mama's bloodlines, and they'll be citing you. Oh, yeah, and they'll say she was black—that's the essential ingredient of your traitor story." Deb threw her hand on her hip. "Benny," she called back to the kitchen, "go ahead and get Jinx's order up!"

Jinx dove into the glass of icy Coke that Deb set before her. After a long moment, she looked up again. "Deb, come on. I don't care that Battis was black. I mean, I do care, but I don't care. She was just as much Indian as you or me."

"Don't you dare try that colorblind crap on me. I know you too well, Jennifer Inez Micco, ever since you was a baby. And I can't say as I've noticed you calling any of your other Indian figures, no matter how mixed with white they were, 'part-Creek' in your column." Deb paused, then dropped the grenade she had been hiding in her apron pocket all along. "Like auntie, like niece, I guess."

"What?" Jinx exploded, causing Sam Sells to slosh his coffee over the top of his chipped ceramic mug. Deb's other morning diners were craning their necks to get a look at who was making the commotion. Her mother would hear about this before ten o'clock, Jinx was sure. "Are you calling my aunt a racist?" Jinx wasn't afraid to use the race card either. If Deb could deal it, she could play it.

But Deb was Deb; she stood her ground. "Angie Micco was a lot of things, some good and some bad. But one thing she wasn't was open-minded about people who were different." She looked intently at Jinx. "Any kind of different."

Jinx chipped her words off the ice of her thoughts, gripped the sweating glass, empty now of soda. "I don't know what you're talking about."

"I think you do, honey. I think you do. Here's your breakfast. Eat up and get on over to the library before you make yourself late."

Jinx hiked over to the slab cement public-library building and stowed her messenger bag. For a part-time job, it wasn't bad, even if only schoolchildren and members of the Saturday ladies' book club found their way into the local branch. The children bounced in like balloons for story time and then were gone in a swirl of color and motion. The ladies' club read historical romances, which Jinx could probably appreciate if they contained just a sliver of irony. She had taken the job more for the books than the people. Books were constant company and had personality to boot. Spending her days at easy book work kept her mind clear for the evenings too, when she did her writing and cataloged her great-aunt's files. Her library income paid the taxes on Angie's house, which didn't sit on tribal land in their checkerboard Oklahoma town where former Creek Nation lots had gone to white residents over the years. It also paid for her fruit-pie habit at Deb's, her Twizzlers habit at the 7-Eleven, and her daily Coca-Colas.

When Angie Micco left her house and everything in it to Jinx, no one in the family had minded. From the time she was a tiny girl, Jinx had gravitated to Aunt Angie, circling her ample form like a small moon to its planet. There were photos of Jinx as a sixth-month-old sitting on Aunt Angie's lap, sucking on the end of her aunt's thick eyeglasses. At family feeds and cookouts, she toddled behind Aunt Angie, clasping soggy fry bread chunks in her fists. Everyone said it was Angie, not the kindergarten teacher, who taught Jinx to read. At picnics in the arbor, the two of them would settle on a blanket all their own, reading old Indian Territory newspapers and reacting in tandem to the goings-on of historical figures Aunt Angie had taught Jinx to know. Except for Jinx's mother, who would pause beside them now and then to smooth back Jinx's hair and refill Angie's coffee mug, the relatives had left them to their studies.

For Jinx's twelfth birthday, Aunt Angie gave her a series of early-edition Creek history books that had been sold by the tribal college after it updated its library collection. When Jinx turned sixteen and finally asked Aunt Angie an Indian history question she couldn't answer with certainty, Aunt Angie had smiled and said it was time for Jinx to leave the nest. At seventeen, Jinx went off to college on scholarship at the University of Tulsa. "That one's a smart cookie, trained by Angie," everyone back home had said. Four years later, Jinx set off for graduate school to pursue her doctorate in history. Aunt Angie, then seventy-six with dyed purplish hair and the same oversized eyeglasses, had ridden shotgun next to Jinx on the cross-country trip to North Carolina, telling Jinx what turns to make and which lane to drive in, even though she herself hadn't driven a day in her life. Eight years later, Jinx had yet to earn her degree. When her mother called to say Aunt Angie was gone, Jinx packed up the notes and files for the dissertation she would never finish and returned straight home to Ocmulgee.

"There you are, Jennifer! I was about to send out the troops!" Emma called when she spotted Jinx in the empty reading room. Jinx's cheery coworker was dressed in a delicate yellow sundress and flat-soled sandals, her hair neatly clipped with a matching barrette. Emma's looks whispered *librarian*, while Jinx's shouted *tomboy*. Jinx sported her favorite oversized cargo khakis and the cherry-red Converse high tops that made some of the older patrons blink in surprise.

"Send *in* the troops?" Jinx said.

"Right! Do you have any plans for the morning? Mindy's day-care group will be here at ten. If you don't mind, I thought I'd take them."

"Knock yourself out," Jinx said. "I've got some returns to process, and the nature section is a mess after that Boy Scout troop rifled through it yesterday."

"Thanks, Jennifer! I just can't wait for the school year to start. Then we'll have classroom visits once a week. All of those kiddies with their new lunchboxes and stuffed pencil cases. They're just so cute."

"Too cute," Jinx said. "I'll be in the back, if you need me."

Jinx made her way to the cramped office area where Emma's cuddly-kittens calendar swung from a bulletin board and her pointelle knit sweater draped the back of a chair. Emma would be busy for a while setting out puzzles and selecting stories for the kids. Their branch director, Marjorie, hardly ever came in on Friday mornings and wouldn't be the wiser. Jinx plopped down in front of the computer and settled in to surf the Internet.

Mary Ann Battis got no hits when she typed it into the Google search bar, but the name of the mission where she had first gone to school returned a series of articles. Jinx opened a link concerning Alabama state historic sites that blurbed the Fort Mitchell Asbury Mission School, next to the photo of a historical marker. The Methodist mission school in the Creek Nation, located on the Georgia-Alabama border, had been destroyed by fire in the early 1800s. Most of the children were relocated to nearby white Christian homes, but advanced students had been transferred to a Moravian mission school in the Cherokee Nation, housed on the estate of a wealthy Cherokee chief named James Hold. When Jinx Googled *James Hold*, a score of tourist websites popped up profiling the "devil-may-care" Cherokee "entrepreneur" and describing his "showplace" plantation on the Georgia "frontier." Jinx clicked on a link about the Hold Plantation museum, this one to a recent newspaper article: "State Cuts Pull Rug from under Cherokees, Friends of the Hold House."

She skimmed the article. The historic Hold Plantation site was being pawned off by the state like a broken turntable. It wasn't as bad as when the United States government had put the Creek Council House up for sale in 1902, but it was bad enough. This plantation was the last place Mary Ann Battis was known to have lived. Traces of her might still exist among the auctioned household items. The home would be sold within a month and would probably fall into some rich white man's hands, just like most Indian land of any value. But maybe the door had not completely closed. Maybe the house was full of old museum documents she could request copies of.

"Story time, children!" Jinx heard Emma sing-songing out in the multipurpose room. "It's *Mary Poppins* today! And then we'll make tissue-paper umbrellas!"

Jinx printed out the pages from her search, then scooped up the pile of book returns. Someone had been on a supernatural-romance binge and was partial to Heather Graham. Someone else—a middle-schooler, she guessed—had finished a summer science project on undersea volcanoes. And someone fond of sticky notes—most likely a gardener—had tabbed several pages in a book called *Dangerous Plants*.

Jinx didn't stop by Deb's that night. She warmed a can of pork and beans and ate it with toast and a hunk of commodity cheese her cousin had brought over. Then she sat in her aunt's desk chair and reread her last week's "Indian Country Yesterday" article. She still didn't see anything wrong with the argument she had advanced that black and black Indian Christian converts like Mary Ann Battis had furthered the cultural assimilation of the tribe. True, her readers could infer that she questioned Battis's choice in shunning Creek family life in exchange for the Christian faith. But her facts were correct—of that Jinx was certain. If Deb Tom wanted to claim that her writing wasn't sensitive enough, that was fine with Jinx. She didn't deal in sanitized history. That was a job for the Pine-Sol lady.

Jinx opened a dog-eared book on the history of the Green Peach War. She compiled more facts in her notebook, glancing up at the windows and walls, distracted by the strange undercurrent in the air. She sighed, craving pie and feeling uneasy. Maybe Aunt Angie had information on Mary Ann Battis in her collection of papers.

Jinx turned to her aunt's filing cabinet. *Battis* was there. The wafer-thin folder had only four microfilmed letters inside, from the Creek Agency records of the Bureau of Indian Affairs. Jinx shifted toward a shelf and pulled down the general Creek history books, searching for *Battis* in the indexes. She found her listed in two studies. The authors disagreed about whether the girl's mother or father had been black and whether her black parent had been enslaved or free. But the authors, like Jinx, agreed that Battis chose to remain with the missionaries while her Indian family suffered the trial of compulsory removal. It was the only conclusion that could be reached from the documentary record. There was nothing new here—nothing Jinx could see.

She closed the file on Chief Isparhecher, opened the top drawer of her great-aunt's metal filing cabinet, and slid the folder back inside. Then she opened the second drawer to put the Battis folder in place.

Jinx looked from drawer to drawer, realizing for the first time that these files were not in alphabetical, chronological, or even thematic order. She slung open every drawer then, running her fingers along the razor-edged folders like a blind person speed-reading Braille. Could it be that her great-aunt's biographical files were organized by race, full-bloods positioned at the top, mixed-bloods placed in the back, and black Creeks stuffed into a segregated second-tier drawer? Could it be that Jinx with her almost-Ph.D. had come along two generations later and maintained the same color-coded filing system? Deb Tom's accusations against her great-aunt—against her—rang in Jinx's head.

"Holy smokes," Jinx said to no one. She abandoned the study, snapping off the painted floral lamp. She brushed her teeth in the subway-tiled bathroom and pulled on a pair of boxer shorts. Her bedroom—her great-aunt's bedroom—was shadowy and still. And then a cool breeze floated through a window, tangling with the flat interior air. Jinx turned in surprise. It was early September in Oklahoma, where even nighttime breezes were sticky and warm. The curtains fluttered as she watched. Jinx had never taken those curtains down, never washed them or dusted the rods. She reached out, gently touching a lace-edged hemline that left a faint trail of dust on her fingertip.

When Jinx walked into Deb's Diner early the next morning with her messenger bag slung over her shoulder, Deb just looked at her for ten still seconds. "Sit," Deb finally said, gesturing toward the counter.

She set a glass of Coke beside Jinx, along with a napkin and fork. Sam Sells was having sausage and biscuits smothered in gravy. He nodded a silent greeting at Jinx from beneath the rim of his John Deere baseball cap. Jinx breathed in relief.

"Nobody talks about Mary Ann Battis much these days, among the freedmen descendants," Deb said. "There's some pain there, I guess, pain still felt from a story long forgotten. Mary Ann's daddy—they called him Battis—was a black man who took his own freedom. I always heard he came through Alabama Creek country on a forged government passport back in the 1790s. And her mama, well, she lost touch with the girl once the family came out here to Indian Territory. Her mama got one letter and never heard tell of poor Mary Ann after that."

"That's some story, Deb," Jinx said. "Sad."

"That's only part of the story. The rest of it, we don't know. But you could find out for all of us. You could head back east. Go to Alabama, where Mary was from. Find her grave. Sit with her for a spell. Get your information from the real source instead of some book."

Jinx didn't dare cut into the fluffy blueberry pancakes that Sadie, one of the waitresses, had delivered to the counter. Deb was looking at her too intensely, waiting to see if Jinx would accept her assignment. Communing with the dead to corroborate a loose oral story was not one of Jinx's usual research methods. But there was that plantation for sale in Georgia, and there were those hypothetical house-museum documents.

"Wait here," Deb said, having made some mysterious decision. "I might have something for you."

Jinx was left to worry and wonder while she packed in mouthfuls of pancake.

When Deb returned, huffing and puffing from her exertions, Jinx was sure she had walked all the way back to her shotgun house down the alley from the restaurant. Deb was holding a wrinkled manila envelope twined shut with a thin red cord.

"What is it?"

Deb leaned forward on the counter, exposing cleavage in the deep V of her neckline. "This was part of my great-grandfather Cow Tom's papers. The family kept them stashed away in a cardboard box all these years. I take them out from time to time and read them, share bits and pieces with the freedmen's descendants groups. I never could make heads or tails of this letter. But I bet you could if you set your mind to it." Deb paused. "It might just be the push you need to finish that dissertation."

Jinx snapped her head up. "I didn't finish because my great-aunt died. I had to come home."

"No, baby. You didn't finish because once things got tough out there, once those university folks challenged what you thought you knew, you tucked tail and ran. Your auntie's death was hard on you, that's true, but it was also a ready excuse for you to give up. You were born to study history, Jinx, born to write about it. You'll soon find out that life's too short not to chase your dreams. Here, hon, open it." She handed the envelope to Jinx.

Stung by Deb's blunt words, Jinx hesitated, but she couldn't resist the call of that envelope. She untwined the thin cord and drew out a saffron page. The paper was cracked and brittle, flaking at her touch like the salted surface of a pretzel stick. She worried about the oil of her fingertips damaging the document. If this had been an archive, she would have been asked to wear white gloves before handling something so fragile. Down the counter, Sam Sells waved to Sadie for a refill of coffee. Behind the counter, Benny fried eggs and wiped his brow with a forearm. Jinx scanned the paper, taking in its prominent features: shape, texture, date, script. Antiquated cursive loops, beautiful in form, trailed across the page.

April 18, 1826

Dear Mother,

I pray this letter reaches you before much more time has passed, whether you be in the West or still here in the East. I hope it can be read to you, for when we last saw one another, neither of us could speak or read the English language. My mind turns to you on this tenth anniversary of the death of my godmother in Christ. I could not accept the loss of her then, as I could not, a lifetime ago, accept the loss of you.

I do not blame you, Mother. Do not blame yourself. You had no means to feed me. The mission school at the fort took me in and placed me among their pupils. At the tender age of eleven years, I was one of the eldest. I learned the ways of civilization and tried my best to be good, but ghosts haunted me at the school; ghouls grasped at me. They pulled my gown in the dark, split my braids in two, unfolded my insides, and stole me from myself. I had a child. She did not survive. What was I to do?

I set the place on fire and watched it burn. They would not let me return to you, would not let me see your face, even when you came to beg for my return, even when my uncle came dressed in white men's clothing to strengthen your entreaties.

And so I was exiled to the Cherokee Rose and given the gift of a second family. I have lately heard the news from my godfather that our lands in Alabama will soon be claimed by that same ravenous horde who settled our lands within the borders of Georgia, and that more of our people will go west. I cannot come to you, Mother, despite my affection, which forever abides. I must remain here always, to do the Lord's work and tend the graves of my other mothers. Even as I write you, I sit in my godmother's chair, reading the pages of her Bible, worn from the tread of her finger: "Whither thou goest I will go, and whither thou lodgest I will lodge. Thou people shall be my people and thy God my God. Whither thou diest, I will die, and there will I be buried."

I seek only to do the bidding of the Lord. I pray that you and my uncle are safe, that my brothers and sisters care for you even as I would have done. I pray that the new land in the West is fertile and rich and that a future may be possible for our people.

Yours forever in the wounds of Christ Jesus,

MAB

Jinx dragged her eyes from the page. *MAB*. Mary Ann Battis.

Deb Tom was watching her with that same intense stare. "We've been waiting over two hundred years to learn what became of our Mary Ann. That's damn sure long enough, even on Indian time. I think you're the one who can find out. The question is, will you?"

Deb was not the first person to ask Jinx for information in the five years since she had been back in Oklahoma. Right away, people had started coming to her with their research questions. "Your great-aunt Angie used to say you'd know this," they'd begin as they put a question to her about a fifth cousin, once removed. "Your aunt Angie said to ask you, if she wasn't here," they'd explain when they inquired about a rift on the nineteenth-century Tribal Council. That was how Jinx came to know that she had inherited not only a house but a role as well: family historian. Because the Creek Nation was one big family of families, all interwoven through the cartilage of kinship and history, and because Jinx was not just Creek, but Cherokee, too, on her father's side, the role of family historian could be the work of a lifetime. Aunt Angie had devoted herself to the study of history. Jinx had failed at it.

Jinx replaced the letter in its envelope and handed it back to Deb without speaking. She reached inside her pocket for a ten-dollar bill, placed it on the counter, and took one last long swig of Coke. Beneath the tinkling of the diner's bell, she made her escape.

"Are you going to Deb's tonight?" Jinx's cousin Victor said on the telephone.

Jinx had spent the afternoon on the back porch of the bungalow typing up her column. Now she was in the living room fiddling with Aunt Angie's ceramic figurine collection.

"I'm getting a little tired of Deb's cooking. I thought I might go to Applebee's or cook at home. Do you and Berta want to come over? I can make Indian tacos."

"Okay, spill it." They had grown up like sister and brother, and Victor could still read her mind.

"Long story or short?" Jinx fingered the fringe on her cutoff blue jeans.

"Short," Victor said.

"I messed up my last column and might have told only part of the truth. Deb Tom is pissed off and wants to send me out on assignment."

" 'Early Christianity in the Creek Nation.' I read that one. A little dry, maybe, but that's no crime. Don't let Deb Tom push you around, Jinx. I know you feel close to her, but there are limits. You don't need to be all torn up about some column. I mean, you didn't lie. You didn't slander anybody."

"Libel. Slander is when the defamation of a person is spoken. Libel is when it's written."

"Fine, you didn't libel anybody. What does she want, anyway, some kind of retraction?"

"She didn't say that, not directly. She wants me to go to the Southeast and research this girl. She wants me to find out what really happened to her."

"A road trip? Now you're talking. Does Deb Tom pay mileage?"

"You don't think I should go, do you?" Jinx said, freezing in front of the figurine shelf.

"I think you want to go, or you wouldn't be upset about it. And I think you could use a vacation. You need to get out of that house. It's like a mausoleum in there. If you don't watch out, twenty years will pass and you'll be on *Hoarding: Buried Alive* with a wall of old newspapers blocking your door. So if Deb Tom is giving you a reason to get out of there for a while, I say you should take it."

"I'd have to get time off from the library," Jinx said, walking into the bedroom to pace in front of her great-aunt's dresser mirror.

"If you give me a week to arrange things, I'll come with you," Victor said. "Where is it we're going?"

Jinx smiled at that. "Georgia."

"What? The Coca-Cola capital of the world, and Jinx Micco's still sitting there? When do we leave?"

"Victor, you're a Hotshot. It's fire season. You can't just take off."

"But *you* can. The children's library will make it without you for a week."

"The library's not just for children, Vic. We have other programs."

"The Saturday ladies. Right."

"How is it that you always end up pissing me off?"

"Because I know you too well, little sister. You've already got Monday off for the holiday, so it's like the weekend hasn't even started yet. Pack up your stuff and come over. We'll chart your route on MapQuest."

Jinx wheedled a week's vacation out of Marjorie and spent the late afternoon making plans in Victor's trailer. If she got as far as the Arkansas border tonight, then did just six hours a day, she would have two days each way for travel and four days in between for the research.

Back at the bungalow, she packed a nylon duffle bag with T-shirts, cargo pants, underwear, and athletic socks. She stuffed her orange canvas messenger bag with the Mary Ann Battis file, a Craig Womack novel, and a Nancy Clue mystery. She stuck her toothbrush and deodorant into a plastic baggie and left a message on her mom's machine telling her not to panic. She didn't contact Deb Tom.

Grabbing a fresh can of Coke and an unopened bag of Twizzlers, Jinx headed out of the quiet house. She locked the door behind her and climbed into her Chevy. It was the same truck she had driven cross-country thirteen years ago, setting off for graduate school with Aunt Angie beside her. Jinx could almost see her now, a ghost riding shotgun, with burgundy curls, soft-veined hands, and thick eyeglasses.

Headlights blazing, gas tank full, Jinx flew out of town.

2

Cheyenne Rosina Cotterell read the auction notice aloud, bracing herself for the onslaught.

"Forty acres?" her friend Toni said in her pushy attorney tone. "You can't be serious about this, Cheyenne. All you'd need next is the mule."

"Fourteen acres," Cheyenne corrected as her girlfriends listened, stunned. "Right below the Cohutta Mountains. It used to be a five-hundred-acre estate, back in the 1800s, but most of the land was parceled out and sold off over the years. The original plantation house is left, some cabins, a peach orchard, and a whole lot of mosquito-ridden river cane. And yes, I am serious. I'm buying the place next week."

"Now I *know* you've lost your mind. You can't live in the mountains, girl. You're 100 percent city." Toni leaned back in her chair and raised the smooth arch of an eyebrow. She savored the crispy end of a sweet potato fry that would probably go straight to her hips.

De'Sha nodded, sipping her Chardonnay.

Layla adjusted her black-frame glasses and skimmed the state auction notice Cheyenne had placed on the tabletop.

Cheyenne eyed her three closest friends, a tableau of black urban chic. Toni wore a sleeveless tangerine sundress that showed off the deep tone of her shoulders and complemented her sultry bleached-blond hair. Layla was dressed in hand-dyed jeans and impossibly high heels, a look that punctuated her short natural haircut and stylish glasses. De'Sha was still wearing her beige crepe suit from work, her hair coiled in shiny black ringlets that touched the collar of her jacket. Cheyenne knew she had thrown a Molotov cocktail into their weekly dinner conversation. The four of them had met in a reading group for single black women a year before and instantly hit it off. Now they got together every Friday night at Aria, a hip new eatery in Buckhead with too many rich desserts on the menu for Cheyenne's taste.

"I thought that place was a public museum for Cherokee history," De'Sha said. "I remember going up there for a field trip when I was in grade school. Is it even habitable? I mean, for a real person?"

"I have to say I agree with them, Cheyenne. This plan is a little unrealistic," Layla said. She was a graduate student in public policy at Georgia Tech and took it upon herself to play the role of the thoughtful one in their group. "Why would you buy an old house up in the boonies? A plantation house, no less. Doesn't the idea freak you out just a little bit? You're doing well at Swag. You just got promoted to lead interior designer. Is this really the right time for a change?" Layla nibbled on a warm ginger cookie with a dollop of fresh organic cream. She had inhaled her meal and moved straight to dessert, indifferent to the effect on her waistline.

Cheyenne took a sip of her lime-freshened tonic water. "When I saw that house advertised for auction, it was like a dream come true. My family, my grandmother's people, came from that part of the state. They probably lived on that plantation. You're right, De'Sha, it was a museum back when we were in school, but the state closed it down. The house has been sitting empty for at least four years while the director of the

Department of Natural Resources weighed what to do with the property. The state can't take care of it anymore. But I can. I've always wanted to design and run a bed-and-breakfast. This, ladies, is my chance."

"But have you thought this all the way through, Chey?" Toni asked, her gold hoop earrings rocking with the emphatic motion of her jaw. "Where would you get your nails done? Where would you get your light Frappuccinos? How would you even find the staff to run the damn place? I hear they have a Dunkin' Donuts up in North Georgia. And a bunch of Billy Bobs. Maybe you could get used to that, but I doubt it. You like expensive coffee and fine men too much."

"Fine men?" Layla pounced. "Did I miss a breakup story when I was away at that conference last week? And does this mean I can have Devon now?" She paused at a look from Toni. "Yes, Toni. I take Cheyenne's leftovers. Her men are always beautiful, and you know I don't have time to meet people while I'm working on my dissertation."

"Girl, that dissertation is working you," Toni said. "What is this, year six?" She took a sip of Fresca and returned her attention to Cheyenne.

Cheyenne forked a leaf of baby arugula. "I know this comes as a shock, but I *am* serious. Atlanta is less than an hour away in good traffic; I can drive back here on Fridays. You'll hardly know I'm gone. And you can come up to the B&B after it's open, relax a little bit." She shot a cool look at Toni.

"If you open a B&B, you can say bye-bye to Fridays and hello to a new identity as Butterfly McQueen," Toni said. "You'll be slaving away twenty-four/seven, washing other folks' linens and handing out maps for hiking trails."

"I have to say I think you've got this all wrong, Toni. She's not Prissy the maid in this story," Layla chimed in. "She's Scarlett O'Hara. Isn't that right, Cheyenne?"

"Which version of *Gone With the Wind* did you watch?" Toni said.

"Tara was a plantation that ran on black slave labor, and the last time I checked, we were all black—even those of us who think they're Indian because they have good hair and a legend."

"We all have good hair, girls," Layla inserted in a warning tone. "Let's not be catty."

Cheyenne ignored Toni's dig and directed her words toward Layla and De'Sha. "I want something big in my life, something romantic. I'm tired of working at a rarified boutique, helping the society set pick out three-hundred-dollar throw pillows. I was meant for more. Buying this plantation house and bringing it back to life, that could give me purpose. I'd be saving part of my history, part of my family's history."

"*If* you're right about that Indian legend," Toni said.

Her friends' expressions ranged from patronizing disbelief to misplaced sympathy. Cheyenne was hurt, but she refused to show it. She knew Toni had always been jealous of her. Toni craved attention, was used to it. But as striking as Toni was, she couldn't hold a candle to Cheyenne. Cheyenne drew open, naked stares from attractive men—and a few women, too. People were transfixed by her willowy figure, toffee-toned skin, and swirling dark tresses. The hair was her inheritance from the mysterious Cherokee ancestor who jealous women including Toni loved to dismiss as fantasy. Most female friends she'd ever had were just like Toni—secretly wishing to see her fail, but hoping her charms would rub off on them like some kind of magical fairy dust. Cheyenne smoothed the skirt of her Lilly Pulitzer floral dress and flicked back the ponytail she had pinned with a rhinestone-studded clip. She was ready to go.

"It sounds like you've made up your mind, Cheyenne," Layla said, reading her body language. "I'll come visit you up there, but only after you've fixed up the place. You know I don't do rustic."

"Let me know if you need a home loan, Chey," De'Sha, a banker, added with a grin.

Cheyenne slid a fifty-dollar bill onto the table. "Desserts are on me," she said, standing.

Cheyenne arrived home late that night, after first stopping to fill the gas tank of her silver sports coupe. She planned to hit I-75 at dawn and beat the other drivers as they headed to quaint inns and cabins in the Blue Ridge Mountains for Labor Day weekend. The Hold House was waiting. She wanted to get a feel for the property before it was auctioned on Tuesday.

Opening the door of her condo and slipping off her pumps, Cheyenne sank her feet into the white shag carpeting. Her glass-walled townhouse in Candler Park was sleek and modern, boasting views of the city skyline. She looked around at the Eames side chairs and angular cranberry couches. Maybe she was 100 percent city, as Toni claimed, but who said she couldn't bring city to the country? The Hold House could be completely redone in a modernist style—straight lines, nickel fixtures, shagreen finishes, textured throw pillows. The contrast between nineteenth-century architecture and the clean look of her interior design would be to die for.

Cheyenne dropped her dress in a tent on the floor, showered, and blew-dry her hair until it fell arrow-straight. She changed into silk pajamas, stepping over the crumpled dress. Gretchen, the domestic help whose visits were a gift from her parents, would be in tomorrow afternoon to tidy up. Cheyenne settled onto the leather couch, tucked her feet beneath her, and turned on Lifetime. The made-for-TV drama about a divorced couple's new lease on marriage after taking in an orphaned child was a repeat. It was Friday night, after all. Nothing was on. Cheyenne flipped through last month's *Cosmo*, then picked up the racy urban romance she was in the middle of. She plunged back into the story of Diamond, the pretty girl who grew up too fast in the Chicago projects, and Jay, the would-be poet turned drug dealer who sold crack only to satisfy Diamond's gold-digging appetites. Cheyenne tried to ignore the hungry ache she felt in the pit of her stomach. A salad at Aria and a Nutri-Grain bar were all she had eaten that day. As she often found in the dim hush of her luxury condo at nighttime, she was starved for more.

Cheyenne had been fooling herself when she pledged to hit the road at dawn. She never woke a minute before nine o'clock. She packed her suitcases and makeup bag, dressed in a skirt and fluttery blouse, then waited in line for ten minutes at the nearest Starbucks drive-through. *Damn holiday travelers.* She sipped her light latte as she peeled onto the highway behind a line of cars. It took her thirty minutes just to clear the city sprawl on the way to her dream house in the foothills. Cheyenne sped up I-75 with the top down on her Mercedes-Benz and a Jackie O–style scarf tied around her head. The view of closely congregated buildings gave way to green space; flat land rose into hills and dipped into shallow valleys.

Cheyenne felt on the verge of a great discovery, one that could change her life. She had always been interested in her grandmother's stories about their Native American heritage, but she hadn't started tracing her roots until after her grandmother's death. There were so many things she wanted to ask, now that it was too late. To compensate, Cheyenne was an avid participant on the *AfriGeneas* and *Roots-Web* genealogy sites, posting queries and checking compulsively for the latest postings to the Cotterell crowd-sourced family tree. She could trace her family history back to the 1860s, but then the trail went cold. That's where her grandmother's stories came in. They explained the gap.

Many times growing up, she had heard her grandmother tell the tale that traced their family's origins. Her grandmother used to say that the Cotterell line had started on a Cherokee plantation two hundred years ago with a female ancestor who married an Indian man. The couple's children hadn't been enrolled in the tribe because of their mixed-race ancestry, but the children's names, along with those of all black Indians on the plantation, were recorded in a secret list that no one had seen since. The Hold Plantation in the North Georgia foothills, the heart of former Cherokee territory, was the only place she had found during her genealogical research that matched the description in her grandmother's story.

Like most other kids in Atlanta, Cheyenne had toured the Hold House once or twice in grade school. But having a chance to own it, to hold it for herself, was only a fantasy until this week. Her parents thought she was obsessed with genealogy because she hadn't found the right man to settle down with. Her father humored her with fabricated interest in the draft charts that filled the pages of her *Black Indian Genealogy Workbook*. Her mother didn't even pretend to care, waving away her grainy prints of family census records. To them, genealogy was a hobby. To her, it was a quest to find the missing pieces of an inner puzzle that could finally tell her who she was. Cheyenne was a throwback, her grandmother used to say, to an unknown branch of the Cotterell family tree. She fully intended to find that branch and brandish it.

3

RUTH MAYES STARED AT THE OCEAN LINER floating across her computer screen, wanting to squash it like a bug. Holland America had slashed its Jamaican cruise fares to drum up ticket sales for the fall season. Pop-up ads nettled her; so did movie trailers. She tended to edit the images she allowed into her head, resenting any loss of control.

She x-ed out the picture of the long white boat, blocking the thoughts it conjured. Reaching for her travel mug, she took a sip of bad office coffee, then pulled off her tortoise-shell glasses and tugged a corkscrew of thick, dark hair. She leaned back into her seat, aligning her butt with the padding, shifting her swivel chair with the movement of her body. Wheeling the chair in close to her desk, Ruth dug her clogs into the floor and glanced at the architectural photographs taped to the backbone of her cubicle. She needed a muse, a muse who knew houses. She needed a story idea.

Ruth rested her head on her forearms. It was four o'clock in the afternoon, one hour until the start of her forced vacation. She had nothing to do and nowhere to go for the next two weeks. What she absolutely could not do was lounge around at home in her basement apartment. When she had time on her hands, the pictures popped into her mind, forming a cloud of memories that overtook her like a storm.

"Ruth, are you feeling all right?" It was Lauren, Ruth's empathetic, India-print-skirted creative director.

"Just fine. Thanks." Ruth straightened her back and popped her glasses onto her nose, taking care not to tangle them in her thicket of curly hair.

Lauren scanned the blank face of Ruth's computer screen. "Good, because I've got an assignment for you. The sisal mat photo spread didn't come through. By five, we need a filler story on floor coverings—something trendy, preferably natural fiber. Look for carpets; see what's new."

"Carpets? Are you kidding me? Fudge, Lauren."

"I only need five hundred words. And don't miss the deadline just so you have a reason to come in Monday. As much as we love you around here, Ruth, we don't want to see you next week. Take the vacation that's coming to you and save your company some money."

Everyone on staff knew *Abode* was suffering. Advertising had plunged in the last year; subscriptions had slowed as readers started cutting back on their leisure-activity budgets. For the first time in its eight-year run as a sleek Minneapolis-based shelter magazine, *Abode* was in the red. Instead of cutting staff or shutting down, senior management was trying an intermediate tack. All of the writers had been asked to take accrued vacation time without pay by December. Ruth, an office junkie who barely alighted at home, had saved up six weeks of vacation in her four years with the magazine. The lost pay would devastate some of her coworkers, but Ruth's mother had left her an ostrich-sized nest egg. For Ruth, it wasn't the money that kicked her heartbeat into high gear, it was the yawn of open time.

"Carpets are cozy. Carpets are colorful," Lauren was saying. "Just the thing for fall. Six hundred words with an ethnic twist. That's all I'm asking."

"I thought you said five hundred."

"Six hundred," Lauren said, patting Ruth's shoulder in encouragement. Ruth shrugged off the touch. "Got it."

When Lauren moved away to make her office rounds like a chipper, bohemian candy striper, Ruth stood to stretch. She walked to the wall of windows at the far side of the industrial loft, touching her hand to the brick and gazing out at the skyscrapers. She cracked one of the windows that had been sealed all summer to trap the air conditioning. The breeze outside was cooler than she expected. She pulled together the buttons of her denim jacket over her Barq's Root Beer T-shirt.

"Ruth! Got a minute?"

The voice came from behind her. She turned her back to the window, brushing dust from her fingertips. It was Justin, the magazine's eco-stylist. He had been asking her out for months. Justin was one of those thirty-something white men with feeling eyes and attractively rumpled, longish hair. She had observed a whole tribe of his nouveau beatnik poet kind at Carleton College when she was in school.

"So . . ." He took a breath. "Since you'll be on vacation for a few weeks coming up, I thought maybe we could try to get together."

Justin was cute, Ruth supposed. Any woman with her head on straight might at least toss him a bone. "Thanks, Justin. That's a sweet idea, but I'm going out of town for work."

"I heard about the late-breaking carpet story. Did you find a good angle? I've been thinking of doing a piece on rugs made out of recycled rubber. There's a growing industry down in Dalton, Georgia, the U.S. carpet capital." He smiled and leaned in. "Maybe we could do the research together. Pitch a feature-story idea to Lauren."

"My carpet piece is just a filler for the November issue. Nothing special. The carpet capital, though, there's a ring to that. Thanks for the lead." Ruth flashed him half a smile before walking away.

She could feel Justin's eyes on her ginger-colored culottes as the soft cotton shaped to her ample hips. It was one of her best features, she knew—her hip line to rump line to firm, strong thighs. The thighs came courtesy of many a long-distance weekend run, the hips and butt from her full-figured mother. Try as she had to lose weight back when she was in summer camp sharing a cabin with a Whitley Gilbert double, or when she was at Carleton rooming with stick girls who complained that the size twos were the first to go from the sales rack, she found that the weekend runs never quite canceled out strong maternal genes. She was a comfortable size fourteen, just a tad slimmer than her mother had been. She still recalled the rounded lines of her mother's shape. "My Gold Coast," her father would say with a proprietary smile, tracing the curve of her mother's hips with cool blue eyes. Watching her mother's expression cloud, Ruth would frown and, for reasons unclear to her small child's mind, cling to her mother's side.

Ruth shut the memory down, slid into her desk chair, and typed "Georgia, rugs, carpets" into the Google search bar. The first few links were carpet-company websites. She scrolled through their menus, jotting down notes. Then she opened a link to a newspaper story about the carpet industry in northwest Georgia, the influx of Latino workers and arrival of Mexican groceries and taquerias. *Thank you, Justin.* This was the kind of angle she needed to type up six hundred words of cotton-candy copy for Lauren. If Justin was *Abode*'s eco-stylist with a regular column to his name, Ruth was its ethno-stylist, but without the title or highlighted byline. She was assigned virtually all of the "ethnic" stories—on drapery inspired by Somali fabrics, the Hmong kitchen garden, new directions in outsider-art furniture design. Ruth ignored the obvious pigeonholing of her de facto job description, which she knew fell to her only because she was black. So far, Lauren had been willing enough to keep her busy on assignment, which Ruth accepted as a trade for the narrow topical scope.

Ruth had a rote method for her filler stories. She started with on-line research, made a few phone calls, conducted lightning interviews, and dashed off a feel-good piece. It took her just under an hour to pound out her story on how workers in the Georgia carpet industry incorporated hints of their Latin heritage into textile designs. It was claptrap, and she knew it. The real story was labor exploitation in the heart of the industrial Sun Belt. But that wasn't the kind of story that would suit the readership of a glossy magazine like *Abode*, with its pho-tos of lovely homes, emerald lawns, and wraparound porches as lacy as push-up bras.

Ruth skimmed her article, "Aztec Influence Colors Georgia Carpet Kingdom," before pushing the *Send* key to whisk it off to Lauren. It was five o'clock, but a few of her fellow writers still hunched over their desks. She dreaded going home to her "garden-level" basement apart-ment, where not even houseplants fought to survive. Ruth tapped her unpolished fingernails on the mousepad, trying to think of a reason to stay late. As she scanned the results of her previous search one last time, her eyes fell on an odd blue link. It was an article in the *Dalton Daily Citizen* dated August 30, 2008:

State Cuts Pull Rug from under Cherokees, Friends of the Hold House

Local residents were saddened to learn that a beloved institution is being dissolved.

Georgia Department of Natural Resources officials said Wednesday that the state-owned Hold Plantation, along with the

Moravian Church mission building on the grounds, will be sold due to the budget crisis.

The Chief Hold House was built in 1804 by James Vann Hold, the son of a Cherokee mother and Scottish father, who rose to become one of the Cherokee Nation's most prominent leaders. The house served as a political and economic center for the Cherokee people until they were forcibly removed from the area by the federal government in the 1830s. It was restored and opened as a state historic site in 1952 but was closed by the DNR in 2002.

The DNR has announced an auction of the Hold House, its contents and its surrounding land for September of this year.

Local volunteers who hoped to raise funds to reopen the Native American house museum are calling the impending sale an "outrage." John Cook, a Tribal Council member of the Cherokee Nation of Oklahoma, agreed, saying, "The Trail of Tears was an effort to eliminate the Cherokee people, and now they are trying to eliminate our culture."

Other tribal members echoed this sentiment. "If there is no interpretation at our Georgia historic sites, who will tell that story?" said Stuart Pickup, a member of the United Keetoowah Band of Cherokees. "The Trail of Tears was an ethnic cleansing. The state of Georgia is adding insult to injury by refusing to tell the public about it. If you don't understand history, you're doomed to repeat it," Pickup said.

Ruth pushed her glasses up to the broad bridge of her nose. She opened a new window in *Ask.com* to confirm what she thought she recalled from her ethnic studies courses. The Cherokees' grueling forced march along the Trail of Tears from the hills of Georgia and North Carolina to Indian Territory in Oklahoma had taken place in the winter of 1838–39. Now, more than 170 years after that crime, an economic crisis was going to finish the job of wiping Cherokee history off the Georgia map.

"Lauren!" Ruth called, jumping out of her seat and grabbing pages from the shared office printer. She plunged into Lauren's office, culottes swirling against her calves. "Am I all set with the carpet story?"

Lauren looked up from her mug of chai tea and the slick proofs fanned across her desk. "Yep. Nice work. Do you have any plans for the holiday weekend?"

"I do now. A new story." Ruth dropped the printed pages next to Lauren's proofs. "About a historic house down south, built by Cherokee Indians in the 1800s and run as a house museum since the 1950s. The state of Georgia closed the museum six years ago and is going to sell the land this month in a public auction."

"And you want to investigate. I can see why. The topic is intriguing, packs an emotional punch. Our readers would appreciate the historic-house focus, and the Indian angle is something they would expect from your byline." Lauren sighed, handing back the pages. "But you know *Abode* can't afford—"

"I'll pay my own expenses."

"That's easy, then. Sold. Take a slew of photos. Good ones. I can't afford to send a photographer down there."

"I will. Thanks, Lauren." Ruth gave her boss a smile, then turned on the heels of her clogs.

Back at her desk, she shut down her MacBook, slipped it into its quilted sleeve, and grabbed her bunchy leather bag. She snatched the travel mug from her desk and stopped to refill it with the dregs of coffee left in the staff kitchen.

As she pushed through the metal door into the clear autumn day, she felt again that hint of coolness. The weather was on the cusp of change. She was going south just in time.

Ruth hurried to her Volkswagen Beetle and plopped her mug into the holder. She would stop by her apartment to throw together a travel bag and ask her upstairs neighbor to collect her mail. She had no one to call, no one who would miss her. Ruth and her father rarely spoke these days. Even if she were to pack up and move away from Minneapolis–St. Paul, her father probably wouldn't notice until Christmastime when she failed to turn up at his high-rise condo for their awkward annual dinner. Her grandparents on both sides had passed away. She had no siblings.

Ruth programmed her GPS with the address of the Chief Hold House and waited for her route to upload. The digital map glowed green in the dashboard. She was headed straight down I-75 to a small, rural town in the state where her mother had been born.

4

As she stretched to wipe the window ledge, Sally Perdue hiked up the baby. Her dust mop, dulled by the grime of countless cleanings that never seemed to make this old house shine, flopped on the end of its stick. From his seat on her hip, the baby lunged for the mop, reaching sideways with a chubby fist. "No, no, baby." Sally's voice was gentle. "This is Mama's, and this is Junior's." She handed him a rattle. He reached again for the mop, his blue eyes tracking dust set in motion by his mother's hand. Dust motes rose like dandelion seeds where they stood on the staircase landing, a space one-third the size of the trailer Sally shared with Eddie Senior.

Sally blew a puff of air through her lips. *Not much more now. Just the stairwell and the hallways, the butler's pantry and foyer. Thank the Lord Eddie Junior takes good naps.* Sally had finished the second floor while he slept in his seat. She had mopped and polished the main floor while he rode on her hip in a fancy made-in-Canada sling she had gotten as a hand-me-down from one of the former docent's daughters.

Sally cooed at her son once, twice, looking into his eyes while he gurgled. She lifted him out of the sling and bent to strap him into the bouncy seat. "Almost finished, Junior. Gotta make it pretty. Somebody's fixin' to buy this place." Sally plopped a kiss on her baby's cheek and popped a pacifier into his mouth. She pressed the button that made the seat rock back and forth, then wiped a palm across her damp hairline.

Raising the sling over her head and stuffing it into her diaper bag, Sally grasped a fold of her T-shirt and flapped it in and out. She cranked the iron handle of a leaded-glass window, hoping for a breeze. The noise of a construction truck rumbled in. *Maybe a digger, maybe a bulldozer. Mason Allen.* Beyond the dip of the elegant hill on which the old plantation house stood, the land was being cleared for a condo development.

Sally touched a hand to the paneled oak wall beside her. Its planes and ridges felt like vertebrae beneath her thumb, fragile and hollow, thinning with age. She had begged for this job back in high school—talked her way into it when she heard the previous cleaning lady had quit in a huff, complaining of an odd smell in the attic that just couldn't be gotten rid of. *A dead bat,* Sally had thought at the time. She had seen worse around her trailer, even before Eddie Senior moved in. The director of the house museum called an exterminator and hired Sally on the spot, desperate to see the place spruced up in time for the garden show that year. The pay was low, but better than what Sally made cleaning at the nursing home. And she had always wondered about this brooding house on the hill, visible for miles. She had been curious about its history even before her fifth-grade class took the standard tour for county kids. If she had made it to college, or even out of high school, before getting together with Eddie Senior, she would have taken some kind of class on Southern history. But working here had given her the next best thing, a chance to soak in all that drama of the past.

The story went that James Vann Hold, the man who built the plantation when this all counted as Indian land, was the handsome son of a full-blood Cherokee mother and European father. Hold got to be filthy rich investing family money in slaves, trading deerskins and crops, and making shady business deals. He was murdered in the prime of manhood, and nobody knew who did it. Sally recalled the script by heart from overhearing the docents. They never really changed it up unless a black person took the tour, in which case they said "servants" instead of "slaves." She had cleaned the place only a year before the state closed it down. She had been hired back today to get the house ready for auction. Sally was glad for the work, such as it was. Lord knew, Eddie Senior took a paying job only when he had a mind to.

Junior dropped his passy. Sally tucked it into her bag and stuck a clean blue one in his mouth. She dusted ornate mirror frames, wiped down silvered glass, swept the formal stairway and long oak halls. When she finished the foyer, she was parched and thought that Junior must be, too. After climbing the stairs to where he sat rocking contentedly on the landing, she pulled out his bottle of formula. *What a good baby.*

The rude honk of a horn blared through the open window. *Shit,* Sally thought. *Eddie.* She flew into motion, lifting Junior and hooking him to her hip with one arm beneath his padded bottom, grabbing the diaper bag in one hand and the bouncy seat in the other. She jogged down the staircase, jostling the baby and his things while the horn bellowed.

"What the hell took you so long, Sally?" Eddie was mad, his face puffing out and in from his worked-up breathing.

"Sorry, Ed, sorry." Sally reached inside the open rear window to unlock the door and throw the bouncy chair inside. She eased into the passenger seat and held Junior out to his daddy. "Could you take him for a spell? I need to lock up."

"Jesus Christ. I thought I told you to be ready when I got here."

"I won't be but a minute."

Sally ran back to the house and opened the double entry doors. She reached for the oval sign that hung on a hook beside the door chime's soundbox. Exiting, she pulled the doors shut behind her, turned the oblong metal lock, and listened for the click. Hearing it, she twined the ribbon of the sign tightly around the neck of a brass doorknob. *Closed*, it read. With her back to Eddie Senior, Eddie Junior, and the winding driveway that led into town, she pressed her hand to the heavy wooden door panel. "Bye, now," she whispered to the house.

"Get a move on, Sally!" Eddie shouted. "This kid of yours is gone and shit his pants."

Sally turned her back to the red-brick mansion, its eaves and porches, porticoes and columns. As she hustled down the broad front steps, a stiff breeze followed her, carrying with it the meadowy scent of late-summer wildflowers. The wind caught and parted Sally's short red hair, cooling the nape of her neck.

While Eddie careened the beat-up car around the circular driveway, the breeze kept on blowing, flipping the sign to read, *Open*.

The drive stretched into a frustrating trek, heightened by Cheyenne's nervous anticipation.

After what felt like two hours, rather than the fifty minutes promised by her GPS, she found herself pulling in front of the Chief Hold House. She eased out of her car and planted her heels in the uneven gravel, taking in the view. Bold, brick, and becoming, the home seemed to greet her like a bridegroom. Cheyenne seized a breath. *Magnificent.* Even the high heat couldn't distract her from this architectural belle.

The Department of Natural Resources had arranged for a local broker to show her the house that afternoon, and a middle-aged woman in a blue pencil skirt and white blouse with a Peter Pan collar was standing in the driveway. Light brown hair hung neatly to her shoulders from a center part. She wore silver earrings and sensible shoes. She leaned in the window of a parked black SUV and smiled flirtatiously at the driver, whose face was hidden from Cheyenne. Cheyenne willed the woman to speed it up. She was desperate to get a look inside. There was no chance the photos posted on the realtor's website did this beauty justice.

Cheyenne undid the silk scarf on her head, shaking loose her dark sheeting of hair. She retied the slip of fabric in a soft knot around her neck and shifted her weight and one hand to her hip. She stood at a polite distance, impatiently biding her time.

"Of course, Mr. Allen," Cheyenne overheard the woman say.

She caught snatches of conversation interspersed with laughter.

"Pro forma . . . required to show it to anyone who makes a request . . .

". . . can't be serious . . .

". . . gorgeous property, good bones . . .

". . . want that river view you promised me . . .

"You have a good holiday, now."

Cheyenne watched as the SUV's window rolled up to seal out the sunlight and the woman straightened her back and cleared the playful look from her face.

"Miss Cotterell?" The woman held out a hand as Cheyenne closed the distance between them. "I'm Lanie Brevard. We spoke on the telephone."

"Yes. Nice to meet you, Lanie. If I may, who was that just leaving?" Cheyenne's voice landed on a nervous high note. Her lips puckered with concern. Someone had scheduled a viewing. *Competition.*

"Oh, him." Lanie Brevard's tone was playful again, as if she were still speaking to the man himself. She cleared her throat. "That was Mr. Allen. Mason Allen. One of the pillars of our town."

Cheyenne frowned. "He's interested in the Hold House?"

"Everyone around here is interested in the Hold House, Miss Cotterell. Surely you've read about the controversy in the papers. The Hold estate has been an economic boon to this town for centuries. With any luck, we'll see its fortunes rise again after the auction next week. Let me show you the house."

She escorted Cheyenne up the wide front steps, dangling a key labeled *Hold* like a forbidden delicacy. The metal parts of the lock released. The broker turned a knob on one of the twin oak doors that held a sign on a ribbon. Cheyenne stepped into the foyer after her. The house had a stale, closed-in smell despite the scent of cleaning products that betrayed a recent mopping. The air felt cool and still, like a root cellar. Cheyenne crossed her arms, stroking her bare skin in the sudden chill.

The broker watched the motion of Cheyenne's hands. "Handmade bond brick," she said. "Keeps the house cooler than a cave. You're from Atlanta? Did I remember that right?"

"You did."

"Mr. Allen does business down in the city every once in a while, but most of us prefer to stay here in the mountains. Our town is just right for us, fits like a hammock. Have you been up this way before?"

"Back in elementary school, we toured the Hold House. It was something like a fifth-grade pilgrimage. And I used to go to summer camp on Fort Mountain. Camp Idlewood?"

"Yes," the broker said. "I've heard of it. Idlewood was an African American camp that started as a school for former slaves, wasn't it?"

"It was a school for fifty years. The camp's founders bought the lot in the 1920s and repurposed the old Freedmen's Bureau buildings. African American families from all over the South, and a few from the North, paid a fortune to send their children there every summer."

"Hmm," the broker said noncommittally. "I believe the buildings are used for crafts and whatnot now. The state purchased the land to expand Fort Mountain State Park—which, by the way, is just one of the gifts of the Allen family to our county."

Lanie Brevard broke off her homage to the Allens and turned to the drawing room. Cheyenne followed, pushing back worry as her Giambattista Valli skirt swirled around her knees. This was it. She was here. Inside the arms of the Hold House. She took in the elaborate carvings on the fireplace mantel, the plaster moldings that framed the walls and ceilings, and the hand-blown windows languidly filtering light.

They exited the drawing room, entered the dining room. She scanned the nine-over-nine leaded-glass panes topped with gold-leaf fixtures in the form of phoenixes rising. Dried pine needles and okra pods rested on the window sills. An old-fashioned brick of tea sat on a saucer made of blue transferware china. The antique textiles and furnishings collected over the years remained in place in the house. Some of the pieces had belonged to the Hold family; others had been donated by wealthy patrons over the years. Cheyenne had read in *Southern Living* that the table settings in the Hold House were replicas of the fragmented dishware uncovered beneath the outdoor kitchen by a state archaeologist in the 1950s. The property would be auctioned with its contents intact, sold "as is." Spacious by nineteenth-century standards, boasting three stories, eight rooms, broad hallways, back and front porches, and a cellar, the house brimmed with the contents of generations. And it could all be hers. It had to be.

Lanie Brevard led Cheyenne through the first floor with chatty narration about the upstanding families who had lived in the home before the museum opened. Cheyenne tried to tune her out. She wanted to focus on the house.

Back in the front hallway, where a half-opened cardboard box held forgotten copies of Chief Hold House brochures, Cheyenne turned with the broker toward the wooden staircase. They mounted the grand oak steps with carved balustrades, reached a large, superfluous landing crafted solely for show, and continued to the second story. At the front of the center hallway, a seating area flowed into a covered veranda that faced the road leading off the estate. Cheyenne turned on the crisp heels of her slender Bottega Veneta sling-backs to make her way to the master bedroom behind Lanie Brevard.

It was divided from the rest of the home by a lateral bridge that echoed the structure and form of the staircase. The oddly placed bridge connected the front and rear of the second story. It rose in an arch from the center hallway and crossed the open space of the downstairs hall. Cheyenne had read that architectural historians debated the reason the bridge had been built. Some said it represented the split sides of James Vann Hold's racial identity; others argued it was Hold's calculated attempt to keep his private life separate from the scrutiny of United States Indian agents and white missionaries.

Cheyenne crossed the elegant arch of the bridge, the sharp edges of her sling-backs digging into the floorboards. She faced the entry to a spacious bedroom and saw a closed doorway farther down the hall— leading up, she supposed, to an attic. She watched as Lanie Brevard unlatched the velvet rope that cordoned off the master bedroom, protecting its heirloom contents from long-gone tourists. Inside, Cheyenne's gaze caught first on the full eastern view of the Blue Ridge, then on the hand-worked lace canopy atop the mahogany bedstead, and next on the folding antique game table splayed with period playing cards. The room had no proper master bath, but one could be added without even knocking down a wall. She moved to a chestnut wardrobe with an inlaid rose motif on the crest. Pulling it gently open, she marveled at the little drawers inside and stroked the silk of the chest's inner lining. Cheyenne breathed in and out, gazing at blue-peaked mountaintops and feeling deep in her bones that this would be her bedroom. She turned to see Lanie Brevard watching, a sharp look in her eye.

"Miss Cotterell, I would be remiss if I didn't tell you just how much work goes into maintaining an old house like this. And you're alone, as

I understand it. This would be quite an undertaking. If you're looking for a vacation property, we have a number of charming cabins and log homes on the market. I could show you a few right now."

Cheyenne's eyes narrowed. The woman was steering her. "I like a challenge, Ms. Brevard," she said. "I like the Hold House."

"I see. Then you have the right to know that members of the original Hold family . . . they tended to die under mysterious circumstances. There's no evidence that this is a stigmatized property per se, but, well, who knows?"

"Mysterious circumstances? Is that right? Did you tell Mr. Allen that story, too?"

"Of course not." The broker waved her hand in the air between them as if the suggestion were ridiculous. "Mason is local. We're pretty close-knit here. I'm sure he knows all there is to know about this house."

A high-pitched peal erupted from the hallway. The sound was not human.

"What was that?" Cheyenne jumped, hand flying to her chest.

"It's bound to be a stray cat. This property is full of them." Lanie Brevard smiled politely. "Like I said, a big undertaking."

Cheyenne fingered the natural pearl in her left ear, dropped her fidgeting hand, and set her chin. "I like cats," she said to the broker. "I've even been thinking about adopting a kitten."

5

Jinx blazed down the interstate in her ruby-red pickup with a public-library audiobook blaring from the speakers. The braid of sweetgrass made for her by Great-Aunt Angie, the one she always traveled with and vowed never to burn, nestled in the crevice where the window met the dash.

She crossed the border into Tennessee at twilight and decided to stay over in Chattanooga on Sunday night. When she saw the billboard for the Chattanooga Choo Choo, the historic train depot converted into a pricey hotel, she imagined a long soak in a cool porcelain tub, plush white towels, and a cache of fancy toiletries. Turning off the highway, she pulled into a Super 8. After stashing her duffle and her messenger bag in a corner of the motel room, she twisted her braid into a knot, showered under the tepid spray, and dressed in jeans, a clean T-shirt, and high-top sneakers.

Jinx had to get back into the truck to find the main drag downtown, where she planned to forage for food and see what there was to see. She scooped up Coke cans, Twizzler wrappers, and used napkins, stuffing them into the crumpled McDonald's bag from that morning. She dumped the trash into a can on the sidewalk and took in the street scene around her. People were out enjoying the warm night air, savoring the last summer holiday weekend. Jinx walked in the path of pairs and groups, passing clothing boutiques, gift shops, and antique stores flanked by potted urns of vibrant late-blooming flowers.

On a quieter corner, she found a used bookshop with the name *Once Upon a Time* stenciled above the entrance. A fat orange cat was sleeping in the display window. Jinx ducked inside. Helping herself to a sugar cookie from the yellow plate on the counter, she started a scan of the bulging shelves. The clerk, a rosy-cheeked older woman dressed up like Mother Goose, complete with downy wings, waved at her. Jinx did a double take before regaining her momentum while biting into a sweet, crisp wafer.

The store didn't have a section on Native American history, but the American history alcove overflowed into stacks on the floor. In the Civil War section, she found an out-of-print biography of Stand Watie, the heralded Cherokee brigadier general in the Civil War. With one foot on a stepstool, she skimmed the first chapter. Watie's story began in southeastern Cherokee territory, where she was headed that weekend. He and his brother Buck had both attended the mission school run by Moravians on the Hold Plantation, the place where Mary Ann Battis had ended up after she set the fire. Jinx flipped to the index. No *Battis* there. But the book was well worth the six-dollar price. It would make for good contextual reading once she pulled into Georgia and found a place to stay for the week.

She tucked the book under her arm and moved down the aisle, thinking about the sugar cookies but not wanting to leave any stone unturned. She was examining the women's history shelves, pulling out books to read their title pages, when she stumbled on a great find: a hardbound volume with needle-thin black lettering. It was a reprint of an old Moravian church history, seven hundred pages long, no contents page, no index, no price. Jinx swung her messenger bag onto her shoulder, holding a book in each hand as she speed-walked to the counter.

"Did you find what you were looking for?" Mother Goose said.

"I did. But this one"—Jinx pushed the navy-blue book across the counter—"doesn't have a price on it." *Let me afford it, let me afford it,* she thought.

Mother Goose studied her face, then the inside front and back covers of the book. "How much do you have?" she said.

"Twenty?"

"Plus six for the biography, plus tax, and it's yours. Take care of it, now."

"Great. Thanks." Jinx dug into the pocket of her blue jeans, came up empty-handed, and unzipped a pocket of her messenger bag. "You know," she said, handing over her only credit card and hoping she wasn't too close to the limit, "the cookies here are top-notch, and the chubby cat is cute. This shop would be perfect if you added a Native American studies section."

Mother Goose raised an eyebrow in surprise, as if to convey that Jinx should have been happy enough with the prices. "I'll take that under advisement," she finally said, ruffling her costume feathers.

The sky was slate dark, the air still warm, when Jinx left the bookshop. Smelling the tang of barbecue and hearing a din in the distance reminded her that she was starved. She followed the smell to a doorway framed by Christmas lights and a mounted speaker that pumped out the voice of Tammy Wynette. Inside, she sat at a brown picnic table covered with a sticky, checked plastic cloth and plotted out the next day's route on her highway map. When her meal arrived, Jinx folded the map and dove into a basket of brown-tipped fries and sauce-slathered ribs.

Once she finished off her food, licked the tips of her fingers, and cleaned up with a wipe, Jinx headed for the wharf. She knew she had to see it before she left Tennessee: the riverside park. Cherokees had camped along the river here, at a place now called Ross's Landing, in preparation for their forced march west to Indian Territory.

Jinx took the boardwalk to the end, where it hung above the water. Blocking out the boisterous sounds of passersby as she stared into the night, she imagined the scene as it might have been 170 years ago. In the summer of 1838, her father's people had been herded here and corralled into rancid camps, where they sickened and died in the sweltering heat before their principal chief, John Ross, secured permission from Washington to allow them to postpone their departure until cooler weather arrived. Jinx pictured her ancestors inside the tent village, a makeshift concentration camp. Old ladies with sagging eyes, grown men with flagging spirits, babies dying of heat exposure against their mothers' mourning breasts. It was as though they were all there with her at the wharf, behind a sheer curtain sewn of nothing but time. She could almost reach out to touch them, to whisper in their ears, to tell them that although it would cost dearly and always, their people would manage to survive.

And so would the slaves of her ancestors, who, though ignored by history, had walked the Trail of Tears alongside them.

6

HE'S NOT HOME, Sally thought with a spike of relief. Only Delta's faded sedan was parked out front in the gravel drive. Delta must be working the holiday, too. Mason Allen hadn't expanded his family's real-estate profits by giving folks time off for Labor Day. She bet he had his Mexican crew working right now in the empty lot that some folks whispered used to be a slave burial ground. Sally pushed Eddie Junior's umbrella stroller, grateful he was still asleep even though the wheels kept catching.

Mason Allen's family home sprawled before her, three white clapboard triangles topped by red-tile eaves. It was an old Cherokee plantation house like the Hold place, built by the Indians before the Trail of Tears. Mason's family won it when the state of Georgia seized Cherokee homes in 1830 and redistributed them to white settlers in a rigged land lottery. Mason had kept the estate pristine, along with the other property he would one day inherit from his daddy. The Allen family used to own as much property as James Hold had in his heyday. They'd even possessed the mountain that dominated the area, back before they donated it to create Fort Mountain State Park. The story went that it took a dinner in the Governor's Mansion with none other than Lady Bird Johnson to convince Old Man Allen to hand the mountain over for conservation and the benefit of the public. But Mason Allen could still have the state park closed when he had a mind to, for hunting parties, social-set picnics, and whatnot. He and everybody else acted like his family still owned half of the county, one of the Blue Ridge Mountains, and practically all of the sky.

Sally leaned forward to heave Junior's stroller onto the porch. She rang the bell of Mason Allen's long white villa.

"Hi, sugar," Delta Jones said to Junior, whose bright blue eyes had just popped open when she answered the door. Delta nudged the door back with her hip, reaching down to unbuckle Junior. She and Sally both knew Mason Allen wouldn't tolerate stroller wheels on his checkerboard parquet flooring. "Come on in, Sally. You want some coffee?"

Delta was wearing her light blue maid's uniform, a cotton dress with buttons lined straight as a ruler down the front. A white apron dusted with flour curved around her ample middle. Her short gray hair was pressed and curled, shining from a recent visit to May Bell's Beauty Shop. Miss Delta always took care with her appearance, even now that she was knocking on the door of her seventy-eighth birthday.

"Yeah, Miss Delta. Thank you, and good morning. You been doing all right? Your hair sure looks nice."

"Thank you, sugar. We had a family picnic on Sunday, and you know I had to go and get my hair done for that," Delta said. "And how about some grits?" she added, looking at the shadows under Sally's eyes.

"Yes, ma'am. I didn't have time to make any breakfast this morning. And Eddie Senior's been real busy lately. Gone a lot."

"Mmm-hmm," Delta said. "I'm through with my baking. Let me take Junior and give him something to eat."

"Thank you, Miss Delta. But remember, now, he can't eat solids yet. Just formula, in the diaper bag."

"Is that what them doctors at the health clinic told you? I raised eight babies of my own and three of the Allens'. A baby can always use some good pot liquor. Chock-full of vitamins. I got some left from yesterday's collards. Now you go on and start that deep-clean. Mason wants us only half the day. Seems like he's cutting back. That stock-market hullabaloo all over the news has the rich white folks running crazy. You know where to find your supplies."

Shit, Sally thought. *That's minus thirty dollars.* She did a cleaning for Mason once a month. She had been counting on a full-day's job for her grocery money.

"Mr. Allen's out this morning?" Sally said, listening for the sound of his footfalls. He lived alone except for Delta on weekdays, and Gus, his three-legged hound dog.

"Afraid not. He's in the study, wrangling with somebody in New York on the telephone. He's been over at the courthouse wheedling old maps of the Hold Plantation out of poor Jasper, who surely would rather be home in bed on the holiday. When Mason came back, he parked his truck in the garage. That's why you didn't see it. Might be he doesn't want people eyeballing his papers. He's a mite more nervous than his daddy. Always thinking somebody's trying to outdo him."

"Too true," Sally said, handing Delta the diaper bag and kissing Junior on the nose. "Miss Delta, you're a lifesaver. I'll clean up quick." She smoothed Junior's downy tuft of strawberry hair. "You be good for Miss Delta, now."

Sally made her way up the sweeping double staircase, lifting the vacuum step by step. Mason had carpeted the stairs an eggshell white to contrast with the dark banister. That staircase was a bear to clean. She would start with the bedrooms.

"The hell I don't have it," Mason was barking as Sally passed his wood-paneled study. "You're my banker, Mort, not my nanny. Don't tell me what I can't spend. I don't care what's going on in that Yankee stock market of yours. Liquidate something if you have to. The condo development by the river is coming along just fine. I got the land for a song, and the units will sell big. We're close enough to Atlanta to draw out the yuppies. It'll generate income by springtime."

Sally peeled back the door of Mason's bedroom. She slipped inside, dragging the vacuum behind her. She freshened the linens on his king-sized bed and dusted the furniture. She used the special cloth he favored for his flat-screen TV, marveling again at the mammoth size of it. Besides the television and a leather lounge chair studded with brass prods, Mason hadn't changed his parents' room when they retired to their Florida vacation home and left him here to run the real-estate business. Sally wiped down the doors of Mason's closet, filled with dark, custom-made jackets ordered from Charleston and one or two seersucker suits for when he wanted to play the part of a gentleman.

"Check with my father?" Mason's voice rose in undulating waves. "I run this company now. Land is what I deal in, Mort. Real estate. And I want that Hold Plantation. Nothing like it's changed hands around here since my granddaddy got charmed by a woman and gave away Fort Mountain. I know a good investment when I see one."

Sally opened the door to the master bathroom and lifted the lid of the john. She sprayed Clorox and started to scrub.

"My father didn't build up this family's fortune for me to come along and lose it. I will not lose it, Mort. It takes risk to play the game. Borrow the money if you have to. It'll sell below value. I'm up against a bunch of Indian lovers and a black Barbie doll."

Sally flushed the toilet and watched a cyclone of chemical blue swirl toward the pipes. She knelt beside the spa bathtub, sprinkled cleanser in, and turned the water on. She scrubbed the rings from Mason's baths in rhythmic circles. Delta couldn't get this house as clean as she used to in her daily ministrations.

Sally felt him before she heard him—Mason's stiff blue jeans sharp against her folded back. Delta ironed them after the wash. Mason liked his creases.

"Sally." His voice was quiet. "Can't you keep it down in here? Can't you hear I'm trying to talk on the telephone?"

Sally turned off the faucet. Water sluiced from her hands and dripped from her forearms. She hated the way Mason always tried to catch her alone, tried to subtly press up against her and breathe in the scent of her hair. She never cleaned for him unless Delta was also in the house. She didn't trust him one lick. Especially now that the Hold House was on the line and the town was wound up tighter than an old grandfather clock. Anything was liable to happen.

"Please be more aware of your surroundings," Mason said. "Important things transpire within these walls. In my father's time, half the county changed hands from conversations started around the Allen dinner table. Between Delta's cornbread and my father's silver tongue, they never knew what hit 'em. This is a special place with a special legacy. We all have to do our part to uphold it." Mason patted Sally's shoulder, turned his back to her, and glanced at his reflection. "I think you missed a spot on this mirror." He stepped back into the hall through the bathroom's second doorway. "Come, Gus," he called, snapping his fingers.

Sally heard the crippled coonhound teetering out from his corner in Mason's paneled study. Folks said it was good of Mason to keep his daddy's hound after it got shot in a hunting accident. But Sally knew Mason liked the company of weaklings. That way, he could be assured that, barring his daddy, he was top dog.

Cheyenne arrived early for the property auction at the Murray County Courthouse on Tuesday. She had spent the weekend in the Room with a View Bed-and-Breakfast on Fort Mountain Road, studying her future competition and fending off repeated offers of rich morning pastries and high-carb fruit.

As she sat in a pew toward the front of the main chamber in the dome-roofed courthouse, adjusting her pearl necklace and checking her cell-phone messages, Cheyenne eyed the anxious crowd slowly gathering around her. The room crackled with expectation. Representatives from the Department of Natural Resources arrived in inexpensive suits and ties, wearing masks of resignation and sporting blunt haircuts. The green-uniformed rank-and-file employees of the Parks and Recreation Division exuded frustration; they had turned out in force to defend their jobs and historic sites. Although the park employees and their supporters would try to have their say after waging a public fight in the newspapers, Cheyenne was sure the private sale would proceed. Decisions had been made at the executive level by the director of the Department of Natural Resources, who was appointed, not elected, and therefore had little to fear from public agitation. Golf courses and fishing lakes—big draws for tourists—would receive the lion's share of state funding in this tight economy. Prizing revenue over what some viewed as sentimental attachment to the past, DNR officials had determined it made good financial sense to sell state history to the highest bidder. The Dahlonega Gold Museum, the Georgia State Archives building, and several other properties were on the chopping block. The Hold House would be only the first historic site to go.

A small group of self-identified Native Americans conversed indignantly in the back of the courtroom. They didn't look any more "Indian" than she did. Cheyenne felt the "Cherokee" contingent watching her with a curiosity akin to judgment. They would never entertain the thought that she might be Cherokee too. Because they were more white than black, they got a pass. Their Cherokee identity was scarcely questioned, while Cheyenne's was openly ridiculed even by her closest friends.

Across the aisle, the real-estate broker, Lanie Brevard, sat with a notepad in her lap. She glanced at Cheyenne and shook her head in a gesture that radiated pity. Cheyenne felt as if the whole room was watching her, as if a spotlight was singling her out and flashing the word *intruder*. She volleyed the stares of the Cherokee contingent, ignored the smug assessment of the broker. She held her head high, coiffed ponytail softly skimming her raw-silk blouse.

Cheyenne's gaze skated to the far corners of the room. She noticed that a spatial division had taken shape. Government officials and white professionals in shirts and ties populated the front of the courthouse. Employees of the Georgia state parks were clustered in the middle. The Cherokee contingent and some onlookers filled in the back. Opposite them on the other side of the courthouse, a few African Americans sat together. An older black woman with pressed gray curls kept a steady, interested gaze on Cheyenne. An older man in overalls sat beside her. A woman in a paisley dress who might have been a schoolteacher had glasses dangling from a chain around her neck. The man next to her was dressed in a park-service uniform but sat apart from his fellow employees. He chatted easily with both women, making them laugh. His cropped hair lay in black waves, framing a sculpted chestnut face with angled cheekbones and a classically firm chin. His dark eyes were serious despite the levity he seemed determined to buoy in the others, as if he wanted those around him to feel safe but harbored private apprehensions.

Cheyenne felt a twinge for him, an uncharacteristic stab of empathy. He probably wanted the auction to go poof at the last minute, for a representative of the Department of Natural Resources to stand and say it was all a mistake. She pulled her gaze away from the park ranger's face, but not before his eyes found hers in the flicker of an instant. Resisting the pull, she fixed her eyes on the lady in front of her, an elderly woman dressed in white after Labor Day.

She tapped the heel of one wine Ferragamo pump against the waxed courthouse floor. It was fifteen minutes past the appointed start time. The clock on her dream was ticking, and she didn't want to see one minute wasted. Her parents had promised a down payment toward the purchase of her first home. It was an extravagance they could afford. Her father was a chief Coca-Cola executive and major stockholder in the company. He and Cheyenne's mother, who came from old Atlanta money, owned a faux Italian villa in Decatur and a summer cottage on Martha's Vineyard. Cheyenne had lived in the carriage house behind the villa during her years at Emory and then while pursuing her M.A. in interior design at Georgia State. Moving to Candler Park had been her declaration of independence, and her parents had applauded the step. They were even more pleased to learn of her intention to use their promise of a house to start a small business. She needed achievements in her life, her mother had opined over drinks at the tennis club, especially if she was going to attract the right sort of man: a doctor, lawyer, or techno whiz with an Ivy League or Morehouse degree.

What was the holdup? Why was this taking so long? Cheyenne shot looks of annoyance at the auctioneer, who stood facing the packed house in a seersucker suit that stretched across his rotund belly. He seemed to be waiting for something to happen. And then it did. A cadre of well-dressed men barreled into the courtroom, moving like they owned the town and everybody in it. One of them, with storm-gray eyes and sandy hair, strode at the head. He had accentuated his tailored suit with a smart tie striped in Georgia Bulldog colors. *A UGA grad. With money. Wait until I tell the ladies about this,* Cheyenne thought. *Billy Bob just got an upgrade.* She took a steadying breath as the men settled into a row that had been left empty, as though reserved for them.

"What are we waiting for, Jasper?" The sandy-haired Bulldog spoke to the auctioneer. But it was apparent to everyone in the room that he was the answer to his own question. They had been waiting for him— because this so-called public auction was preordained. Cheyenne looked at Lanie Brevard, recalling their conversation the day before and the fragments she had overheard. *Mason Allen. Pillar of the town.* He turned just then to find her with his slate-gray eyes. He gave her an appraising look and didn't quite smile. Cheyenne gripped the Blackberry in her hands. She knew determination when she saw it. He was there to steal the Hold House out from under her.

The auction began, the buzz of nervous conversation drowned out by the rhythmic calling of the auctioneer. Cheyenne sat on the edge of her bench, stiff and alert. She had accompanied her mother to Christie's auctions and watched expensive jewelry and curios changing hands, but she had never done this alone before, never made a bid for herself on something as large as a house.

"And who will start the bidding at one hundred thousand dollars? One hundred thousand for the house on the hillside and fifteen lush acres of prime Georgia farmland," the auctioneer intoned.

A man in a cowboy hat representing the Cherokee contingent bid first, lifting his hand with a pointed index finger. A low murmur of approval sounded from the back of the courthouse. This group was determined to keep the home out of private hands with the donated funds it had raised in its community campaign, which probably included many of the onlookers in the room that day.

Mason Allen casually threw his hand up, raising the bid to two hundred thousand.

Cheyenne bided her time, waiting to see what would happen next.

The man in the cowboy hat looked encouraged, and answered the auctioneer's prompt for an increase of fifty thousand dollars.

Mason Allen appeared cool in his Brooks Brothers tie. "Three hundred thousand, Jasper," he said with quiet finality.

The Cherokee contingent fell back against their benches, defeated. Everyone who followed the local news knew they had raised only three hundred thousand dollars—an impressive figure, but clearly not enough.

The courthouse went silent.

"I have three hundred thousand dollars, three hundred thousand dollars. Who will make it four for this one-of-a-kind plantation property?"

"Four hundred thousand." Cheyenne's voice was high and shaky, like the ring of a wineglass touched to a tabletop by jittery fingertips.

Turning in his seat to look behind him, Mason Allen fixed his steely eyes on her face. He raised a hand at the auctioneer and coolly pledged half a million dollars.

Cheyenne knew the outcome was now uncertain. Her parents had set her limit at five hundred thousand, and even that was too much in their view. Just like Cheyenne, they had seen the Hold property photos online—visual evidence of the lapse in care, overgrown shrubbery, and provincial town services. But those photos didn't do the house justice. You had to be there to grasp its value. You had to feel the spirit of the house.

Cheyenne tapped the buttons of her Blackberry as she worded a hasty text message to her father and waited for his answer. "Going bid is 500k. Great investment. Go to 600, Daddy?"

Her cell phone beeped, and she lifted her hand with a cautious smile.

Mason Allen's face reddened. He raised his hand like an ax splitting wood. He never took his eyes from hers as he bid seven hundred, eight hundred, nine hundred thousand, more. Cheyenne saw her opponent's emotions rising with each sharp cut of his palm in the air. He could be running out of rope. They could be close to the end.

Cheyenne's fingers flew across the face of her phone. She didn't want to give her father time to call or text her mother, who surely would have nipped this little adventure in the bud hundreds of thousands of dollars ago. But she had always been her father's favorite, his pretty little princess.

She seized on the thought. "Daddy," she typed out, "it can be all mine for 1.5. A castle for your princess. I've never wanted anything more."

Seconds that felt like minutes passed. Her cell phone beeped.

Cheyenne was stunned as she uttered aloud the astounding figure. No one had predicted the house would go for so much. That amount could have bought a mansion in Savannah's famed historic district.

Mason Allen sat back, breathing like a steam engine, his face bright red. Cheyenne heard a collective gasp from the room. She had won her dream house, to have and to hold. And the Big Man on Campus had been bested, maybe for the first time in his life. Her stomach tightened with the promise and the anxiety of it.

Mason Allen turned to his shocked associates with a look that could not contain his rage. He stood and strode down the courtroom aisle with a confidence born of privilege. The other men followed. The state employees craned their necks. Lanie Brevard wilted with patent disappointment.

When Mason passed the bench where Cheyenne sat, flushed by her public triumph, he paused to hold out a hand to her. "Congratulations, Miss Cotterell. The Hold House is quite a prize. Be sure to sleep tight, and don't let the bedbugs bite." He chuckled at his own words, making show of his good sportsmanship.

She bent into her seat, instinctively ducking her head like prey, then raised her eyes back to his. She was the kind of woman who got what she wanted. He had just seen proof of that. "Don't worry. Mr. Allen, is it? I can take care of myself."

"Please, this way." The auctioneer was speaking to Cheyenne, motioning her toward the rear doors to handle the paperwork in a private meeting room with a horde of shell-shocked attorneys and state representatives. Cheyenne stood, smoothing the red-wine silk of her knee-length skirt. She held her shoulders upright and headed toward the auctioneer with a sashaying walk. She didn't look back at Mason Allen, who stood beside her empty bench, hands clenched at his sides.

"Well, now." Cheyenne heard a voice like rustling autumn leaves as she passed. It was the elderly woman with silver hair and maple-syrup-colored skin. Her light blue dress was like a costume out of time, a 1950s-style maid's uniform. "Just look at you, sugar."

"Excuse me?" Cheyenne said.

"Just look at you. I'm Delta Jones. Lived here all my life. And I have to tell you I ain't never seen nothing like that before. The Allens bumped down a notch. Where are you from? Who are your people?"

Cheyenne saw pride shining in the woman's eyes, pride directed toward her. She offered her hand and introduced herself.

"Owning the Hold House is more than a notion," Delta Jones said. "Funny thing about that place. No one can seem to hold on to it, no matter how bad they want to. The family that built it lost it to the state of Georgia before they got shoved west on that Trail of Tears. Georgia militia men smoked them out, set fire to the place because the head of the militia himself wanted that property so bad. The Cherokees got pushed on out of here at gunpoint. Meanwhile, the Georgia militiaman lost the house."

"Well, I'm not intending to go anywhere, Mrs. Jones," Cheyenne said, clutching her Burberry handbag and looking toward the door where the attorneys waited. She knew the park ranger with the serious eyes was standing behind Mrs. Jones, listening to their exchange. She didn't want to make eye contact, to learn what she would see in his face. Surely not the kind of pride that the elderly Mrs. Jones exuded, a racial pride she remembered from her grandmother's generation of black Southern women. No. The ranger's job was on the line, and his side, the state employees, had not even had one chip to play. He had lost to her, just like Mason Allen. Would she see anger? Resentment? Outrage? Cheyenne chanced a glance. Up this close, the ranger's eyes were magnetic, so dark and intense that they rivaled the nighttime sky.

He shook his head—in disbelief, or maybe confusion—when their eyes finally met. "Come on, Miss Delta," he said in a Southern accent thicker and deeper than what Cheyenne was used to in Atlanta. "Let me drive you back to work."

Fine. That was fine with her. She didn't need to know his name. She would probably never even see him again. Maids and park workers were not exactly in her social set. The Hold House auction had brought out all sorts of people, and now they would scatter again to the places where they belonged.

"Watch yourself, sugar," Mrs. Jones called as the ranger gently led her away, touching an elbow to guide her toward the courtroom doors. "Things ain't always what they seem on the face of it. Shallow waters run out. Still waters run deep."

7

JINX SLEPT IN AT THE SUPER 8, called her cousin and her mom to tell them she was still alive, and found an IHOP for lunch because she would eat pancakes anytime.

By late afternoon, she crossed the state line and found the town of Chatsworth, Georgia, sister city to the historic township of Hold Hill, where the Hold Plantation and Moravian mission were located. She followed Highway 411 through the center of town, passing an old inn, boarded up and abandoned, with a massive sign of a caricatured Indian advertising the Chief Hold Hotel. She drove past a brick law office, a flat-roofed diner, and a dive called Chief Hold Video and Tanning that shared a lot with a Marathon gas station. Indian kitsch was always weirdest in places where Native Americans used to be. Jinx rolled her eyes, pulling into the gas station. She had read online that a few motels were located in town, mostly along the main road into the mountains. She would grab a fresh Coke and ask for directions.

"You're not looking for the Hold House, are you?" the girl behind

the counter said. She held out her hand to take Jinx's money for Twizzlers, Coke, and beef jerky. "Because it's all closed down now. No more
tours. We used to get a lot of Indians coming through to visit the place
back when I worked there part-time. Cherokees and Poarch Creeks,
mainly. Are you from North Carolina? Alabama?" The woman was in
her early twenties. She had a bright Southern drawl and rambunctious-
ly curly strawberry hair pinned back at her temples with clip barrettes.
Her sunny smile contrasted with the circles beneath her eyes.

"Oklahoma," Jinx said. "How come there are no more tours?"

"The museum closed a few years ago because of the state budget,
but folks around here held out hope it might reopen someday. The state
auctioned off the place this morning. It's a sad case, to tell you the truth.
It wasn't just General Scott who ran the Cherokees out of this valley.
The local militia was in on it up to their ears. The way I see it, the state
of Georgia is guilty for the part we played. The least we could do is keep
the Hold House open as a show of respect that the Indians were here
before any of us white folks. But I'm going on too much. I always do
that, Eddie says." The young woman handed Jinx her change and shook
her head as though correcting herself.

"Eddie sounds like an idiot," Jinx said, smiling at her.

The woman blinked in surprise, then grinned. "Well, don't tell his
mama that. She'll quit babysitting for me Tuesdays and Thursdays.
Want to drink that now?" She handed Jinx an old-fashioned bottle
opener and leaned forward on the counter.

Jinx popped the top on her frosted Coca-Cola, cradling the thick
green glass. "Heaven," she said, taking a swig. "I'm Jennifer Micco."

"Sally Perdue, no kin to the governor. And I guess you could say I'm
a history buff."

"Nice to meet you, Sally. So who bought the house? Do you know?"

Sally Perdue glanced around the store. Except for a couple in biking
shorts quibbling over the various brands of bottled water and a lone

teenager lurking around the explicit magazines, it was empty. "Well, Mason Allen tried to buy the house. He's a real-estate man and builder whose family goes a long way back in these parts. He spent a month placing ads in the paper about his big plan to build a housing development on the old Hold property. The Cherokee Chieftains Club, he was calling it, 'where the streets are lined with gold.'"

"Sounds a little over the top." Jinx sipped her Coke.

"Not really, not around here. We had our very own gold rush in 1829, when nuggets were discovered on Cherokee land. There's a legend around here that gold is still buried somewhere on the Hold property. They say it dates back to the ancient Indian mound builders who had a village at Etowah. But no one's ever found anything. Allen liked the idea of it, I guess—the symbol of the gold. The development was supposed to be real fancy, with a clubhouse in the original building, half-a-million-dollar homes scattered around it, and a golf course in the old corn and wheat fields. I bet he's steamed he couldn't get his hands on that land. Somebody else bought it right out from under him. A woman from Atlanta." Sally whispered, "A black woman."

Jinx's eyebrows shot up. "Really? Has she moved in yet?"

"She came to town last weekend. Drives a Mercedes." Sally winked. "Looks like she's got what it takes to give Mason Allen a run for his money."

Jinx was quiet, recalibrating.

"You know," Sally continued, "maybe she'd let you see the place. Wouldn't hurt to ask. It's just up the road, past the four-way stoplight. You'll go up a hill and turn right at the iron gates."

"Thanks," Jinx said. "Could you recommend a place to stay around here? For cheap?"

"How long are you fixin' to be in town?"

"Just a few days."

"There's a bed-and-breakfast way up the mountain road, before you reach the entrance to Fort Mountain Park. That'll run you at least a hundred a night. But if you want cheap, I have a neighbor who rents a room in his cabin. He clears out and stays in his tent. Charges thirty bucks a day, and that includes a fair share of whatever he's got in the fridge."

"Is he a good guy?" Jinx said.

"The best. Used to work at the Hold House before they shut it down. Now he gets by how he can, like most of us."

"How would I find this place?"

"It's halfway up the mountain road. A log cabin with a green door and a vegetable garden out front, just past the Ball Fruit Stand that looks like it's falling apart."

"A fruit stand?"

"The Ball Fruit Stand. The sign fell off its hooks, but you can still make out the lettering. My grandparents used to own it, but they lost the land due to taxes. Oh, here! Try this." Sally reached below the counter and handed Jinx a canning jar wrapped in a decorative red-checked square of cloth. "Strawberry preserves. I learned how to make homemade jams from my grandma. They used to sell the freshest fruit at that stand, sweet and juicy like you wouldn't believe, a lot of it grown right over in the Hold House orchards. There's still plenty of good fruit there, even though the state let the grounds go to pot. You just gotta hike through the high grass and brambles. My jams are pretty popular around town. My boss pretends like he doesn't know I'm selling them, in exchange for jars for his wife. She likes the peach."

"This looks delicious," Jinx said. "How much do you charge?"

"It's a gift. Stop back in before you leave town and say hello." Sally reached for Jinx's empty Coke bottle. "I'll take that for you."

"Thank you. I'll be sure to do that," Jinx said, grabbing her plastic bag of snacks, along with the jar of jam. The teen was loafing his way to the counter with a computer gaming magazine. Jinx headed for the exit.

"If you stay at Adam Battis's cabin, tell him I sent you," Sally called. "I live just up the road from him, in a white trailer."

Jinx stopped in her tracks. Adam *Battis?* Then, through the convenience-store window cluttered with decals and obscured by two-liter Sprite bottles, Jinx saw the lot suddenly fill. Three men pulled up in a roar of sound: engines, brakes, and revved-up voices. Rifles hung at the rear of their vehicles. A dead doe, her neck nearly severed, flopped in one of the truck beds. The men jumped from their cabs, cloaked in Day-Glo hunting vests. They yanked the gasoline hoses free and filled their tanks.

The teenager squeezed past Jinx, who had frozen in place, holding the door ajar.

"Speak of the devil," Sally Perdue said. "Mason Allen hunting with firearms before the season's open. He must be madder than hell today."

Taking her cue from Sally, who had gone rigid as a scarecrow, Jinx fixed her eyes on the man striding toward the building. He pushed past her as if she were invisible. The smell of sweat mixed with cologne escaped his skin in the tight space of the doorway. Jinx backed into a rack of free advertising circulars, watching the other two men follow in the first's footsteps.

"Why didn't you get him, Mase?" one of the men called out while he grabbed a six-pack from the cooler. The couple in biking shorts made their way to the checkout with bottles of Evian and pouches of granola.

"I told you I didn't have the angle, Tom," the first man responded in a low voice.

"Lay off, Tom," the third man said. "Mason's had a tough day. Probably doesn't feel right hunting in the Hold House woods now that somebody else holds the deed."

Mason Allen's face went red as he turned to his fellow. "If I didn't feel right hunting in those woods, I wouldn't have suggested it, Frank. I still own all the property around the Hold estate, which is more than any other man in this town can say. I'll hunt any place I damn well please. Nothing's changed."

"Sure, Mase," the third man said. "We know that. Why don't you come over to the house tonight? I'll have Jules clean up the deer. We'll have venison, some good draft pints, and Betty's fresh chess pie. We can shoot some pool in the billiard room and relax."

Jinx watched Mason Allen's temper drain. He had accepted the peace offering.

"She won't last in that big old house," the second man said. "Wild animals in the woods. Weeds and vermin."

"Right," said Mason Allen. "She won't last a week."

With a last glance toward Sally, who was ringing up the couple's things, Jinx hustled to her truck. Turning out of the parking lot, she headed in the direction of a tree-covered mountain jutting into the sky.

Jinx followed the two-lane road through town, past chicken coops and an old sawmill. As the road climbed, the buildings and yards spread farther apart beside it. A forest sprang up to her left, throwing shade. Jinx spotted a dilapidated ruin of white wood and lattice, where a faded, peeling sign on the ground pictured a blush-orange peach on the stem: *Ball Fruit Stand*. She peered into breaks in the trees beyond the stand and spotted a small log cabin with dark green shutters and a porch set with two red rocking chairs. She turned down the dirt road, passing raised garden beds crowded with cornstalks, sunflowers, and tomatoes. She passed a small woodshed and parked by an old pump well.

"Hello?" Jinx called into the yard. No one answered. She climbed the porch steps and knocked on the closed screen door. Nothing. A handwritten Guests Check Here sign was taped to a tin mailbox on the porch floor. Jinx opened the lid. An envelope was inside. "Instructions for Guests," it read. The note invited visitors to use the enclosed key to let themselves in, to put a sign on the front door, and to leave thirty dollars in the box; it also provided a number to call if they needed anything. *Trusting guy*, Jinx thought. *Or crazy guy.* She rifled through the supply of mini-flashlights and one-size-fits-all rain ponchos in the mailbox and saw a stack of creased motel-style Do Not Disturb signs. She was too curious to turn around and leave, too strapped to pay B&B prices. Besides, Adam Battis had to come home sometime, and Jinx wanted to find out exactly who he was. She pulled the key out of the envelope and unlocked the cabin door.

The building was designed with an open layout of around six hundred square feet. A loft bed with a futon underneath was built into the wall to the left of the entry door. A sign taped to the futon frame read, *For Guests.* A stone fireplace was the focal point, encircled by a plaid sofa and ladder-back wooden chair. Outdated gas appliances and a scratched round table and chairs made up a kitchen area in the rear corner. The space was neat and clean and smelled like pine trees. There was little clutter to offer clues about the man who lived here—no photographs on the dresser, no pictures on the wall, no dirty dishes in the sink. A bag of dry cat food hunched on the kitchen counter, but she saw no sign of a cat.

Instead of trinkets or photos or pets, this man collected books. Built-in bookshelves sandwiched the fireplace and wrapped around the living-room walls. The titles were labeled by category, then by genre— *Fiction: Literary, Mystery, Speculative; Nonfiction: Religion, Science, Mythology.* The bookshelf by the futon was labeled *Local Interest* and held books on Cherokee history, Georgia history, plantation architecture, Southern gardening, and the Appalachian Trail. Brochures and maps had a home on the shelf, along with a laminated field guide to birds and a bin of vintage postcards marked at a dollar each. Between Mother Goose at the bookstore, Sally at the gas station, and the mysterious

Adam Battis, Southern hospitality had reached heights of eccentricity Jinx had never imagined.

She went out to get her duffle and messenger bags, then hung the Do Not Disturb sign on the front door. She rummaged in the fridge and cupboards and made herself buttered toast with gobs of Sally's homemade jam, uttering an involuntary "Hmm" as she bit into a piece. Jinx washed her dishes and made up the futon with the striped bed-sheets folded at the foot. She heaved the heavy church history out of her duffle bag and situated two bed pillows along the back of the futon. Sitting up against them, she pushed her legs in front of her and listened for the sound of a car approaching. She would read while she waited for Adam Battis to appear. She had a few questions she'd like to ask him about a girl named Mary Ann.

Jinx opened the book to the title page: *A History of the United Brethren in America, Inclusive of Abstracts of the Hold Hill Mission of the Cherokee Nation, 1815–1825, kept by our brethren and sisters who journeyed into the darkness of the heathen Indian lands.* She skimmed the chronicle of church events in Eastern Europe, Pennsylvania, and North Carolina, making her way toward the section on the Cherokee mission on the Hold Plantation:

> What follows is an accounting of the Hold Hill Mission to the Cherokees. The chronicle is based on the diary of Missionary Anna Rosina Kliest Gamble, as recalled by her favorite pupil and Indian sister in Christ, Mary Ann Battis, who gave the story in a letter to the clerk of the Church before her death in 1886. The diary of Mrs. Gamble, known only to her pupil, is lost now to history. It was, the Indian sister related, full of anecdotes, sometimes even of thrilling interest, particularly those in reference to the celebrated James Hold & his contemporaries. After her mother's early death, Mrs. Gamble was raised to great success in the Bethlehem orphanage and boarding school. She taught sixteen years in the Female Academy at

Bethlehem. Later in life, she was a very efficient help in the Missionary labors of Br. John Gamble and became the Hold Hill Mission's chief diarist. It is to be regretted that Mrs. Gamble had no biographer, & even astonishing that she was not her own, as she was passionately fond of her pen & wrote about almost everything, excepting herself. Her command of English, both written and spoken, was exceptional. Her gifted mind possessed a poetic fancy. She left many pages of manuscript, which we fear have been lost. Gathered here is all that remains, as recalled by her devoted pupil.

An immediate picture of Mrs. Gamble affixed itself to Jinx's mind—based, she guessed, on her brief encounter with Moravian history in graduate school, as well as a hazy image of Laura Ingalls Wilder's mother from the *Little House on the Prairie* television show. She envisioned a kindly middle-aged woman with graying light brown hair swept up into a modest bun. On top of Mrs. Gamble's head rested a thin covering trimmed with hand-worked lace. Contented with her conjured image, Jinx continued to read:

After the restoration of peace following the Cherokee War with the English in 1760, it was decided by the Church to establish a Mission among the Cherokees, but the Indians were not then receptive. In the wake of the American War of Independence, which changed the balance of power in the region, our ambassadors received a friendly reception from James Hold, a chief of the upper Cherokee towns, who said if the Brethren should open a grammar school for their children, we might come and make a trial of teaching the Gospel also. The upper chiefs came to our ambassadors, bid them welcome, & shook them by the right hand as a sign of friendship. James Hold appropriated land for the use of the Mission & directed his Negroes to assist our Brethren in enlarging an existing cabin. According to the instructions agreed upon in the meeting, we were not to concentrate on the Indians alone but to give some attention to the half Indians and the Negroes also, many of whom were slaves.

At last the Revd. John Gamble, an experienced and faithful Minister of the Brethren's Church, who had already been on a visit to Hold Hill and was well known to Mr. James Hold, felt himself called upon to accept an appointment as principal Missionary from our Church to the Cherokees. His respected wife, who had entered into the married state but a few months before, after having served for many years as principal Tutoress in the School for young ladies at Bethlehem in Pennsylvania, accompanied him. Mrs. Gamble had, two years prior, accompanied the Revd. Loskiel in a visit to our Indian Congregation in Ohio. Her mind opened to the plight of the Aborigines of America, she found herself called into Mission service. Out of interest and care for the Indians, she joined herself to Mr. Gamble, who sought a spouse to assist him in our Missionary labours amongst the Cherokees. There, by the Lord's blessings, Mrs. Gamble's gifts proved a particular benefit for the Scholars at Hold Hill.

Besides providing food and raiment for the scholars, keeping school daily, acting as physician, entertaining visitors, writing letters, & on Sunday teaching the Gospel, Mrs. Gamble, kept, in the midst of this wilderness, a botanic garden, containing many exotic and medicinal plants listed by their Linnaean names. To her friends at Salem and Pennsylvania, besides, Mrs. Gamble sent between twelve and fourteen hundred specimens of dried plants, & near a hundred packets of seeds, several minerals, specimens of all the Indian manufactures of cane and a number of other curiosities.

In early March, 1815, the Gambles arrived at Hold Hill, the plantation of Mr. Hold, which is about eighty miles from Tellico Blockhouse, Tennessee. Mr. Hold was a half Indian but in his dress & color & conduct was quite like a white man. Mr. Hold had there two wives, who kept busy spinning and weaving cotton. He had ninety Negroes and a German overseer who took care of the plantation. Mr. Hold had about one hundred heads of horses. He traded mostly to Charleston and Augusta, & many people came from afar to trade with him.

Mr. Hold resided in a fine brick house, the first of its kind in the Cherokee country, with a dignified doorway and bridge-like stairway that was much wondered upon by visitors. Hold's house had a large and spacious yard with many beautiful roses and shade trees, & somewhere in this yard, it was rumored, lay a hidden treasure. The Georgia settlers say it is a trench of pure gold buried by the mound building Indians who dwelled in this valley in ancient times. These stories have never been confirmed. Beyond Hold's home and fields, his mill at the creek, & his ferry at the Conasauga, all was perfectly wild.

Jinx forgot she was reading as she tunneled deeper into the world of the 1800s. Afternoon sunlight speckled the windows, filtered through a bank of pines. Unseen birds called from perches high in the treetops. Jinx drifted off to sleep with the weighty book pressed to her chest, reducing her breathing to shallow draws of dreamlike air.

8

CHEYENNE FINGERED THE FINE LACE CURTAINS flowing against the glass in the Hold House master bedroom. She opened the chestnut wardrobe, unzipped her Louis Vuitton suitcase, and lifted out her dresses, blouses, and skirts. As she put her things carefully away, Cheyenne imagined what life was like two hundred years ago, when the home was illuminated only by candlelight and the man of the house would have come home riding a steed. She pictured Chief James Hold, dark and chiseled like the male models on the covers of her historical romance novels. The house was still. The room was quiet around her except for the scratching that seemed to come from behind one of the many shut doors.

She smoothed back the dampening hair at her forehead. She left the room, crossed the odd interior bridge, and descended the staircase, thrilling again to the echo of her heels on the floorboards of her dream house. She made her way into the drawing room, approached a window, and drew back the golden curtains. Her eyes fell on the ornate furnishings, on the fine film of dust. She thought fleetingly of something she had heard once on *The View*: 80 percent of dust is made up of dead skin cells that people shed in the daily course of life, which meant that in any person's home—on the dusty bookshelves and window sills—were bits and pieces of the resident's former self. Did dust from a thousand lives settle into the crevices of an old house like this one, forming sediment as deep as an archaeological pit? Cheyenne didn't want to think so.

She untied another of her Jackie O scarves and let the hair of her ponytail fall gently to her shoulders. And before she knew what she intended, she found herself dusting the room. The silk scarf, thin and delicate, fluttered in Cheyenne's hand, caressing the indentations of the carved fireplace mantel. Dust rose and fell again onto the oak floorboards, soft as a newborn snowfall. Through the windows, she could see that dusk had stolen in and settled itself upon the grounds. High in the cottonwood trees, katydids hummed. Cheyenne draped her sullied scarf across the Tiffany fireplace screen. She was stunned at the lateness of the hour. She had skipped every meal that day and was starting to feel it. She wondered if she would still be able to find a takeout salad in town.

Cheyenne stepped out of the Hold House into an evening humid after the day's long heat. She locked the front doors behind her with the heavy notched key that Lanie Brevard had handed to her at the courthouse. Sweat pooled in the hollow between her breasts beneath the wine-colored silk. September was turning out to be one of the hottest on record in Georgia, with temperatures hovering in the nineties.

As she stood on the wide front porch fanning herself with an open hand, Cheyenne heard a rustling in a bank of azalea bushes. She narrowed her eyes, scanning the shrubbery for rabbits, opossums, or rabid raccoons and vowing to buy a can of pepper spray at the next opportunity. But this was no small animal. The man who emerged from behind a utility shed raised his hand in a gesture of greeting—or maybe guilt, given that he was trespassing.

Cheyenne squinted in the dark, her heart racing to catch her panic. She backed into the porch's shadows and fumbled for the door key. Forged of heavy brass like the others on the ring, the key felt like a rock in her fist. She aimed it, hand shaking, at the waiting lock. But what had been easy a moment ago seemed impossible now. The lock resisted as the stranger approached. He walked the curving stone path beside the overgrown formal garden, then stopped twenty feet away from the front porch. Cheyenne fished the Blackberry from her purse, stabbed 911, then swore aloud in a whisper. Her cell phone got no signal here. The nearby mountains and steep dip to the river made her new plantation house a pre-tech lockbox. She realized just how vulnerable these isolated fourteen acres made her.

"Excuse me, ma'am," the man said. "I didn't mean to startle you. I didn't realize you had moved in yet."

His deep voice and green uniform were little data feeds that let Cheyenne take a breath. She paused with a finger hanging over her useless cell phone. She recognized this man. The park ranger.

"The name's Adam, Battis," he said, standing at a distance, slowly rolling the vowels on his tongue. "I'm with the Georgia Parks and Recreation unit of the Department of Natural Resources. I work here— used to, that is. The Hold House was my responsibility, and since I live close by, I've been keeping an eye on the place ever since they closed it."

Cheyenne took in all she could of him through the evening shadows. He was tall and stood with a wide-legged stance that projected subtle confidence, an ease in his own skin. His eyes flashed through the dusk with a dark intensity. He was holding a bag of cat food and a Maglite. *Cat food?* She zoomed in on this random detail, putting aside for a second the thought that he lived nearby, a possible comfort or possible threat.

"We met this afternoon, didn't we? Almost. Cheyenne Cotterell. Why are you carrying pet food?"

"For the feral cats. This plantation's full of them, mostly in the out-buildings, though one or two have been known to slip inside the main house. They're wild, I know. They can hunt. But I don't like to think of them being out here on their own for too long. I should've waited 'til daylight to come by, but I didn't know anyone had moved in yet," he repeated. "Need some help with that?"

Cheyenne knew he meant the lock. What she didn't know was whether he was a Good Samaritan or a disgruntled ex-employee who might go postal. Everyone who worked at the Hold House had been fired or reassigned when the place closed. There was bound to be some bad blood out there, some resentment at the recent turn of events.

"No! No thank you. I was just double-checking things, double-checking the doors. My husband and I wanted to make sure the house was locked up tight for the night."

The man looked skeptical, then amused, or so Cheyenne thought, trying to read his eyes.

"I understand." He paused. "And if that husband of yours deserves you, he probably ought to give you a ring."

Cheyenne turned her back on him. She heard the tease of a smile in his voice and knew he had seen right through her. She felt a tug. He was sharp. And fine. And unemployed. But she would probably never see him again. She considered turning to face him, offering him an inviting smile. Being a beauty had always made her bold. She was comfortable with one-night stands, and in fact preferred them. Until she found the one she would marry and make her mother happy with, men were like throw pillows: necessary clutter. She could have this country ranger dumbstruck and panting in less than five seconds and be back at work on her dream home in the morning.

Cheyenne rolled her shoulders back and turned to hit Adam with her irresistible full-lipped smile. Her loose mane of straight hair flew as she turned, spilling loosely across her breasts. It took her only a second, instead of the five she had planned on, to realize that something had changed. The path before her was empty. The ranger was already gone.

The shock Cheyenne felt was disarming. When before had a man failed to linger as she walked away, failed to steal just one more look at her? Maybe he was gay. She bit the corner of her lip, fit her key into the lock, pushed on the doors. The strangeness of the evening hadn't diluted her hunger. It had made the gnawing in her stomach grow worse. She sat on the teal divan in the drawing room, replaying the scene in her mind until thirty minutes had passed. She was giving Adam the park ranger plenty of time to clear out of her yard. There was no way she wanted to lay eyes on him now. There was also no chance she would find a decent restaurant open this late. She would have to locate a grocery store if she wanted to eat anything at all. Cheyenne sighed, grabbed her purse, and headed for the Piggly Wiggly.

The city of Dalton was twenty minutes west of the Chief Hold House. Twenty minutes just to reach a facsimile of civilization. The Room with a View Bed-and-Breakfast, where Cheyenne had stayed on Fort Mountain Road, stocked a cooler of grocery items in its gift shop. Now Cheyenne could see why. She would have to do something similar when she transformed the Hold House—serve breakfast and afternoon tea to her guests and run a high-end commissary.

She pulled her sports coupe into the lot at the Piggly Wiggly, a name that conjured warring thoughts of three dancing little pigs and roasted pork loin. Popular culture had lately decided pork was "the other white meat," but Cheyenne didn't trust it. She had given up pork chops and steak years ago, along with baked goods, potatoes, rice, and cheese. She had caught on early that her looks were something special, that she was, as her mother said, a true natural beauty. And true beauty had to be protected, just like fine art and architectural landmarks.

Cheyenne had learned that lesson well. In sixth grade, when she had started filling out, her mother noticed a ripple of flesh across Cheyenne's stomach. "Oh, no, honey," she had said. "We're not having that. Hold that belly in. A true beauty like you can't afford fat." So Cheyenne had held it in, every day, until she forgot what it felt like not to clasp her muscles like a knot of tightly coiled rope. As she entered high school, and her breasts took shape and hips flared out, her stomach remained as flat as a girl's. She made sure of that. When her body struck back at her, it was with hunger, a clutch at the gut that couldn't be satiated with all the rice cakes in the world. Like the clawing feeling of emptiness she felt right now that had brought her to the Piggly Wiggly.

The parking lot was nearly vacant. Cheyenne parked two spaces from a green Ford truck that looked like it belonged in an old car show. She eased out into the evening, feeling the sticky residue of the day's heat. From the seat of an idling motorcycle, a young man eyed her. He was white with bad-boy tattoos, rumpled hair, and thick eyelashes. Back in Atlanta with the safety of her friends nearby, she might have done him if they had met in a trendy club. Her mother wouldn't have approved, of course. Her mother wanted her married yesterday to a black man from a black family that was wealthy and fair-skinned, just like theirs. The guy with the tattoos smiled at her, letting his eyes roll over her figure. Cheyenne avoided his gaze, stepping quickly away.

The sliding doors swooshed. She entered the cool space, thinking this had been new once. Now it just looked tired, worn, and grungy, a grocery store past its prime. She picked up a basket and headed for the produce aisle, holding her purse on the elbow of her other arm. Cheyenne skimmed the signs. Where were the organics? She would give anything for a Whole Foods right now. After five minutes, she gave up, settling for pre-bagged iceberg lettuce, floppy celery sticks, and wan tomatoes that should have had a few more days in the sun.

"Good evening, Piggly Wiggly customers," a canned voice came over the loudspeaker. "Our store will be closing in fifteen minutes. Please bring your final selections to a register, and have a good night."

Cheyenne looked at her paltry basket. She would have made a poor wife back in the Cherokees' day, when the men hunted and the women gathered fruits and nuts. She lifted a bag of wilted sprouts and found unsalted California almonds. She hurried to the dairy aisle, where she fingered a package of low-fat dip.

"You only live once. Go for the good stuff," a deep voice said behind her.

Cheyenne whirled. Adam the park ranger. The third time today. He had already changed since she saw him prowling her grounds. His wavy hair glistened from a shower. He smelled like Irish Spring and pinesap. He had discarded the park-service uniform and was dressed in worn blue jeans, a dark green T-shirt, and brown leather sandals. She felt disheveled next to him, rumpled and sweaty, even though he was in Levis and she was in Donna Karan silk. She also felt as if she had been caught doing something shameful.

"The dip," he explained. "You can do better than low-fat."

"I don't really eat dip," Cheyenne said. "I was just looking for the soy milk."

"The milk is that way." He pointed down the wall.

"Of course. Thanks." Cheyenne worked to regain her bearings. This was not how things went with her. She was calm. She was poised. She wrapped men around her little finger. Cheyenne rolled her shoulders straight, accentuating the swell of her breasts. "Adam, I'm afraid I may have been rude when you came to the house tonight. I wasn't expecting anyone, and I'm not especially familiar with the area."

"I made a mistake coming by." He leaned down, resting his elbows on his cart, bringing his eyes to her level. Cheyenne took in the cart's contents: pork chops, drumsticks, brown rice, cereal, eggs, tortilla chips, olive oil, cat food. "I should have known I might startle you. I just assumed you'd be going back to Atlanta and coming up next weekend to start making the place your own."

"How did you know I'm from Atlanta?"

"It's a small town. People talk. Plus, you look it."

"I look what?" Cheyenne flipped her gleaming hair and let it fall back into place. Adam watched the motion with something behind his eyes, something she wasn't used to. Amusement.

"Rich," he said.

"Well." Cheyenne puffed herself up, shocked by his bluntness. "There are a few people with money around here, too, I've noticed."

"We've got our kingpins. But mostly, people who live here full-time struggle to get by."

Cheyenne's eyes dropped. "About the Hold House. You said you used to work there. I hope you understand that the state would have sold it no matter what, whether it was me who bought it or someone else."

"Oh, believe me, I understand. What are your plans for the house? Weekend getaway? Rental property?"

"No," Cheyenne said. "Nothing like that." She felt as if she should explain, as though she needed to defend her actions. A word came to mind that she had never associated with herself: *shallow*. It's what that elderly woman, Delta Jones, had said to her in the courthouse, spouting riddles like some kind of sphinx. *Shallow waters run out. Still waters run deep.* Cheyenne took a breath. "I've been dreaming about that house for a long time. My family history starts at that place—at least I'm fairly certain it does. I believe my ancestor was once the mistress on the Hold Plantation. I'm going to take care of it now, renovate it, and run a bed-and-breakfast there. It will be better than it ever was before."

Adam's brow wrinkled, as if he were trying to remember some buried fact. Cheyenne couldn't read the expression in his eyes.

"So . . . you're planning to stay here full-time," he said.

"That's right. And I'm sure I'll need help on the place. Employees. Maybe I could hire you back, once I get things off the ground."

Adam's dark eyes flashed. "Thanks for the thought," he said. "I'm doing all right on my own. But you know, there is one thing. A favor."

Cheyenne's eyes widened. Her long lashes fluttered. He wanted something from her. She was dying to hear what.

"I have a friend. Her name is Sally Perdue. She's accustomed to picking fruit—peaches and apples, mostly—in the orchards on the Hold property. I've been taking care of the trees since the museum closed, and they're in good shape, producing well. It would crush Sally if she didn't have access to the land anymore."

Cheyenne blinked. Not exactly what she was expecting. "What does your friend look like?"

Adam's eyebrow rose.

"So I'll know her when I see her."

"Redhead, blue eyes, petite," he answered.

Well, well, Cheyenne thought. *First Mason Allen and now Sally Perdue. More competition.* Who would have guessed that a Podunk town would present her with a challenge? Toni, Layla, and De'Sha would get a smug laugh out of this one. Cheyenne Cotterell passed over for a Southern Little Orphan Annie—red-haired, probably spunky, and poor enough to steal fruit.

"I'd like to meet her," Cheyenne lied. "In the meantime, please tell Sally she can borrow all the fruit she'd like."

"Thanks, I will," Adam said. "But a person doesn't really borrow fruit, right? Once you've got it, you don't give it back."

"Of course. And that's exactly how I feel about the Hold House," Cheyenne said. "They're closing at nine o'clock. We'd better go pay."

With one last glance at Adam the park ranger and his night-sky eyes, Cheyenne whisked her basket to the checkout aisle.

Back at the house, she closed and locked the oversized doors and scooted a box of museum brochures against them for good measure. Running into Adam had made her feel uneasy for the second time that night, as if a familiar item didn't quite fit her anymore, like a pair of favorite leather shoes that had shifted their perfect shape over time. But of course it wasn't the shoes that changed in a case like that. It was the wearer. Locked inside her new old house, alone and a little shaken, Cheyenne considered what to do next. The house felt huge, wide, and empty, as if it were yawning into the hillside. She flipped on a light switch in every room as she walked through the first floor, eating a handful of almonds as she went. She drank a glass of water, then rinsed her face in the single sink of the three-quarter bath. She retrieved the scarf she had used to dust the drawing room, rinsed and wrung out the fabric, and hung it on a hook.

Through the small bathroom window, Cheyenne heard the rumble of a four-wheel-drive fade into the night. Her ears pricked. A truck or SUV had been nearby, maybe as close as the parking lot that the museum used to operate. Had Adam the park ranger followed her home in the vintage green Ford? Now, that would be interesting. But if he had thought to pursue her, he had changed his mind. The yard outside was quiet.

Cheyenne breathed a sigh of relief tinged with disappointment, climbed the stairs, and crossed the interior bridge. Back in the bedroom of Chief James Hold, she kicked off her pumps and unclasped the waistband of her skirt. Briskly rubbing her chilled upper arms, she changed into satin pajamas the color of ripe apricots. Her thoughts went to Sally

Perdue, to Adam Battis, to Delta Jones. It felt wrong, almost rude, to jump inside the bedsheets. She really didn't know this house very well. Cheyenne frowned, wondering why she felt such reserve with a building when she had slipped between scores of men's sheets on the first date.

She stood again, scanning the room, looking for an answer. In the far corner, she discovered a linen press with a frayed patchwork quilt inside. She unfolded the faded covering and wrapped it around her shoulders, then curled up on top of the canopy bed. Except for the distant creaks and sighs of the settling foundation, the house grew quiet around her. Cheyenne allowed her eyes to close and leaned into the pillows, trying to ignore the feeling that she wasn't alone.

9

ADAM BATTIS HADN'T COME BACK to his cabin last night, at least not as far as Jinx could tell. She showered, dressed, and ate a bowl of his Honey Nut Cheerios while she called her cousin on her cell phone.

"Geez, Jinx, what time is it?" Victor said. Jinx could imagine him running his hand through his long, tangled hair.

"Nine o'clock my time. Eight o'clock yours."

"Oh, you're cruel."

"You should be up anyway. You have fires to fight."

"Not today I don't. So what's going on? Did you find the plantation? Do they still sell Cokes with the original cocaine formula down there?"

"That's obscene."

"But accurate. Look it up on the Internet."

"I haven't found the plantation yet, but I did luck into a couple of local connections. I'm staying at some guy's cabin. He may be able to tell me something about the history."

"Some guy's place? You? Now I know the Coke is drugged."

"He rents it out, Victor. I haven't even met him yet. I need to track him down after I visit the plantation today."

"Sounds like you found the yellow brick road. You know what they say: follow it. Everything is fine out here, since you didn't ask. I'm holding down the fort at Aunt Angie's House of Curious Antiquities."

Jinx sighed. "Why do I call you?"

"Because you can't help yourself. Take care down there, little sister."

After the call, Jinx drove down the mountain road, passed the Marathon station, and came across the wrought-iron gates Sally had described. She turned in through the elaborate ironwork opening, followed the long paved road, and inched beneath oak trees draped in the kudzu so pervasive that people thought it was native to the South. She drove toward a gravel lot half a mile ahead, where a white Volkswagen was already parked. Farther in the distance but within walking range of the lot, a svelte Mercedes sports coupe nestled in front of a big brick house. The new owner, it appeared, was at home. And she had company.

Blackberry in one hand and Burberry bag in the other, Cheyenne pushed on the doors. She stepped onto the wide front porch, leaned against a column, and was surprised to nearly trip on something beneath it. An old-fashioned picnic basket had been tucked beside the base of the column. She stooped, opened the wooden lid, and peeled back the cotton dishtowel. Inside were golden corn muffins, fresh red tomatoes, Vidalia onions, loose-leaf lettuce, citrus vinaigrette, a bottle of milk imprinted with the name of a local dairy, and homemade strawberry jam. The note attached read, "Welcome. Adam. P.S. Sorry no soy."

Cheyenne brought her lips together, then smiled to herself. His gift was surprising, discriminating, and . . . gallant. It almost made her want to rise to the occasion and eat a homemade muffin slathered in butter.

Almost, but not quite. She lifted the basket with both hands and glanced toward the distant gates. Two cars had appeared from out of nowhere. A Volkswagen Beetle sat idling in the lot. A rusty red pickup was crawling up the road. And to the left of the house, where she had seen Adam walking last night, her azaleas had been beheaded. Cheyenne sucked in a breath. The beautiful shrubs that had framed her front yard were barren at the tops, their lush leaves and pink flowers lopped off like a bad haircut. Someone had taken a weed-whacker or hedge trimmer to them. Someone with time, a ladder, and a grudge. *Oh, my God. Who could have done this?* Cheyenne's thoughts turned again to Adam. *No. Impossible.* When she had seen him in the yard, the azaleas were intact. This had happened while she was gone, while they were both at the grocery store. Or it had happened while she slept, after she heard the vehicle. Cheyenne tried to arrange the pieces in her mind. And then a woman was stepping out of the car in the parking lot, and the truck was inching closer along the drive.

Ruth switched off the engine and emerged from her car as if from a cocoon. A wall of wet heat smacked her in the face, steaming her tortoise-shell glasses. It had to be eighty degrees out there, and it was only late morning. She stared blindly, then thought to pull the glasses off, wiping them on her T-shirt and placing them on her nose. She was standing in a gravel lot beside a small, abandoned shed meant for a parking attendant. Before her, a gravel road stretched like a ribbon toward a stately brick building. Ruth squinted at the house through the leaves of oak trees that followed the line of the road. It appeared reserved, withholding in its elegance, facing north from atop a hill. Classic in structure, the house revealed elements of the Federal and Georgian architectural styles. Every built facet from windows to porches to tripod eaves was perfectly proportioned to signify authority. This was the house of a patriarch, turned soft at the edges from old age and experience.

The road made a graceful loop before the house, rejoined itself, and wound out toward the iron gates. A woman stood on the porch holding a picnic basket, staring in her direction. Ruth thought better of driving beyond the public lot. That might seem presumptuous. She would leave her car and approach the house on foot. She started up the path. When she passed the fifth oak, Ruth caught a glimpse of the woman's features, which were coming together in a sickeningly familiar way. Her heart gave a little kick. *Could it be? Of course not. Maybe. Shoot!* By the tenth oak, she knew for sure. Dressed in a flattering lemon tank dress was Ruth's best friend from summer camp—the best friend she couldn't stand. The woman's hair was brushed back into a shiny ponytail. A cluster of gems glimmered from the center of her headband. A classic Black American Princess, BAP, from birth, Cheyenne Cotterell had finally gone and gotten herself a tiara.

"Ruthie Mayes! That can't be you!" Cheyenne pounced with the grace of a hungry feline, crossing the distance between them and throwing her arms around Ruth. "I just can't believe it. After all these years. You look exactly the same, girl! Just your natural self. And you still have that great full figure, I see. I can't tell you how good it is to see an old friend here, someone I know and trust."

Ruth cringed at the nickname she had shed years ago, pronounced in that lightly lacquered Southern accent. Cheyenne Cotterell was exactly the same, too: exquisitely polished, perfectly shaped, and swinging impossibly straight, dark hair that Ruth had always suspected was a weave. It was just like Cheyenne to bury a dig in the rut of a compliment. To Cheyenne, *natural* meant *uncouth*, and *full-figured* was *fat*.

"Now, tell me everything. What brings you back to Georgia? I know it's not to finally meet your grandparents, God rest them. Wait, I know!

You came to tour the Hold House. How ironic!" She laughed. "This old place is mine now. And let me tell you, I could use some company."

"Yours?" Ruth said, hoping she hadn't heard right.

"Mine. As of yesterday. Buying it seemed like the perfect opportunity to start a boutique B&B and explore my Indian roots. I had a successful career and all the men I could want in the city, but life is short, now that we're over thirty. I needed something more. So here I am, the proud new owner of a Cherokee plantation. But why am I blathering on about my boring life? What's up with you, girl? What have you been doing with yourself these last ten years? Don't even try to book a hotel room while you're in this teacup town. I insist you stay with me."

The rush of words was overwhelmingly familiar—the coyness, the bossiness, the sickeningly sweet narcissism that stunk like rotting flowers left in the vase too long. Ruth looked over her shoulder at her getaway car. She needed to extricate herself before this got any worse.

Cheyenne followed Ruth's gaze. "Is she with you?" She gestured toward a woman stepping from the pickup beside Ruth's Beetle. Dressed in rumpled shorts, with a long, dark braid looped around the back of her neck, the woman held her hand up to her forehead like a visor, taking in the scene.

"No," Ruth said with interest. "I've never seen her before."

"Another tourist, I bet. The house museum's been closed for years, but I've been warned they keep on coming to gawk at the exterior. Let's go in and catch up. She'll figure it out." Cheyenne started up the stairs to the veranda.

Ruth glanced back at the woman, who had slung a messenger bag over her shoulder and was loping on long, lean legs toward the house, a look of purpose on her face. "She's already seen us standing here. To walk off would be rude, Cheyenne. Why don't we wait a minute, and you can explain that the place is closed."

"Ruthie, there's a sign. It says *Closed*. I'm sure that woman can read."

Ruth scowled. Cheyenne had always talked down to her—a high-school queen bee addressing the friendless fat girl. Ruth bristled at the memory of feeling dependent, the new kid at camp desperately needing help to fit in. After her mother's death, her father had sent her to Idlewood, a summer tradition in her mother's family. He said she would learn about her African American culture there. But Ruth had known he just wanted to be rid of her, especially as she grew older and began to mirror her mother's looks. She had resented being sent away by her father and then being claimed as a project by Cheyenne, the only one at camp who would toss her a bone, because their grandparents had known each other. Cheyenne ruled Idlewood. Whatever she wore set the trend. Whatever she said went. Whichever boy she wanted to date was hers for the taking. Even the counselors loved her. And now Cheyenne owned a famous riverfront home, while Ruth still lived in a basement apartment and went to a coin-op laundry. She'd left behind the painful memories of childhood a decade ago, and she hadn't come all this way to relive them now.

Sighing, Ruth did the math. Seventeen hours back to Minneapolis. Six weeks in her empty apartment. The loss of the most interesting story she had come across at *Abode*. And there was that woman, whose purposeful look had given Ruth an inner jolt. Something about the woman's stance, the ease of her limbs in motion, made Ruth want to know more.

Ruth gave in and followed Cheyenne up to the imposing entryway. The windows on either side of the doors cut sunlight into diamond-shaped patterns. The front lock was oblong and intricate, shielded by a slender cover. Etched into the rounded knob below the lock was the barely discernible outline of a rose. With one last curious glance at the stranger walking the alley of oaks, Ruth trailed Cheyenne into the waiting house.

Jinx fanned herself in the heat, following the gravel path, shifting the weight of her messenger bag from one shoulder to the other. She reached the doorway through which the women had vanished and pressed her thumb to the antique bell. The chime echoed through the walls. Moments later, the doors swung open. Two arresting African American women faced her across the threshold. The woman to the right with her hand on the knob was poised and svelte and had classically lovely features, a coffee-and-cream complexion, and a crisp ponytail that caressed the nape of her neck. Jinx could picture her on the cover of a bridal magazine, holding a single white lily and dripping pearls. This one grasped the doorknob possessively—she must be the woman who had bought the house. The other was shorter and generously figured, her tight, animated curls spilling over a cloth headband to loop around the tops of her ears. Her skin was a rich, powdery cinnamon. Her eyes, a semisweet chocolate-brown, overwhelmed tortoiseshell glasses that sat off-kilter on the bridge of her nose. Jinx looked a second too long at those eyes, deeply dark and withholding.

"Can I help you?" said Ponytail with a look of piqued interest as she took in Jinx's Gathering of Nations powwow T-shirt.

"I hope so. I'm Jennifer Micco. I'm a writer from Oklahoma doing research on Creek and Cherokee history. I understand you're the new owner of the site. I was hoping to talk with you about the history of this house and the Christian mission that used to be on the property."

"I see. And you're with what publication?"

"The *Muscogee Nation News*, my tribal newspaper. I write a history column. The Moravian mission school that used to operate here educated a member of my tribe. I'd like to write an in-depth story on her. I know the house is closed to the public now, but I thought there might be some records related to the mission here, and that I might be permitted to take a look."

"Who would have thought my little plantation would attract all this attention so soon? Ruth here is a writer, too. She was just telling me about the story she wants to do for a home-and-garden magazine based in Minneapolis. We were about to discuss my plans to renovate the property and reopen the house as a boutique bed-and-breakfast. Three is the magic number, they say. Why don't you come in and join us?" She opened one of the double doors wide enough for Jinx to peer down the hardwood hallway. Then she stepped back inside with Chocolate Eyes frowning beside her.

As she crossed the threshold behind the oddly coupled pair, Jinx felt a sudden coolness, like a winter wind riding the back of a warm autumn breeze. She looked over her shoulder toward the road, feeling unsettled as Ponytail sent the front doors swinging shut. Jinx followed the women through the foyer and entered a spacious formal room made extravagant with intricate woodwork designs. Artisanal carvings of snakes and panthers wrapped around the mantel; small alabaster roses embellished the wall moldings. A gilded mirror flashed the reflection of Jinx in her carpenter shorts, Chocolate Eyes in a long denim skirt, and Ponytail in a slip of a dress. Wide windows flanked the mirror and the elaborate fireplace, allowing views to the lush hillside and stately lane of oaks.

"Please, sit down."

Ponytail gestured toward a seat, lifted a crystal pitcher, and set about pouring water into drinking glasses. She arranged the tumblers on a Victorian folding tray whose copper joints creaked under the weight of the heirloom service. She eased into a straight-backed chair with forearms carved like cat claws and smoothed the lap of her un-wrinkled dress. Chocolate Eyes, who had yet to speak, sat on the edge of a damask divan looking ready to stand and bolt at any moment. Her legs were crossed at the knee, and she tapped one foot in the air, dangling a leather clog until it threatened to drop. Jinx found herself focusing on the woman's lips, wondering what her first words would be.

"Please," Ponytail repeated.

Jinx took the seat across from her host, a mahogany chair with elaborately carved cutouts and a scroll design on its chartreuse cushion.

"We've put the cart before the horse, haven't we? I'm Cheyenne Cotterell. This is my old friend Ruthie Mayes. Welcome to the Hold House, Jennifer." She extended a slender hand into the cool air between them.

"Thanks for letting me take up your time like this. It's very generous of you." Jinx's eyes darted around the room, landing on the stiff, dark furnishings with richly colored upholstery, the oil paintings depicting women holding vases, and the two of them sitting awkwardly before her, seething with hidden emotion.

"I'm Ruth Mayes," Chocolate Eyes said, curtly correcting her friend's introduction. "No one calls me Ruthie anymore." She sat with a straight spine, leaning slightly forward to reach out a hand to Jinx. Her hand, in contrast to her distant eyes, was soft and warm. She quickly withdrew it.

"So where in Oklahoma do you come from, Jennifer?" Cheyenne asked, ignoring her friend's interjection. "Are you a Cherokee Indian, by any chance?"

"I'm Creek on my mom's side, Cherokee on my dad's," Jinx said, annoyed. Who went around asking if people were Cherokee 'Indians'? What other kind of Cherokee was there? "I live in Ocmulgee; it's not too far from Muskogee, if you're familiar with the state. Are you from around here?"

"I'm from Atlanta, but my Native American ancestors are from this plantation. That was my ulterior motive for buying the house—to uncover my family history while I run a luxury bed-and-breakfast. Ruth's family is from the area, too. Our grandparents knew each other in Atlanta, and so did their grandparents before them. There weren't many free people of color back in the day, and they were a tight-knit community. Many of them also had Indian ancestry. I wouldn't be surprised if

Ruthie is a little bit Cherokee, too, though she doesn't show it the way I do. Everybody says you can see the Indian in my hair." She stroked her ponytail.

Jinx watched Ruth scowl. "That's . . . interesting. And how do you know your family was Cherokee? Aside from the hair, I mean."

Cheyenne tilted her chin up and inserted an over-the-shoulder pony-tail toss. "My family must have been among the group who hid out in the Georgia hills during the Trail of Tears. They didn't go to Oklahoma, and they were never in North Carolina. My grandmother always said we came from a Cherokee plantation right here in this area. It took me years to pinpoint it. I look the way I do because of our Indian heritage. That's why my grandmother named me Cheyenne. She didn't want me to ever forget."

"Cherokee and Cheyenne . . . Right . . . because they both start with *Ch*," Jinx said. Cherokee Princess Syndrome pissed her off. This woman was probably about as Indian as that Chief Hold Hotel sign on the road leading into town. Jinx saw a smile start at the corners of Ruth's full lips. This was getting a little mean, and Chocolate Eyes was enjoying it. As much as she wanted to see that smile, Jinx knew she should check her-self. She shouldn't disrespect anybody's grandma, even the grandma of a black Indian wannabe. And she certainly didn't need to make enemies if she wanted access to this place.

Cheyenne spoke into the awkward silence. "We're not on the Cherokee Nation Dawes Rolls, if that's what you're really asking. But as a historian, surely you know those government lists are completely unreliable."

"*Completely* is an overstatement. The Dawes Rolls are fairly reli-able. No record is ever perfect. And I didn't say I was a historian." Jinx glanced at the silent Ruth, who sat with her elbow pressed against a tufted teal pillow, observing the undercurrents of the conversation.

"I've kept you two waiting entirely too long for the grand tour,"

Cheyenne announced with polish, as if this were a natural follow-on. She was so smooth at wiping away any hint of discord that Jinx wondered if she had trained for high teas and debutante balls at some kind of finishing school. "I have an architect on retainer in Atlanta. He'll draw up the remodeling plans over the next month. I expect to keep the house and furnishings intact for the most part, though I'll want to do some modernizing and add full-sized baths. I'll preserve the reception hall where you entered, keep this drawing room as is." Cheyenne stood. "Ladies, follow me. Feel free to take as many photos as you like, but please do seek my permission before printing them in your publications. I plan on promoting this house just so, to draw the right kind of client base."

Cheyenne swept toward the doorway. Jinx fell in next to Ruth, noticing that up close she smelled like cherries. Ruth flashed Jinx a little smile that didn't quite melt her eyes. *Dark-chocolate-covered cherries,* Jinx thought.

"How did you find out about this place?" Jinx asked her.

"I was doing some online research for a story about carpets, of all things. I stumbled on to a local newspaper article that said the house museum was being sold and Cherokees were protesting. I thought it was an issue that should be publicized, and I had some vacation time coming, so I drove down here to check it out. What about you?"

Jinx felt a chill prick her neck. "I read that article. John Cook was quoted? Stuart Pickup? My dad knows those guys' families. I'm researching a teenage girl for my column, a Creek student who lived here in the 1800s. She had a troubled life, and a woman I know back home wants to find out what happened to her."

"A friend of yours?" Ruth said.

Good, Jinx thought. *She's curious about me.* That made them even. "An elder, kind of a friend, and a heck of a cook. She makes the absolute best cherry pies. I almost got my doctorate in history, and I write a column on historical issues, so folks at home sort of give me homework assignments."

"Your mission, if you choose to accept it?" Ruth said with a grin.

Jinx smiled back at her. "Right. A lot of people really care about this stuff—what happened in the past, and why. It's almost as though they feel we live in parallel worlds, like the past is always with us in the present."

"Are you one of those people?"

"I guess so. I guess I am. My great-aunt taught me to see things that way. Tribal history was her life. She died five years ago."

"It sounds like you and your great-aunt were close. You must miss her. I'm sorry for you that she's gone." Ruth's eyes took on a darker cast, sincere and shadowed. Jinx found it hard to look away.

"Thank you. We were." Their joined gazes held. Jinx thought that Ruth might say more, until she suddenly turned, breaking the connection.

"This way, ladies." Cheyenne gestured like Vanna White as she exited the drawing room, sharp-heeled sling-backs clicking on the old oak floors. A velvet rope, unhooked from its mooring, hung loose in the hallway. "This is the formal dining room. Beyond it is a butler's pantry with a modern kitchen nook—microwave, mini-fridge, hot plate—and beyond that a three-quarter bath."

Jinx took in the room. Fold upon fold of gold silk drapery flowed around the windows. A portrait of a brooding, dark-haired man dressed in a deep blue vest and red velvet jacket hung above the fireplace. The dining table was lavishly set below a brass chandelier topped with white candles.

"James Hold?" Jinx asked, facing the oversized portrait that made her feel as though the eyes were evaluating her.

Cheyenne nodded. "That's him. Handsome devil. He built this estate from the ground up and ran it until his death in 1816. He got to be the richest man in the Cherokee Nation, and most of upper Georgia, too. This plantation sat right at the crossroads, the frontier line where Georgia and Cherokee country met. James was murdered in a nearby tavern—drinking brandy, the story goes."

"Who killed him?" Jinx said.

"Who indeed?" Cheyenne answered.

"That galley kitchen must have been added later," Ruth said, surveying the layout of the space. "In a house like this, the kitchen would have been outside originally."

"That's right," Cheyenne said, sounding more than a little condescending. "The kitchen was located out back when the home was built, to protect the house from fire. Then the kitchen structure became the Moravian missionaries' cabin, where they lived and held worship services. The plantation kitchen was rebuilt in the basement of this building, a practice James Hold would have seen in the Savannah homes he visited on business. The park-service staff added the kitchenette for the sake of convenience during their events. They used the original kitchen outside as storage space. I'm planning to have it connected to the main house through a glass breezeway that will frame out the garden and river below the property."

"I passed that river on the highway," Ruth said. "More than once. It's not easy to find this place. My GPS went schizo."

"I'll update the signage, Ruth, of course. The Conasauga River was a major thoroughfare in James Hold's day. He operated a ferry and trading post along its banks. His plantation stretched much farther then, encompassing most of the historic township."

Cheyenne led them through the rear parlor, then exited the open French doors to wind back into the center hallway.

"This is the home's only phone right now." She gestured to a walnut secretary holding a coal-black telephone that looked as ancient as the house. "And you won't get a cell-phone signal or an Internet connection here, I'm afraid. Feel free to use the house phone for local calls. For long distance, you'll need a calling card, either your own or mine, which I'd be glad to let you use until I get a new phone system installed."

Cheyenne sashayed toward the main staircase, which rose, made a graceful turn, then rose again to a second story. At the top, the staircase stretched into a wooden archway—a footbridge indoors. The sight was so odd that Jinx half-expected the floorboards to shift under her feet, morphing into a mountain stream or the River Styx.

"This bridge is the most famous architectural feature of the house," Cheyenne said. "The only other one like it in Georgia is in Savannah, in the Owens-Thomas House. But Hold built his much earlier. And these are the second-floor bedrooms. This one would have been used as a children's or guest room." The room contained a pencil-post bed swathed in a coverlet of handmade lace, a satin-covered slip chair, and a dark mahogany sleigh bed. "You two are welcome to stay at the house while you're working on your stories. There are two beds here, if you don't mind sharing a room."

Cheyenne led them across the bridge.

"The master bedroom," she said, showing them a room aglow with sunlight. "Lovely, isn't it? James Hold and his favorite wife would have slept here."

Jinx stepped inside the room. Behind a floral folding screen with an air of the Orient in its design, she saw a suitcase lying open. Fluted skirts danced from sateen-lined hangers in an unlatched wooden armoire. A tall and gleaming chest of drawers held personal emollients and high-gloss cosmetics. A cashmere wrap was neatly folded across a needlepoint footstool. Cheyenne had wasted no time moving right in.

"Does that lead to the attic?" Ruth asked. Hanging back at the threshold, she pointed to a narrow door at the end of the hall, catty-corner to the master bedroom.

"It must," Cheyenne answered. "I haven't ventured up yet. There are so many nice parts of the house to see."

"May I?" Ruth cracked the door before Cheyenne could answer. And since Jinx immediately followed Ruth, Cheyenne had little choice but to bring up the rear of her hijacked grand tour.

The door led into a small closet full of mops with dingy heads, straw brooms, empty spray bottles, and dustcloths. Peering into the darkness over Ruth's shoulder, Jinx saw steps behind the clutter—steep, narrow, spindly steps with cobwebs at the corners. A dank smell—caused perhaps by a moldy rag or dead mouse—wafted from the top of the stairwell. A row of dusty woven baskets dangled from a field of hooks along one wall of the stairway. The baskets emitted a faint scent of tumbled earth that cut the stifling air of the closet. Jinx watched as Ruth drew closer to the baskets, sinking into the darkness.

"Beautiful." Ruth bent toward one of the baskets, stroking the dual-toned weave with her forefinger. Particles of pale dust dotted her fingertip like the powder of a cabbage butterfly wing. "What are these made of?"

"River cane," Cheyenne said. "The place is overrun with it."

"This weave is so intricate, the cane so thick. It's hard to imagine someone could work with this material, let alone make something so exquisite out of it," Ruth said. "My mother had one like this when I was growing up. She kept flower seeds in it—her 'heirloom seeds,' she called them."

Jinx fixed her attention on Ruth, on those pensive dark chocolate eyes. So Ruth's mother was a gardener, or used to be. Ruth spoke of her in the past tense. "That's a sifter," Jinx said. "Your mother was sorting with it, I'll bet. Separating the good seeds from the bad, the ones she wanted from the ones she didn't." Jinx watched Ruth suck a shallow breath, swallowing some squall of feeling before it could escape.

Cheyenne cleared her throat with a studied delicacy. "The third story is unfinished," she said. "I was told the museum never made use of it.

I'll have to start from scratch up there, gut the place. It might work well as a family suite. You can stick kids and their hassled parents anywhere. But you didn't come all this way to stare at brooms and buckets. Let's go outside, ladies. I'll show you the gardens."

Cheyenne turned and trooped down the maze of halls and stairways, past the rear parlor and toward the back exit.

"The servants' entrance," Cheyenne said.

"You mean the slaves' entrance, right?" Ruth said. "This was a working plantation. Blacks were owned as property here."

"You always were a suspicious one, Ruthie," Cheyenne said. "Expecting a boogeyman to leap out of the shadows. But I assure you this place is just what it seems: paradise."

10

Irritated by Cheyenne's smooth evasion, Ruth marched outside. Of course Cheyenne had dismissed Ruth's point out of hand. Cheyenne believed *her* family could never have been slaves. In Cheyenne's overactive imagination, her ancestor would have been the master's free wife of color, presiding over a group of well-treated "servants" who were happy to toil in "paradise". She needed more drama, more fanfare, more bling, so she threw in the Cherokee ancestor bit for good measure. Ruth's thoughts were spiraling into a Cheyenne-induced eddy when she stepped onto the wide-plank porch. The unkempt land before her spilled into a sea of green where tousled flowers stretched across the crest of the hill. Cheyenne was rambling on to Jennifer Micco about her Indian roots. Ruth ignored her, awed by the garden.

She focused on the swamp sunflowers, snowy asters, salvias, and sedums intertwining with abandon in the untamed yard. Butterfly weed and Indian blanket blazed in vibrant hues. Wild white roses sprang up among the colorful wildflowers, tingeing the stiff hillside breeze with a sweet, old-fashioned perfume. Each bloom—beside a gate, beneath a tree, along a path—was full and brilliant, knowing it would soon burn out with the full onslaught of autumn. Ruth's trust in this garden was immediate. She felt something as she stood before these plants, sewn from seed generations ago and still growing, still thriving, even though their gardener had long since turned to dust. Ruth breathed in, thinking for the first time in years of the fragrant musk that used to cling to her mother's ebony skin: lily of the valley mixed with perspiration from long hours spent gardening in their double-lot yard. Ruth sank into the memory of her mother's scent and stepped off the porch, her tin-can heart creaking open.

She crossed a patch of dirt and waded into the garden. Her feet found a path of gray river stones that meandered to the edge, winding between a weathered cabin and a row of dilapidated dependency buildings. She stopped when she could go no farther, where the slope took a steep dive to the river. The wildflowers faded into a grove of river cane that crowded out the sunlight, with thin stalks shooting up into a mass of feathery tufts all the way down to the water's edge. The reeds were as tall as trees and had the likeness of bamboo, lovely and primitive as they swayed, whispering in the wind. It was a wonder this canebrake had not been chopped down like most of the others across the region. It was a wonder the cane here had been allowed to live. *Shh, shh,* the cane stalks seemed to whisper to her. *Shh, shh.*

Ruth breathed in the loamy smell of river water flowing at the bottom of the incline. Mud. Fish. Sunlight. A picture of the St. Paul house where she had spent her early childhood flooded her quiet mind. She remembered those long hours in the garden, many hours like one unbroken thread. She remembered her mother looking out from beneath the brim of her rattan hat, smiling at her, smiling at Ruthie, the little girl. Ruthie had always been underfoot, tracing ant trails, mixing mud pies, scouting for rain-soaked worms along the garden's edge, never knowing how much her mother was teaching her there, or that it would all disappear like a faded sepia photograph. That garden was the laboratory where her mother had developed the natural products of Canebrake Botanicals, her wildly successful body-care company. That garden was also their private haven, their secret place away from the prison-like house.

Gazing at the canebrake that girdled the Hold Plantation, Ruth recognized the likeness. Around the perimeter of their yard, in soil made rich by the Mississippi River, her mother had nursed river cane from her home state of Georgia. She had never taken Ruth to meet their Georgia relatives, had never taken her to see their family's homeplace, but surely her mother had missed it, loved it, wished she could return to it. Why else had she struggled to grow a little piece of Georgia in her frigid Minnesota yard? Ruth tore her glasses off. The garden blurred before her eyes, the raw pattern of color and light revealing hidden shapes. She returned the glasses to her nose, smudged and wet, and glanced back at the others.

"How much land did the Holds control?" Jennifer was asking Cheyenne where the two stood talking in the shade of the porch.

"Some say a thousand acres, some say four thousand," Cheyenne answered. "Right outside the house here was the plantation's working yard, where servants did their outdoor tasks—laundering, soap making, log sawing, corn shucking. The state never altered this area, but I'll have it landscaped and put in outdoor patio seating. Past the work yard was the flower garden, and then the vegetable and herb gardens. There's no water view now, but when I have the cane cut back, the vista will be spectacular."

"Where were the slave quarters?" Ruth called out, mostly to needle Cheyenne.

Cheyenne sighed. "Not every black person who lived here was a slave, Ruthie. The servants' quarters haven't survived. In the 1950s, the state had an archaeological survey done. They speculated that there must have been at least twenty cabins on the grounds to support a work force of nearly a hundred people. Those cabins were probably located a mile out, where the cornfields met the mill."

"Have you thought about reconstructing the slave cabins?" Jennifer said.

"Really, ladies. People don't want to pay to think about racial prejudice on their weekend excursions. They want to relax, and I want to pamper my customers, not preach to them." Cheyenne tossed a hand to a hip, switching her slight weight from one wedged heel to the other.

At the mention of racial prejudice, Jennifer's expression flickered. She jumped off the porch, maneuvering through the overgrown blooms. "Can I join you?" she said to Ruth. Strands of dark hair had escaped her braid and were fluttering around her striking face. Her cargo shorts were wrinkled, her T-shirt curled at the edge. And she was smiling with a warmth that crinkled the corners of her eyes.

Ruth didn't gravitate to people, not socially or romantically. She never let them close enough to discover there was a hole inside her. But Jennifer Micco was down-to-earth, direct, and smart. And she was one of the few human beings, male or female, apparently unaffected by Cheyenne's manicured charms. "Yes," Ruth said, startled by the way she blurted it out. "I was just looking at the garden, thinking it has a theme. Roses are growing everywhere, though they're hard to spot at first. Look, you can see rambler roses, tea roses, English roses, even the powder-pink Cinderella roses my mother used to call 'the babies of the rose family.' It looks like someone planted them ages ago. Others were added over time. And see those wild Cherokee roses? The ones still in bloom? Give them an inch and they'll take a mile. They love to grow in places people have left behind, kind of like memories. This is a rose garden, hidden among the weeds and wildflowers, and it's been here for years."

"I didn't realize you knew so much about gardens, Ruth." Cheyenne had managed to reach them on her ridiculous wedge heels. "Maybe you take after your mother after all. It's surprising how much a child can pick up in those early formative years. You'll find this tidbit interesting. I read a *Georgia Backroads* magazine article that included interviews with people who worked at the Hold House years ago. One of the interviewees was a black woman who said she picked cotton on the place as a girl, back when it was used for sharecropping in the forties. She said the blacks who lived around here then—before the white residents made it an official historic township, increased property values, and drove most of them out—used to call this estate 'the Cherokee Rose Plantation.' The name never made it on to any map or formal brochure."

"The Cherokee Rose," Ruth repeated, ignoring Cheyenne's comment about her childhood as her eyes traced the shape of the rose garden.

"Jennifer, this is what you're looking for," Cheyenne said, stepping along a fieldstone path and indicating the rough cabin built behind the main house. "The original kitchen for the home. It was refashioned as a missionary station, the one you asked about." She gestured toward a row of stout batten-board sheds that sat across from the kitchen and formed an enclosure of the rear acreage. "Those were the corncrib, smokehouse, and weaving house."

"And what about that?" Jennifer pointed past the southeastern edge of the garden, where a little oddly shaped shelter crouched among the cane stalks. It was made of mud or clay and crowned by a conical roof. The sun shone hard on its walls and dry thatch top, as if the roof made of reeds could still absorb sunlight, converting the rays into chlorophyll, into energy, into life. Wild sevenbark hydrangea with ivory blooms trailed the perimeter of the spherical house, interspersed with milkweed plants laced with monarch butterflies.

"An oddity, according to the state archaeologist," Cheyenne said, one hand slanted upward to protect her face from the sun. "It's not a structure James Hold would have built. His style was more classically European."

"It's old," Jennifer said. "Maybe even eighteenth century. I bet it predates James Hold's time altogether."

"It could be African-influenced," Ruth said, thinking that her years of being assigned the ethnic stories at *Abode* might actually be paying off now. "West African houses were round. Some of the slaves here might have remembered how to construct them."

"Or it could be an early Cherokee winter lodge," Jennifer said. "They were round houses, too. In fact, it could be a hybrid of forms."

Ruth stared at the habitation in the cane, wondering who had lived there. Had they found a sanctuary in that little earthen house? Or had it been a prison cell? She wanted to go to the structure, to touch its walls, to see what secrets lay inside. Her thoughts flashed to her colleagues in the retro brick loft of the magazine's offices. They would eat their hearts out to see this place—a classic plantation wreathed by gardens with a wattle-and-daub indigenous lodge tucked out back. And her heart could be eaten out, too, if she let it, devoured by the melancholy beauty of a place that pulled her back in time.

"Why don't you ladies take a walk around, if you'd like?" Cheyenne said. "I'll go find some food. It's long past lunchtime, and I know Ruth must be famished. She never was one to skip a meal. We can have a light picnic in the garden, and I'll tell you about my ideas for the B&B's opening weekend." Cheyenne pivoted and headed toward the house, her ponytail swinging and her slip dress swaying in the breeze.

Ruth felt a touch on her arm. Jennifer was watching as if she knew, as if she understood the way it felt to be constantly reminded you weren't as good as somebody else.

"Want to check out the old kitchen with me? It sounds like we have a common interest. I like my meals, too." Jennifer smiled, then walked ahead of Ruth toward the decaying building, making a path of parted stems for them both to tread.

Ruth followed, stooping to examine the outlines of a former vegetable and herb garden. A brown-backed box turtle showed its face and blinked at her. She watched it disappear behind a watercress leaf, then thrust in her hand, parting hedge mustard from shepherd's-purse. Four pairs of beaded eyes peered back at her—two turtles instead of one, tucked together like the twin hearts of the lopseed plant that grew around the exterior of the weathered cabin.

Jennifer pushed through lopseed stalks to enter the low-slung doorway. Ruth tripped over a threshold warped by the elements, righted her clog, and stumbled inside behind her. The cabin smelled like a pine forest after a rain: damp wood, wet moss, sodden earth, balsam. The walls were made of unpeeled log that had once been whitewashed. The floors were nothing more than raw, packed earth. The windows were encrusted with dirt streaked by long-dried raindrops. The only pure shaft of light, dancing with dust and pollen, shone through the open doorway.

The first room was the largest of three, occupying the full front width of the cabin. This was the original cooking space, judging by its size and features. A massive chimney built of rocks rose against one wall. A hunk of tree trunk served as a mantel. Carved into the wood in the center of the trunk was a faded cross formed in the leaves of the tree of life. At the base of the chimney, a deep fireplace took up a third of the room. This had been the Hold family's hearth, the place where their meals were prepared. A slave had probably worked here, or perhaps even lived here. A ruddy brick oven, a later addition, had been built into the opposite wall, surrounded by shelving fashioned from elm. But any cooking elements once stowed on those shelves—cast-iron pots or trivets or cooling stands—had been lost or sold away.

Jennifer lowered herself to the floor, sitting cross-legged. Ruth sat beside her, facing the open door.

"It's incredible," Jennifer said, "to think that people lived here centuries ago, cooked here, prayed here, shared their lives. Mary Ann Battis, the girl I'm looking for, could have sat where we're sitting now, some year, some day, in the 1800s."

Ruth looked at Jennifer for a long moment, at her dark, thoughtful eyes. She was suddenly aware of the sweet clover smell of Jennifer's skin. In the silence, she could hear the sound of Jennifer's breathing—steady, rhythmic, alive.

"The girl you're looking for," Ruth repeated.

"Well . . ." Jennifer paused, her eyes questioning. "One of them. And I think it's time you know that my friends back home call me Jinx."

"Jinx?"

"Buy me a Coke." Jinx smiled.

Ruth laughed out loud, remembering the childhood saying for when two people blurted out the same word at the same time, almost as if by magic. Jennifer was looking at her, flirting with her, leaning in close to her. Ruth didn't know what to do, and so she closed her eyes. When Jennifer kissed her, the touch was tentative at first. Ruth fell into the softness, the clover-scented warmth. She slid her glasses off and placed them on the dirt floor beside her. She eased her arms back, resting her weight on her palms. *Shh, shh*, the river cane whispered from the hillside. *Shh, shh. Come. Go back. Come. Go back.* The rustling echoed in her eardrums, sounding like a voice that had traveled across a great distance. Ruth snapped open her eyes, pulled her cheek from Jennifer's hair, and peered over Jennifer's shoulder.

"What's wrong?" Jennifer said.

And that's when Ruth saw the girl.

She was fourteen, maybe fifteen, with long, awkward string-bean limbs, honeycomb-colored skin, and brilliant brown eyes. The girl's hair hung to her back in a thick trunk of braid, tied off at the base with ribbon. She stood just beyond the cabin doorway in moccasin-covered feet, staring directly at Ruth. Ruth straightened and drew in a breath of shock. She tried to swallow, reached for her glasses, and managed to settle them askew on her nose. She looked up again at the doorway to find the girl was gone . . . if she had ever been there. *Shh, shh.*

Ruth focused only on breathing and then put her mind to work. She was exhausted and under stress. She hadn't slept well on the road. And she had arrived at her destination to find that her queen-bee summer-camp bunkmate, a person she had never been fond of, now owned the place she had lost sleep trying to get to. On top of that, a cute girl she liked seemed to like her back, which threw her into a head spin of giddy angst. It was as though she had careened into an adolescent anxiety dream. And to top it all off, now she was seeing strange things. The girl in the door was a trick of the eye, a trick of the light, a trick of her mind. Ruth had only to blink her eyes to make the girl disappear—just as she had for all those years with the memories of her mother, just as she had with the loss that had hulled the seed of her life.

She looked up to find Jennifer watching with a look of concern and maybe hurt feelings.

"Jennifer . . . ," Ruth started.

"Jinx. Ruth, I'm sorry if . . ."

"*Bon appétit*, ladies!" Cheyenne called from the flagstone path in the garden.

Part II
Talking Leaves

They were women then
My mama's generation ...
How they battered down
Doors
And ironed
Starched white
Shirts
How they led
Armies
Headragged Generals
Across mined
Fields ...

Alice Walker,
"Women," *In Search of Our
Mothers' Gardens*

11

ADAM HAD BEEN WORKING in his garden all morning, staking the cornstalks, thumping the pumpkins, and pulling invasive weeds. The quar-
ter of an acre in front of his cabin that he had devoted to his hobby kept
him and more than a few neighbors in fresh produce all fall. He and
Sally usually chose a slow weekend to can the tomatoes in his shed with
a college football game blaring in the background. Those jars, with their
satisfying pops as they sealed, made for pretty good pizza and spaghetti
sauces come wintertime. The tomatoes Adam grew ranged from tiny
grapes and romas to a purple, bulging heirloom variety planted from
seeds saved by his mother and passed down from his grandmother.

The heat had gotten to him hours ago despite the shade provided
by his over-eager sunflowers, which stood like yellow umbrellas on stilts
along the perimeter of the fence. Adam had stripped off his T-shirt to
fling it across a stump by the woodshed. He took another swig from a

water bottle that was sweating as hard as he was. The outdoor work soothed him, especially in a week like this, when everything seemed awry. The Hold House buyer was far from what he had expected. He thought he would be dealing with Mason Allen, who was tough but practical to the core—avaricious, certainly, but the devil Adam knew. Instead, he found himself tangling with a stranger—a sexy, snobby, gutsy stranger who seemed entranced by the place but for some reason had it in for azaleas. Adam shrugged into a smile. She was a puzzle, that one.

The sound of the telephone inside his cabin grabbed his attention. He wanted to ignore it but knew it must be Sally. She was at home on Wednesdays if she didn't have a cleaning job, and she must have spotted him in the yard through the window of her trailer. Adam stood, the ache in his knees telling him it was past time to call it quits for the day anyway. He grabbed his damp shirt and water bottle, kicked off his Nikes, and walked inside his snug log home. Shaded by pine needles, the cabin was cool around him. It smelled like the coffee he had brewed that morning and left in the pot just in case—and like the pleasantly foreign scents of a stranger, the shampoo and lotion of his overnight renter, who had eaten cold cereal and left while he was out in the tent.

"Yep?" he said, holding the telephone to his ear.

"What in the world are you doing out there in the heat of the day?"

"Hey, Sally. How's Junior?"

"Napping. I know a thing or two about sunstroke, Adam Battis, and don't think because you're black you can't get it."

"So you're babysitting me now, too?"

"Somebody has to, since your mama's moved to Dalton and the whole town's gone nuts over the sale of the Hold House. Now tell me. What's going on over there? I know you've been to see her."

Adam paused. "I did happen to run into the new owner, Cheyenne Cotterell, at the supermarket. She says she wants to operate a bed-and-breakfast and live here year-round. She also said you can pick fruit in the orchards, just like you have been."

"That was your doing, I know. Thanks for thinking of me. So, did you tell her?"

"Tell her what?"

"Adam, don't play dumb. Did you tell her you hope to rent some land on the place and restore the cabin your grandmother grew up in?"

Adam sighed and took a gulp of water. "It didn't come up."

"Of course it didn't *come* up. You have to *bring* it up. Lord knows, you've got just as much claim to that plantation as anybody else. More than anybody else. Mason just wanted to develop the land. He didn't really care about it. And the new owner, she sounds like she just wants to run a business. You have roots here, Adam. You belong to the place."

"Well, this woman says she has roots, too, that she had ancestors on the plantation. Mason might have rented to me if I could have convinced him that having me run the orchards would have turned him a profit. But this one? No. She's a romantic with backbone. She doesn't want anybody crowding in on her dream."

Sally was quiet for a moment. Adam imagined her biting the fleshy tip of her thumb, like she did when she was deliberating.

"And does she?"

"Does she what?"

"Have a history on the plantation? Because your grandparents—my grandparents, all of those old folks—said your own family was there going back at least three generations."

"I don't know her history, Sally. I'm not even sure if she does."

"When's the last time you worked on your family history research, anyhow?"

"I set that aside a year ago. I told you that. I looked into it, called the Cherokee Nation in Oklahoma and tried to see if the Battises were listed on the Cherokee freedmen rolls. They weren't."

"You gave up pretty easily, then. One phone call. You haven't rented that cabin out and slept in your tent for years just to save twenty-five thousand dollars for nothing."

"It wouldn't make any difference now. The property is gone. Nobody cares if my ancestors lived there."

"You never know what might make a difference," Sally said. "Or who might care. Tell you what. Come over here for lunch. I haven't seen hide nor hair of Eddie Senior since Saturday. It'll be you and me—and Junior, if he wakes up. We can watch *The Young and The Restless*, eat bologna sandwiches, and feel a whole lot better in less than an hour flat."

Cheyenne had found a spot, shaded and bucolic, beneath a white peach tree. She spread out a patchwork quilt and busied herself preparing a picnic like a fussy, copper-toned Martha Stewart. She laid out china from the Hold House pantry, corn muffins, a cake of butter, a fresh tossed salad, and dressing. She placed a pitcher of cool water on top of a tin tray and set out drinking glasses.

Ruth sat on the edge of the textile island, tucking her denim skirt around her calves. Jinx found a place a short space away and rested quietly, watching her. Cheyenne knelt on a throw pillow.

"Thanks, Cheyenne," Jinx said. "This looks tasty."

"I can't take much credit. The basket was a gift from a neighbor. Funny, he didn't leave me any way to contact him. It would be impolite not to say thank you." Cheyenne nibbled at the crust of a muffin top, then placed it back on her plate and reached for her water.

Jinx spread butter and jam on a muffin, glancing regularly at Ruth, who was staring into the cane field. "Are you okay, Ruth?" she finally asked.

"She's right," Cheyenne said. "You aren't eating, Ruthie. That isn't like you. You always used to dig right in, like you were starved for a home-cooked meal. I assumed that father of yours couldn't cook and wouldn't hire someone who could."

"I've had plenty of home-cooked meals, Cheyenne," Ruth snapped.

"Well, that tone seems uncalled for," Cheyenne said. "I didn't mean to touch a nerve." She turned to Jinx and lowered her voice. "Ruth's mother died when she was a girl. Her father raised her alone. I don't think she's ever gotten over it."

"What the hell are you doing?" Ruth said, her voice going rigid.

"I'm just trying to explain to Jennifer why you might be acting so strangely. I'm sure being down here in Georgia makes you think about your mother. I just thought we should all be direct."

"Should I be direct and talk about how you're an anorexic who lives on water and lettuce leaves because you have body-image issues?"

Cheyenne looked stunned. She touched a hand to the pearl strand hanging around her neck.

"I didn't think so," Ruth said. "My mother's death is just like your eating disorder—nobody else's business."

"I do *not* have an eating disorder, Ruth. I maintain a healthy diet. Maybe you should worry about your own weight problem. It would do you good to eat a few lettuce leaves."

"I'm happy with my size, Cheyenne, and my looks, even though you never thought I should be."

"Are we really doing this? Reverting back to tenth grade, comparing our figures and fighting over who's the cutest? You never appreciated what I tried to do for you, Ruth. You never fit in at camp, or anywhere else, as far as I could tell. But you've always resented my trying to help, as if it wasn't my business, the messed-up situation you grew up in. Well, down here in the South, everything is everybody's business. It was never a secret, how your mother died."

"My mother's death was an accident," Ruth said.

"And you always were the only one who believed that story. How you could stick with your father all those years afterward, how you could stay in touch with him now that you're grown, I will never understand."

"What was I supposed to do, Cheyenne? Go back to Georgia, where my relatives were estranged or dead? Back to Idlewood reunions, where you turned up your noses because I was mixed and grew up somewhere else?"

"Being biracial had nothing to do with it, Ruth. That father of yours sent you to camp to learn to be black part-time, but it couldn't make up for your mother leaving and taking you out of your community."

"So what if my mother married a white man? So what if she moved away? You always thought you were all that, so bougie, butt in the air, as if Georgia's black elite didn't start out as slaves to rich white folks, the ones who had townhouses in Savannah and summer houses near the mountains. It wasn't only Cherokees who lived up here. I bet your family does descend from an old North Georgia plantation just like you've been claiming for years—a white plantation. The only difference between my family history and yours is that my white father married my black mother." Ruth stared hard at Cheyenne, who didn't flinch.

"You don't know who your people are or where you belong," Cheyenne said. "And you never will."

"All right, you two," Jinx inserted, her body tense. "I think you've both drawn enough blood for one afternoon picnic."

Ruth looked down at her plate, hands shaking. "Maybe my mother didn't want to leave Georgia. Maybe folks made her feel like she didn't belong anymore, like she couldn't come back home to her family, no matter what her life had turned out to be." She rose unsteadily to her feet, avoiding Jinx's searching eyes. "I need to get out of here," she said.

Jinx didn't finish her food. She realized too, given what she just heard, that Cheyenne had never intended to eat more than a bite or two anyway.

She helped Cheyenne pack up the picnic basket and carry the

things into the house, said a polite goodbye, and started up her truck. It felt like a week instead of two days since she had arrived in Georgia; it felt like months since she had received a dressing down by Deb Tom. The longer she spent in this place, the odder things seemed, and the more her research, Ruth's arrival, and Cheyenne's purchase of that house seemed beyond coincidence. But what was she thinking? That they had been gathered here for a reason? And if so, by whom, and for what purpose? *Holy smokes.* She sounded nuts.

Jinx had never considered herself superstitious. She trusted what she could read and analyze; she was a by-the-book girl. But sometimes she felt things that weren't really there—like the Cherokee travelers at Ross's Landing, and the thing askew in Aunt Angie's house that wouldn't let her rest. Something had happened to Ruth in the missionary cabin that afternoon, Jinx was sure of it. Something extraordinary enough to make Ruth go still as a statue, to cloud her face with fear and confusion, to trigger feelings from the past. Poor Ruth. Where would she go from here? And when would she come back? Because they had all started something that day—or something had started them—and it needed to be finished. *Three is the magic number,* Cheyenne had said in the drawing room. That was true in the fairy tales of Western culture. But in the old world of Southern Indian medicine and power, four was the number of ritual magic. Jinx, Ruth, and Cheyenne had already been called to the plantation, which meant that a fourth person was still to arrive. Or maybe the fourth person was already there, and Ruth Mayes knew it.

The moment Jinx crossed the threshold, she had sensed something wrong with that house. It made Ruth sad and vulnerable. It provoked Ruth and Cheyenne's anger. It made Jinx feel the loss of all the chances she had never taken—chances to build relationships, to push her intellect, to live outside of Aunt Angie's shadow. It was why Jinx had kissed Ruth too soon, why she had kissed her at all. That plantation, or the thing that animated it, was obsessed with emotions of the past. Jinx felt an internal chill. What kind of supernatural mess had Deb Tom gotten her into? This was a realm, she was certain, that Angie had never entered and could not have prepared her for.

Jinx could turn toward the highway. She could get out of town. She could fly toward the safety of her Oklahoma bungalow and maintain the lines of order that her great-aunt had established for her. She could leave this mess behind, drop the search for Mary Ann, forget about Ruth, outrageous Cheyenne, and that dark and moody plantation. Instead, she found herself driving up the mountain road. Maybe her inscrutable host would be at the cabin this time.

She knocked on the pine green frame of the screen, peering in through the open door. The smell of meat sizzling in a frying pan wafted out to her.

A tall African American man with close-cut hair, serious eyes, and handsome features came to the doorway with a dishtowel in his hands. "You must be my mystery guest," he said in a deep Southern drawl. "I wondered if you were planning to pay up. I'm Adam Battis. Come on in."

"Hi, Adam. You don't know how glad I am to finally meet you. I'm Jennifer Micco." She reached out a hand to shake his free one and placed her messenger bag on the floor. "I was just out for the afternoon. I was hoping to stay three nights, and I was going to leave the money I owe."

"I'm only kidding you. Sally Perdue said you're cool. She said you came out here to see the Hold House. She wanted me to ask if you liked the jam. Did you?"

"It was incredible," Jinx said, following Adam into the kitchen area, where he pulled a second plate out of the paneled cupboard.

"I always keep her strawberry jam on tap—that or wild strawberries from my garden. We have a belief in my family that having strawberries in your house helps to maintain good relations. You need that kind of guarantee when you've got strangers coming and going the way I do."

"That comes from a Cherokee legend," Jinx said, "about a man and woman who argue. The woman runs away, and the man finds her by following a trail of strawberry flowers. They make up and agree never to let their differences separate them again. The strawberry plant is a reminder to keep the peace, to care for others."

Adam Battis gave her a contemplative look. "Have a seat and join me for dinner, Jennifer. Want a beer?"

"I'll take Coke, if you have it. And that would be nice. Thanks."

Jinx slid into a ladder-back chair while Adam brought over two plates heaped with oven-baked fries and pork chop sandwiches. He set a can of Coke beside her and a Michelob Light in front of an empty chair that he promptly folded his lean frame into.

"This looks great," Jinx said, thinking he was a man whose cooking Deb Tom would respect. She squirted ketchup onto her fries.

"You know your mythology," Adam said, sipping his beer.

"So do you. That's a great collection of books you have over there. I noticed that the mythology section is particularly broad—Native American, Greek, Roman."

"What are we without our stories?" he said. "The big ones. The ones that tell us who we are. I majored in classics in college, went on to study forestry, then took a job with the park service so I could stay in the area."

"You're from here originally?"

"I grew up right on this mountain. My father worked at the mill; my mother sold cakes and cookies to the tourists. My grandfolks, they came from the Hold place. It was called the Cherokee Rose Plantation back then. Growing up, I heard so many stories about its history. I always wanted to work there, and then I did. I used to manage the grounds and physical operations at the house museum."

And then they shut the museum and threw you out of a job, forcing you to run a hostel out of your cabin. "Historic-site caretaker by day, mythology scholar by night," Jinx said. "That sounds like my work schedule back home in Oklahoma. I work at a public library part-time and do tribal research and writing in my free time. What made you stay around here when you lost your job?"

"I belong here. I have a responsibility to this place, no matter who owns the land on paper." He took a messy bite of his pork chop, smothered in onions and mashed between two slices of soft white bread. "What brings you to the Hold House?"

"That's something I was hoping to tell you about—to ask you about, in fact. Have you heard of Mary Ann Battis, a young Creek girl who studied at the mission station on the grounds of the Hold Plantation?"

"Heard of her? Sure have. She was my great-great-great-grandmother. Her son, Adam Battis, is who I'm named after. But I never heard anybody say she was Creek. I always assumed she was black and Cherokee. Why the interest in my family tree?"

"Mary Ann Battis was Muscogee Creek. I'm Muscogee, too. People back home are curious about her history, and I do historical research, so I was commissioned, so to speak. I'm here to find out more about her story."

"So you're telling me your 'people,' whoever that means, want to hear all about some black Indian girl from Georgia? I'd be surprised if Mary Ann is a big topic of interest out there, unless you're trying to make an example out of her for one of those legal cases where freed people's descendants get disenrolled from the tribe, their voting rights stripped like it was 1940s Mississippi."

"I'm not involved in anything like that," Jinx said. "I'm not the tribal citizenship police, and I don't want to be. Indians are Indians, regardless of skin color."

"That's what your family thinks?"

"That's what *I* think. And my cousin who's like a brother to me, and a lot of other people I know."

Adam looked at Jinx for a long moment. "So what is it you've found out about my ancestor in the course of this . . . research?"

"Not much yet, I'll admit. I know she was a student at the Asbury Mission School in Alabama, and then at the Moravian mission here on the Hold estate. Her mother was Muscogee, and her father was a black man. When her mother, uncle, and siblings were sent west during the first stage of the Creek Removal in the 1820s, she stayed on here with the missionaries. No one knows why she stayed behind instead of going to Indian Territory with her family. Did you hear any stories about her when you were growing up?" Jinx took a swig of Coke from her can.

"Only that she came to Georgia by herself in the 1800s, took up with a traveling preacher, and never made it out to Indian Territory. She died on the Hold estate just after Reconstruction," Adam said, starting on his fries. "It wasn't so unusual for black Indian people to use their skin color as a shield back then. Soldiers were rounding up Indians for removal, but even though they thought they knew what an 'Indian' looked like, they regularly missed the mark. I guess it was the one time in U.S. history when passing for black was a tactical advantage."

"Is she buried on the plantation?" Jinx asked.

"Nah. There's an old black cemetery called the Strangers' Graveyard a mile past the Conasauga. Folks buried loved ones there during Jim Crow, when the official town cemetery was closed to them. None of the graves were marked—just a big rock here, an unusual tree there. Back in James Hold's day, slaves who were sickly and died young, or slaves who caused trouble, by breaking the tools or running away, were worked 'til they dropped, then buried beyond the main estate. It could be that's how the Strangers' Graveyard started, as a burial ground for castoff slaves of the Holds. Mary Ann was laid to rest in that ground, I've always heard."

"Do you know where the black cemetery is?" Jinx said. "I'd like to see it."

"Sure I know, but I can't take you there. A man named Mason Allen bought and fenced off the property several months ago."

"What a shame," Jinx said, shaking her head. "There should be ways to protect that land. I remember hearing about a slave burial ground in New York that was saved from demolition. It takes research, a lot of people working together, but it can be done. I bet you could find evidence of the burial ground's existence in the WPA slave narratives."

"That Roosevelt project from the Depression? I thought that was just make-work for unemployed writers." Adam leaned forward, his elbows propped on the table.

"The Federal Writers' Project was just one of the ways to try to get people working again. And the WPA narratives are actual oral histories taken with former slaves by government employees. The narratives are filtered through the questions of the interviewers—often white interviewers talking to black interviewees—but they can be revealing of some of the details of enslaved people's lives. Mary Ann was a free Indian, so I never looked for her there. But former slaves from this area, I bet they'd be represented."

Jinx watched Adam's eyes light with interest, then fade with resignation.

"Mason's already got the foundation in place for his time-share condos with river views," he said. "It's too late to save the graves. If things had worked out the way Mason wanted, he'd own land on both sides of the river—the Strangers' Graveyard and the Hold Plantation, too. There's a local legend about gold hidden on that property. Gold lust never died down around here after the rush of 1829, and it's picking up again now, with all this talk of a great recession. Folks want wealth they can touch. Same old story. Greed. If Mason Allen had won the Hold estate at auction, he might have made a fortune down the line finding gold—or, more likely, selling the dream of hidden treasure."

"So you're saying her bones have been disturbed. All of their bones."

Adam looked at Jinx. "That's what I'm saying." The legs of his chair made an ugly sound on the floor as he stood and reached for the dirty plates.

The house felt empty to Cheyenne now. It had been sort of nice talking with average people who could understand her love for this place. Jennifer Micco was steeped in the history of the plantation and had hung on Cheyenne's every word. Ruth, although she was annoying about it, knew the architectural elements and could identify the plants. Both of them had been eager to learn more about the house, and Cheyenne could have gone on for hours before the big blow-up over Ruthie's mother. And now Cheyenne was alone again, tiny worries pricking her like mosquitoes. She washed the plates from the picnic in sudsy water, taking care not to chip her nails. Maybe she shouldn't have selected good china from the butler's pantry for an outdoor meal, but this was her home now, and she was going to use the things in it. Cheyenne dried her hands on a paper towel, thinking she needed to purchase nice linens. She sighed and made her way up to the master bedroom, where she changed into a watermelon running suit, white tank top, and matching tennis shoes.

On the plus side, now that she was alone, she finally had time to dig around the house and grounds, inspect her azalea bushes up close, and find those fruit orchards that Adam the park ranger had gone on about.

She started her exploration in the foyer, looking through the literature. She rooted through the stacked boxes by the door and drew out an array of Chief Hold House booklets.

Cheyenne flopped onto the teal divan, where a sour-faced Ruthie Mayes had sat that morning. She had been glad to see Ruth again, the friend she had lost touch with years ago, though she had long suspected the distance between them was not accidental. Ruth had pulled away from her, even with all they had in common. They were both secret keepers, with stories that couldn't be easily told. Cheyenne's secret was benign, even kind of sexy. Possessing Indian heritage added to the fascination that people seemed to feel for her. But having your father kill your mother and never be charged for it, well, that was something else entirely. The Minnesota newspapers had covered the story of Ruth's mother's drowning on a cruise ship under suspicious circumstances. Cheyenne was only ten at the time, but she still remembered the gossiping ladies at her grandmother's church, the flowers on their elaborate hats shaking madly with the pitch of their agitated voices. And the next summer, Ruthie had turned up at Idlewood, the same camp both their mothers had attended when they were girls. Cheyenne befriended Ruth at first sight. She felt sorry for her. Ruth needed Cheyenne—someone pretty, someone popular—to help her fit in. And now she was back, needing Cheyenne's friendship again, even though she didn't know it.

Cheyenne opened one of the booklets—a history of the restoration of the Hold House. When the first house museum tour took place in 1952, the cost was fifty cents for adults and twenty-five for children. She should have placards made showcasing those darling prices, painted signs in vintage lettering that she could hang inside the guest rooms. Cheyenne wondered what those first paying guests would have thought about the $1.5 million price tag.

She felt another pinch of anxiety in her gut. Her parents wanted this to work for her, but they were also cautious. They hadn't expected to spend nearly so much on a property, and neither had Cheyenne. Her parents had borrowed half the money by taking out a second mortgage on their cottage at the Vineyard, and they intended to pass that debt along to her, once she got her hospitality business up and running. She needed to make this bed-and-breakfast shine, or she might have to sell the place. She was working within a tight margin. Nothing could go wrong. The stories Jennifer and Ruth were writing could be important for publicity when she opened her doors for the winter holiday season. *Ruth.* That girl was clearly unstable. Accusing Cheyenne of being anorexic or bulimic or whatever. Running off because she couldn't face the truth about her own history. Cheyenne tossed the booklet onto a cushion and stood. She thought of Layla, De'Sha, and Toni back in Atlanta. It was Wednesday. She could drive down on Friday, meet them for dinner at Aria, and stay overnight at her condo. She could drive by Swag and pick up some linens and nice kitchen things for the Hold House.

As she paced in front of the towering windows and carved fireplace, hips swinging and thoughts turning, Cheyenne caught a glimpse of herself in the ornate mirror above the mantel. She paused, smiling at her reflection, at the smooth hair and alluring face, the svelte body that was hers and yet not hers. She moistened her lips to make them glisten, reflecting the lush pink of her tracksuit.

And that's when she saw them: the roaches in the fireplace. Cheyenne swallowed a yelp. Two-dozen well-fed cockroaches with shiny backs were squirming and crawling inside the grate. One or two had scuttled out beyond the ceramic enclosure to traverse the ornate Turkish rug. Cheyenne choked at the sight of them—thick, black, tentacles reaching. She hated bugs. And cockroaches went beyond bugs. They belonged to a wholly separate category of disgustingness. Her eyes darted around the room, and then she began to see more. A roach was clinging to the hem of the curtain next to the fireplace. Three were climbing the Tiffany glass fireplace screen. One was crawling on the window next to the mantel.

Okay, okay. Calm down. Think. Maybe she should have had the house inspected. Of course she should have, if she had been smart. But she had let passion overtake her and had led her parents to believe that she was taking every precaution. But if the home was bug-infested, wouldn't she have seen at least one roach when she toured it with the broker? Wouldn't she have seen them in the galley kitchen when she stored her groceries last night?

This was no ongoing infestation. These creeping, crawling germ carriers had been imported. She thought of the azaleas and put the two scenes together. Twice when she was out of the house, strange things had happened. Today, when the three of them were touring the grounds, she had left the back door unlocked. Someone could have walked right in. Someone was trying to intimidate her. Someone who wanted her out of the house. What had Mason Allen said in the courtroom yesterday? *Don't let the bedbugs bite.* Cheyenne calmed her breathing. First she needed insecticide—make that an exterminator. Then she needed to have a chat with Mr. Mason Allen.

As Cheyenne backed away from the mantel, praying the bugs wouldn't get far, she heard a scratching sound in the hallway. She backed against the wall of the drawing room and peered around the doorframe. A tabby cat the color of orange sorbet sat on its haunches, tail flicking side to side with agitation. The cat's fur was long and spiky, its bright eyes keen. It meowed once, then stretched its paws forward to roll into a four-legged stance. The cat slowly ambled toward her, lean and sleek.

"What the hell?" Cheyenne said quietly, so as not to shock it. *Okay, okay. Not so strange. Not so terrible.* She had feral cats on the property. Adam fed them. She knew this. An exterminator could handle those, too, if she were to ask.

The cat appealed to her with its round jade eyes. Cheyenne backed up a step. The cat, taking this as a sign, bounded past her into the drawing room and leapt at the window, grasping a fat roach in its paw. The cat snapped the roach in its mouth, then went for one on the curtain hem. Cheyenne was mortified. The only saving grace was that no one else was there to see a feral feline dining on vermin in her parlor.

"Good kitty. Sorbet. Good kitty," she whispered to the animal as she grabbed her shoulder bag and ran for the door.

Ruth stepped over brittle twigs, looking at the faded buildings that once made up Camp Idlewood. Released from the Hold Plantation's wrought-iron gates, she had headed blindly for the steep mountain road. After passing the abandoned fruit stand that had seemed dimly familiar, she had felt the mountainside rise beneath her tires. To the right, the road had offered breathtaking vistas where tourists gathered at pull-outs to gape at the misty valley below. And now she was here, at the place where she had spent ten successive summers between the ages of nine and eighteen.

The campus looked smaller now, its handful of Adirondack-style log structures scattered over five acres of cleared forestland. Fort Mountain State Park had purchased the land some time ago, and the buildings seemed to be in use as some kind of crafts and nature center. Ruth made her way to the old dining hall, with its metal crank windows that slowly wound open. She breathed in the familiar smell of live pines and felt her clogs sink into the forest floor. She sat on the steps of the dining hall, tucking her denim skirt around her, peering beyond the campus clearing into the dense woods.

Since the early 1900s, Idlewood had been a tradition among Southern black families with means, a place where girls imagined themselves as future debutantes and boys expected to make connections that would set them up for the future. She had been Little Orphan Ruthie there, viewed as a charity case and put in a bunk with Cheyenne Cotterell. She had no choice but to listen in on Cheyenne's fanciful tales about the foremother who was the wife of a Cherokee chief, about how Cheyenne dreamed of what it would be like to meet her ancestor and learn what she had experienced back then. Since Cheyenne came from a well-positioned Atlanta family, her Cherokee heritage made for an embarrassment of genealogical riches. Ruth couldn't hate her father and late mother for reducing her life to ashes, so she had hated Cheyenne instead. Cheyenne in her skinny pink tanks and J. Crew short shorts, her straight, penny-shiny ponytail doing its jaunty swing. Cheyenne with a gaggle of girls flocking around and a gang of boys gawking behind. Cheyenne and her perfect existence.

Ruth remembered the first time she heard Cheyenne throwing up her grilled cheese and fries in a toilet of the bunk room—how satisfying it had felt, how clarifying, to know Miss Princess found perfection only through fakery and self-abuse. She felt a twinge of remorse at the harsh thought, but only a twinge. Cheyenne was just the same now. Fake and perfect, finally the mistress of her Cherokee plantation, just as she had always dreamed. She deserved to live with a ghost, or whatever that girl Ruth saw had been. It wouldn't be the first time Cheyenne had lived with a lifeless roommate. But what about Jinx? The thought rushed over Ruth in a wave: she had not only left Cheyenne to some unnamable fate, she had left Jinx at the Cherokee Rose with no explanation or warning.

She stood and brushed off the seat of her skirt. She looked again at the empty camp buildings, allowing the thoughts that had tortured her many years ago to push through the surface of her long resistance: her mother had walked these dirt pathways; her mother had slept inside these cabins; her mother had been a girl here, safe and free.

It didn't take Ruth long to narrow the list of places where Jinx might be staying. There was one option: Room with a View Bed-and-Breakfast. She stopped in at the desk, inquired after Jinx, and learned about a cabin rental near the Ball Fruit Stand.

"Battis. Adam Battis," the man said to Ruth, holding out a lightly callused hand. He was a hunk with smoky dark eyes and muscled arms that, from the looks of his place, came honestly from hard work out of doors. She felt a twinge of jealousy. What did Jinx think about Adam Battis and his biceps? *Wait.* She knew that name, and not just because of Jinx's research subject. She vaguely remembered this house.

"Your mother used to sell amazing cookies in front of this house," she said. "I went to summer camp here. I'm Ruth Mayes."

"Camp Idlewood. Sure. Never could afford to go there myself. My mother lives in Dalton now, with her sister. I'll pass along your compliment."

"You didn't miss much. Idlewood wasn't all it was cracked up to be."

"I don't doubt it. What can I help you with? Are you looking for a room? I'm full tonight, I'm afraid, but there's a B&B a few miles up the road."

"I'm looking for a person. Jennifer Micco?" She sometimes goes by Jinx."

"Jennifer? Yep, she's here. Are you two together?"

"Not exactly."

"Yes," Jinx interrupted, pulling the door back to stand beside Adam. "I'm glad you didn't get too far away, Ruth."

Ruth looked from Adam to Jinx, at the easy way Jinx held the doorknob.

Adam was watching Ruth, his gaze perceptive. "Come on in. Jennifer's renting the place for a few nights. I just do the cooking sometimes and then head out to my tent. There's dinner left, if you're hungry."

Ruth followed them inside the rustic cabin lined with shelves of multicolored books. She settled in at the scuffed kitchen table while Adam warmed up something that smelled deliciously hearty. He poured himself and Ruth cups of decaf coffee and set a fresh can of Coke in front of Jinx.

"What brings you back to Fort Mountain, Ruth?" Adam said.

"I'm a magazine writer, here to do research on the closure of the

Hold House and the future of the historic site."

Adam chuckled, shaking his head. "So you're researching my lost job, and Jennifer's researching my dead ancestors. It sure is reassuring to know that the press and professors are on the case."

"I'm no professor," Jinx said. "I write for myself and for my tribe, not a bunch of close-minded academics."

"Right . . . ," Adam said slowly, cautiously. He took a sip of coffee. "And you two were down at the Hold House today. You met the new owner."

"Cheyenne Cotterell," Ruth said, her voice going flat.

"Cheyenne Cotterell," Adam repeated. "She is something."

He was smitten, Ruth saw immediately. Just like all the rest of them.

"A strong woman," Adam said. "She's got grit. Mason Allen gave her a hard time at the courthouse auction, but she stood her ground. Allen's used to being top dog around here. Comes from a powerful family, and had crazy luck in the real-estate market before the bubble burst. Allen saw this little northwest town as the next big development opportunity. He built luxury cabins up here in the mountains for Atlanta executives, owns an RV park for motor tourists down by the highway, and has condos under way by the river. He was planning to build a housing development for rich suburbanites on the Hold estate. He's a lot like old James Hold, to tell you the truth. A cold-hearted businessman. I've heard rumors that Allen was the one who put the parks commissioner up to auctioning off the Hold land in the first place. He thought he'd be the one to buy it. He didn't count on Ms. Cotterell."

Ruth listened with annoyance as she nibbled an oven fry and cut into her pork chop. He made Cheyenne Cotterell sound like Scarlett O'Hara trying to save Tara. But even if he was blinded by Cheyenne's charms, Ruth had to admit that Adam could cook. The tender pork chop met her tongue in a burst of savory flavor.

"What do you think Allen will do, now that he's lost his bid?" Jinx said.

"He won't give up, I can tell you that. Maybe he'll wait her out and see if she'll sell. It's not easy to run a big place like the Hold House."

"Adam used to manage operations when the house was open to the public," Jinx said to Ruth. "But doesn't it piss you off," she said, looking back at Adam, "that your family comes from that plantation, and other people can fight over it because they have the money?"

"Cheyenne claims her ancestor came from the Hold place, too." Ruth realized too late that this sounded like a defense.

"That's what she told me," Adam said.

"She insists her ancestor lived there, a black woman or black Cherokee," Ruth added. "Depending on Cheyenne's mood, the story gets more elaborate. She says her grandmother told her about a secret list of black Indians, the descendants of this woman, who were kicked out of the tribe because they were mixed-race. The list is supposed to be hidden somewhere, along with an equally secret treasure. It sounds like the BET version of an Indiana Jones plot to me. How likely is it that some prissy black interior designer is descended from rich Cherokees?"

"Unlikely, maybe, but not impossible," Adam said. "And I wouldn't call Cheyenne prissy."

"Of course you wouldn't," Ruth said. "You just met her, and you're already under her spell." She saw a grin tug at the corner of Jinx's mouth. "What?" Ruth snapped at her.

"You cast a pretty mean spell yourself, Ruth Mayes," Jinx said from across the table. "But you're too busy fixating on Cheyenne to realize it."

Ruth felt her earlobes warm beneath the bevy of spiral curls that covered them.

Adam shook his head, smiling. "I sure wish my friend Sally were with us. She would love this. Historical drama. Romantic mystery. Right here in our little town."

Ruth's mouth flew open. "Fine," she said. "Maybe what Cheyenne says is possible. But James Hold was a slave owner. They don't have such a good reputation as a class. It's much more likely that he owned

Cheyenne's supposed ancestor, a black slave woman, than that he married her and gave her the keys to the big house."

"And there's a third possibility," Jinx said. "If Cheyenne's ancestor was a slave, Hold could have owned her and slept with her. It happened in my tribe, though some people like to pretend it didn't." She looked at Adam. "Was James Hold ever known to take up with black women, consensually or not?"

Adam hesitated. "I've heard tell that anything was possible with him."

"Cheyenne told us Hold was murdered," Ruth said. "Does anybody know who killed him, or why?"

"Historians say it was his old friend turned enemy, Alexander Sands," Adam said. "The story goes that James went out riding one day with the Lighthorsemen, the Cherokee Nation militia, to chase down horse thieves. He came across Alexander, who insulted him. Well, old James Hold was not the type to tolerate disrespect. He whipped Alexander right in front of the Lighthorsemen. The next thing anybody knew, Hold was shot dead at Buffington's Tavern."

"Is that what you think?" Jinx asked. "That Sands did it?"

"Maybe Sands pulled the trigger. Maybe not. I do know plenty of people had a reason to want Hold dead." Adam spoke with a sober expression, eyes fixed on his coffee cup.

"Like Mary Ann Battis?" Jinx said, seizing on the silence behind Adam's words. "Would she have wanted him dead? I know she set fire to the mission station in Alabama. She seems like a tough, troubled girl who might do anything when pushed too far."

"She was barely fourteen when she came to the Hold Plantation. According to our family stories, she had a baby to take care of right away. Guess she felt she was trapped here."

Ruth's mind filled with an image: the flowing skirt, the dangling ribbons, the dim pearly light. A teenage girl stood on the line between this world and the next. River cane stalks whispered in the background. *Come. Come back.*

"We have to go back to the Hold House," Ruth said to Jinx. "Now."

12

ADAM SAT IN HIS BLUE CANVAS TENT with the flap tied open. The air outside had shifted since suppertime, carrying the faint scent of a coming rain. It was a small tent designed for one or two people. He shared the space with his sleeping bag, an empty crate that doubled as a bedside table, a stack of books, and his laptop computer, which sometimes did and sometimes didn't catch a wireless Internet signal from the Room with a View Bed-and-Breakfast up the road.

As soon as his company left that night, he'd tidied up the cabin and prepared it for Jennifer Micco's return. He didn't know what time she'd be back, given the odd circumstances of her departure, but she had rented the space. It was hers. Besides breaks for showers and meals, he stayed in his tent when he had a renter. That was the deal. What did they call it on the radio? The sharing economy? Folks in economic straits were turning to sharing more often these days to make ends meet. Adam did well with this arrangement, especially in the summer months. Since there was no mortgage on the cabin thanks to his parents—a mill worker and a cook—Adam's expenses went to food, utility bills, student loans, his mint-condition 1980 Ford Bronco, and quality gardening tools. The rest he used to take his mother out to dinner once a month and to stock his savings account.

When the state closed the museum six years ago, Adam had been twenty-seven, four years out of his forestry master's program and working at the Hold House. Once he was out of the job he loved, he'd started renting his cabin, saving his earnings in the hope that he might be able to buy the Hold place someday—or if not buy it, at least rent land around the old mission cabin. This was where his grandmother had grown up, and boy, did she have stories. The family member he was named for, Adam Battis, was born in that cabin, where his great-great-great-grandmother Mary Ann had lived. His grandmother said they descended from two lines: one African American, one Cherokee. Exactly how those lines got crossed, she hadn't known, or hadn't seen fit to tell him. But she always said two proud bloodlines linked together were stronger than one alone.

Adam sighed and stretched his legs on the thin canvas that did nothing to cushion his muscles from the hard ground beneath. He would help Cheyenne if she'd let him, and tend the fruit trees for Sally, but the hope of living there one day, of restoring his family's cabin, was a notion he would have to let go of. Even knowing what he knew now, he didn't have the heart to try to force Cheyenne's hand. Adam took a gulp from his water bottle and lifted his laptop back onto his thighs.

The WPA slave narratives were searchable online, digitized by the Library of Congress. Adam had found the website an hour ago and was still pondering the import of what he had discovered there. He flipped open the black lid of his laptop, reread the electronic pages he had been struggling to absorb. Five former slaves from the Hold Plantation in

Murray County, Georgia, had been interviewed in 1932. The interviewer had asked questions about their owner, food rations, physical treatment, and what they thought of Abraham Lincoln. A man named Michael Gamble was among the five interviewees. He had been born in 1850 and listed Michael and Hettie Gamble as his parents. Michael Gamble told the interviewer his family had lived in the refurbished barn of the mission station, right alongside Miss Mary Ann Battis. Miss Battis, Gamble explained to the confused interviewer, had helped raise two children on the Cherokee Rose Plantation, neither of whom was hers. One of them, Isaac Cotterell, was the child of a local black preacher. The other, Adam Battis, was the illegitimate son of a young slave and none other than Chief James Hold himself.

Ruth gazed out on the shadowed oaks and the burnished brick structure. The Hold House was nearly dark. Only a small arc of light shone from the master bedroom window, casting a dim, eerie glow. Ruth parked her Beetle, imagining Cheyenne ensconced in a cluster of pillows in the high canopy bed. Knowing Cheyenne, she was probably wearing two-hundred-dollar pajamas and a sateen eye mask to match.

Ruth waited for Jinx to exit the car. They rounded the house beneath a full white moon. A breeze rustled the branches, sending warm ripples through the humid air. They picked their way through weeds and wildflowers to the missionary cabin situated behind the big house. Ruth used her iPhone for illumination. It shone like a firefly as she held it out before her. Jinx carried a heavy black flashlight that she had retrieved from her truck back at Adam's. She swung it as she walked with that steady, loping stride, dark braid swaying like the grasses beneath their feet.

Ruth ducked into the cabin ahead of Jinx.

"What are we looking for?" Jinx said.

"I'm not sure. I just knew I had to come back." Ruth moved to the spot where they had sat earlier that day. She lowered herself to the ground facing the doorway, nudging her glasses higher when they slipped down her nose.

Jinx squatted beside her. "What?" she said gently. "What happened here, Ruth? I mean, besides between the two of us. What did you see today?"

Ruth turned to face her. She hesitated. "I saw a girl around the age of fourteen. She was like a flicker, a shimmer, in the sunlight. I heard a sound, a sort of voice, calling me. I've never believed in ghosts before. Not that I was closed to it, but I always thought if ghosts were real, my mother would come back to me somehow."

Jinx sank into a sitting position. She reached out to touch Ruth's back. Her fingers were warm and comforting through the thin cotton of the Chococat T-shirt Ruth wore. Ruth leaned into Jinx, letting their shoulders touch.

"Maybe your mother *is* coming back, in a way you didn't expect," Jinx said. "Ruth, your mother is part of you. You can acknowledge her presence as much or as little as you choose to."

"You're still close with your great-aunt," Ruth said.

"She's always been my guiding light. But as much as I loved her, will always love her, I'm starting to realize she didn't see everything clearly. She wouldn't have liked me being here with you like this, for instance."

"Because I'm a woman."

"And because you're not Creek." Jinx paused. "Correction. Because you're African American. Aunt Angie had a rigid view of the order of things. But there are variations on tradition. I want to do what she did, to help our people by telling our history, but I need to do it in my own way."

Ruth nodded in the darkness, unfolding the knot of her fist and offering an open hand to Jinx. Jinx took Ruth's hand in hers. They sat together breathing, feeling the humid air around them, smelling the dirt of the cabin floor and the raw wood of the walls. The breeze outside rustled the river cane.

Ruth peered at the open doorway where she had seen the girl, where she had tripped the first time she entered the cabin. She sucked in her breath. "The threshold," she said. She leapt to her feet and moved to the doorway. She brushed her hands across the wooden frame, feeling the flow of the grain. "She was standing right here," Ruth said, "the image, the girl. What if she wanted to show me something? What if she had a message?"

She dropped to the floor, inching her hand across the sill. The single plank lay unevenly across the dirt floor. Why use a wooden door sill on a dirt floor? Ruth shoved her glasses up, squinting in the white light that Jinx was shining on the ground. Near the end of the plank, the floor dipped, forming a subtle indenture.

"I need a tool," Ruth said. "Something to dig with."

Jinx was already gone, shining her flashlight through the dust-coated rooms.

"Here," she said. "I found these in a back room." She handed Ruth a gardening trowel and kept the spade.

They dug at the dip in the ground. Two inches deep. Three to four inches wide. The dirt softened and fell away beneath their tools. They reached a hollow space.

"It's a ground safe, a keeping pit." Ruth's words tumbled over each other. "Slaves used to dig them in their quarters, to store food and hide treasured items, sort of like a safe-deposit box."

Jinx laid the flashlight at the edge of the hole and reached a hand inside. She pulled out a conch shell, six silver buttons, a small glass vial, and a pair of green spectacles. Below those was a wooden box. She paused, looking at Ruth.

"Go ahead," Ruth whispered.

Jinx pulled the box out of the ground and gently wiped the dirt from its surface. It was fashioned of light chestnut wood with intricate floral carvings.

"How lovely," Ruth said.

She reached over to Jinx's lap and unhooked the small metal clasp, lifting the tight lid open. A square of scarlet silk was spread inside. Jinx unfurled the folds of the cloth. A sheath of manuscript pages, brittle and thin, nestled within the fabric.

"I don't believe this is happening," Jinx said.

"Neither do I. Take out a page." Ruth grabbed the flashlight from the ground and directed the beam toward Jinx.

Jinx's hand shook as she reached for the sheet of curled paper. The amber edge flaked at her touch. She stilled her hand and read aloud.

The Diary of a Mission to the Cherokees, by Anna Rosina Gamble, Sister in Christ

February 14, 1815

The rain fell and would not stop. It continued, unabated, throughout the last portion of our long journey southward. We passed through the mountains beneath the clear blue of sky, but entered Virginia with the drops constantly upon our backs. It was a bone chilling rain. My husband directed the trembling horses from the front of the wagon, his dark hat a covering over his thoughts. My skirts gathered about my knees, weighted down by the torrent. My sogged hair escaped its pins and hung about my shivering shoulders. From time to time, my husband chanced to glance at me, observing my discomfort. But he did not choose to speak or slow our pace. A higher calling urged us onward. We are expected within two weeks in the territory of the Cherokee Indians, where we will endeavor to spread God's word.

Only when the wagon's wheels stuck fast in the mud did he see fit to stop. He sloshed down to the ground in his boots, and with the help of a stranger, freed us. With our horses fatigued, and us besides, we consented to rest at an inn near Knoxville, the great center city of the Southwest Territory. We retired to our room before supper. My shoes had filled so with water that I thought they were buckets. My hair hung about my face like melted beeswax. I helped my husband to undress first and prepared his coat for drying while he studied his Bible by the fireside. Peeling off my skirt and petticoat, I lay them beside the fire to dry. I cast my gaze about the chamber, from dripping skirts to silent spouse, wishing for the simple comforts of home.

I stared into the nascent flames, bright in the dimness, and reflected on all that I had left behind. I sacrificed my post as head teacher to the girls of Bethlehem village in order to answer this sacred calling. When John Gamble was named Head Missionary to the Cherokee Indians, a selection approved by the Lot, our earthly interpreter of Divine will, the elders of the Church agreed that Mr. Gamble should marry in order to ensure the success of the endeavor. Two women from his town of Salem were tried, but failed to gain the Lot's approval. And then, recalling that I had accompanied Brother Loskiel as his secretary on a journey to the Ohio Indians, the elders approached me, my father and mother having both passed on many years before. Upon hearing what my marriage should be—a partnership for the work and glory of Christ—I agreed to wed at the late age of forty years. The Lot approved. There was neither necessity nor time for courtship. I relocated from Pennsylvania to the merchant village of Salem, North Carolina. There, in our foremost Southern Moravian town, I found a neatness and simplicity that could not fail but to excite the feelings. The buildings were remarkably trim, the gardens pretty, and the streets neatly paved. A noxious weed or tangled grass could not be found, for everything was kept in perfect order. We dwelled in Salem for the better part of a year as we prepared to depart, and many dear friendships were sewn there.

This journey from Salem to the Cherokee nation is the first that I have taken with my husband. How I miss my countrywomen of Salem. How I fondly recall my students of Bethlehem and the specimen garden beyond the schoolyard where we assayed a menagerie of plants. I have packed with me seeds and seedlings, tucked within a burlap wrap which I have not had to moisten due to the constant rain. I have also brought, in linen pockets sewn by my skillful students, a small collection of my favorite tomes: The Book of Common Prayer, An Introduction to Botany, A Botanical Arrangement of British Plants, and Paradise Lost. Besides my good husband, these books will be my only faithful company in the heathen land. And more books yet will be sent, together with sundry supplies, once we have safely arrived in Cherokee country. My sacrifice of the comforts of home is a requirement of this mission, and one that I make willingly. For I have long desired to venture again into the unknown wild, taking the Light of our Savior to the aborigines of America.

I stood and turned the clothing beside the fire in the bedchamber of the inn, lit the candles, and prepared the beds for sleeping. The room smelled of damp and the musk of its former inhabitants. How I wished I could have brought with me a servant to ease the labor of our travels. But none could be spared by the Church, and my husband has been directed to rent one from Mr. Hold, who, we are told, is a very wealthy planter of his tribe with many Negroes to spare. Besides being an aid with the housework, such a servant might also be predisposed to understanding the Indians' tongue, of which we have no knowledge.

I folded the woolen blankets back, making a sleeve of warmth for my husband. He settled himself and consented to close his piercing grey-green eyes. When his breathing aligned into a regular pattern of sound and silence, I peeled away the cool, wet underthings that modesty had precluded me from freeing myself of. I lay my soaked shift and stockings beside the fire, pulled on a dry cotton gown, and braided my tangled hair. I turned to the second bed, grasped the blanket, and had only begun to rest myself when my husband called my name. His voice was low within the silent room, and yet cloaked by that firmness that underwrote his character. I turned toward him. His eyes were stern upon me. I rose and answered his call.

Jinx looked up from the wreck of a page and into Ruth's eyes. "I know this woman," she said. "The missionary, Anna Rosina Gamble. I found a reprint of an old Moravian Church history at a secondhand bookstore in Tennessee. It included a summary of Anna Rosina's work in Cherokee territory, as recounted by her student. That student was Mary Ann Battis. The book said Anna Rosina kept a diary of her time on the plantation, a full-length manuscript that was lost."

"Well, it's not lost anymore," Ruth said. "And someone always knew where it was."

"Mary Ann," Jinx said. "The girl you saw. She must have hidden it when she lived here. But she never told the church about it. She kept it secret from them. I wonder why."

"Keep going," Ruth said.

She leaned over Jinx's lap, squinting at the barely legible manuscript pages. The curling script faded into the paper like so many watermarks. How could Jinx make it out, the faded, looping words, the *s*'s that looked like *f*'s, the disappeared punctuation marks? Ruth tried to read along, tried to follow with her eyes as Jinx picked up the story with the next diary entry.

Jinx stumbled in her reading at first and then caught a rhythm, the particular cadence of Anna Rosina Gamble's lines. Ruth gave up trying to read along and closed her eyes, letting Jinx's smooth voice carry the story. She felt the hard dirt floor beneath her legs, the humid evening air around her, the paintbrush end of Jinx's braid brushing her arm. She breathed in the smell of the manuscript pages, a scent like crushed leaves, a scent like sifting baskets. Plant matter. Jinx read on, her voice the breeze, her voice the river cane. *Shh, shh.*

March 3, 1815

The journey to Cherokee territory was tedious and slow, with many difficulties to be endured. The greater therefore was our relief when on the first day of March we safely reached the Cherokee settlement called Hold Hill. At evenfall, we were directed to Mr. Hold's plantation by a wandering, paperless Negro, who, when Mr. Gamble inquired, indicated through signs, for he spoke only the Indians' tongue, that he was a free man. Mr. Hold's plantation is a broad swath of land, consisting of a rough set of buildings chiseled out of the wilderness between the woods and a field of river cane so tall that one cannot see beyond it. His own house, a fine and fancy brick affair just recently built, is impressive indeed for this country. We have been told that his is the most profitable and civilized of all the Cherokee establishments, for Mr. Hold has put his plantation profits into the development of various mercantile establishments. He owns two trading posts and ferries besides, and seeks to establish a gristmill.

Upon our arrival, Mr. Gamble climbed down from the wagon, removing his hat for less than an instant while he wiped perspiration from his folded brow. The nearness of the river's flow makes the air here wet, with or without a rainfall. Mr. Gamble has the thin, drawn face of a man always thinking: of what should be done, what must be done, and how it should best be accomplished. Every aspect of his existence is drawn and quartered through the chastening prism of duty. He is held in much esteem by our Church for these qualities of single mindedness and dogged self discipline. He directed me to remain in the wagon and approached a cabin with glass paned windows situated along the road to the main house. There he met Mr. Geiger, Mr. Hold's business manager. I breathed a relieving sigh at the sight of Mr. Geiger, standing at the cabin door in woolen breeches. He is a white man, and German by descent as we Moravians are.

I let my worrying fingers come to rest upon my lap. The details of our stay here have been prearranged by elders of our Church and the Cherokee Agent for the U. States, Return Jonathan Meigs. Agent Meigs pledged to help support our labors from the national Dept. of War funds. The remainder of our support comes from our brethren and sisters in Christ and the profit of whatever goods we might barter with the Indians. The chiefs in council of the Cherokee nation have consented to have a Christian mission, provided that a school should teach their children the English language. Our Church elders insist that such a school, if it be established, must instruct in religion as well as English, and must room and board the children in order to extricate them from the daily influence of their heathen households. None other than the prominent Mr. Hold himself has offered to host the mission on the grounds of his estate.

When Mr. Gamble inquired about water and food for our horses, Mr. Geiger called for servants from the barn. The two men, bulky as barrels and darker skinned than soot, set down our trunks on the dusty, red road and then led our horses away. Mr. Geiger conversed with my husband in English, the language of preference here next to the Indians' tongue, explaining that Mr. Hold was away on business in Charleston, Carolina, and that we should stay in the main house until a cabin of our own can be prepared.

We were accompanied to Mr. Hold's home, where upon we met his wives, as Mr. Hold and the Indians here practice the sin of adultery as if it is indeed a virtue, customarily keeping for themselves more than one wife, and sometimes as many as five. Mr. Hold has two wives—a younger one, who is quite lovely and speaks the English language much, the daughter of a Cherokee woman and an English trader; and an elder wife, who speaks only her native tongue and is said to be the younger one's half sister. The younger Mrs. Hold lives with her husband in the brick house. The elder Mrs. Hold, having her own peculiar dwelling in a cleared spot within the river cane, was merely visiting the home of her husband on the day that we arrived. It appeared, however, that the elder wife took precedence over the younger even in the house that was not her own, for she was the one who bid us to come inside. She gave us gifts of woven cloth and a basket of dried, dark berries, which I judged to fall within the Rubus genus. The younger wife directed a Negro girl of perhaps twelve, who then heated water in a kettle suspended above the fire and made us a refreshment of tea. There was no sugar, for Mr. Hold had not returned from his latest trading venture. Nor was there honey or anything nearly so sweet. To accompany our tea, we were served plain cornbread and a sour hominy meal that reeked of lye.

The contrast embedded in this place is striking. The house, which had stood the better part of a year, according to Mr. Geiger, boasts glass windows, triple stories, and verandas to channel the breeze. On the inside, however, it feels much like the rough hewn dwellings of the Carolina country folk, having none of the refinement of our Moravian village structures. The rooms are full of dirt and confusion. The walls smell of hominy and wood smoke, and the air is thick with the residue of too many bodies in motion. My husband and I sleep on mats beside the fire in the rear most parlor of the house, for there are neither bedrooms nor beds to spare in this large abode. The younger

Mrs. Hold retires in a room on the second floor in the evenings, and the elder Mrs. Hold continues her visit mainly to survey us, sleeping in a spare room in the upper chamber. Various men and women whose names we were never told sleep and visit within the house as if it is an outdoor camp, bringing in food from the separated kitchen, taking their meals in any room they please, and clogging the already fetid air with the swill of pipe smoke.

A host of children also scamper through the house, feeding themselves from a large pot of stew nursed on top of the fireplace coals and otherwise running around the plantation grounds unchecked. When they frolic out of doors, which for them is a constant pastime, the children graze directly from the edible trees and plant life. I am told that the pink blossoms of the Eastern Redbud shrub (Cercis canadensis), are as delightful a treat to these children as pastry cakes to the youths of Bethlehem. There is no school for the Indian children here to attend, and no discipline is exacted from them, so that they dash to and fro like wayward field mice with the Negro children as their sole companions. Some of these Indian youngsters, I have learned, belong to Mr. Hold by paternity. The others are his nieces and nephews, the children of his sisters. The younger Mrs. Hold retains the rosy cheeked blush of unblemished youth. She appears to be less than eighteen years and has no children of her own. The majority of Mr. Hold's children, we are told, live in their mothers' respective towns, for Hold had other wives before, or in addition to, the two whom we have met.

The familial life of these Indians is a complete confusion. No one of organized mind could unwind these tangled genealogical registers. Besides the unnamed persons, upward of twenty of whom seem to regularly dwell here, sundry Indians visit the place from day to day, some, but not all, being distant relatives of the Holds. Many a night we must share our sleeping spot beside the fire, rendering what should have been a fine parlor cramped and malodorous.

March 8, 1815

This tedious phase of our stay has lasted for nearly a week, while we await Mr. Hold's return from southern Carolina. During the days, Mr. Gamble studies the lay of the place, walking about the plantation with Mr. Geiger as his guide. If we were back at home in Salem or my beloved Bethlehem, I too should walk freely about. But here, at my husband's direction, I stay behind, shut up like an invalid in the hazy home of the Holds, with only Christ Jesus, and you, Dear Diary, as my interlocutors.

The younger Mrs. Hold does not often speak, but smiles politely and keeps about her work of spinning thread and weaving cotton in what would be called the drawing room in a proper house of this size. The skills she displays have been lately learned by some of the mixed blood women in this country. The older Mrs. Hold, by contrast, speaks quite freely in my presence. I must confess that the cutting syllables of the Indians' language grate on my ears, like a wind sharpened twig repeatedly scraping against the bubbled glass of a windowpane. The constant flow of voluble, unintelligible sound is reminiscent of the mythical Sibyls. I wonder, as Mrs. Hold mutters her incantations, if they are not directed in protest of our presence here. Most of these people, we have been warned by Agent Meigs, believe in ancient superstitions, in beings above and below this world, in witches taking human form, in magic, medicine men, and ancestor ghosts. Many would be loath to learn the Gospel of the Lord, the one true Savior. Showing them the Light will require dedication and steadfast resolve, qualities which my husband possesses in abundance. But even as the older wife shakes her finger and mutters in a repelling, guttural hum, the younger Mrs. Hold has already begun to touch my heart. Her actions toward me are reserved, it is true. She does not consent to pray with me upon invitation. Nevertheless, she possesses a politeness of manners inculcated, it must be surmised, by her English father. This, together with a light behind her amber eyes that burns intensely when she sets about a given task, instills in me the hope that she might someday be won for the Lord.

A high screech sounded from the rear of the cabin, breaking the rhythm of Jinx's voice. Ruth started where she sat.

"A barn cat," Jinx said, looking up from the page. A streak of matted black fur flashed along the back wall, then faded into the shadows. "This is amazing," she said. "A historian's dream. I wonder if anyone's ever seen a diary like it, with such an intimate view of a plantation owned by Indians."

"We should find Cheyenne," Ruth sighed, annoyed but certain. "She'll want to hear this, too."

"You're right. Nice thought." Jinx gave Ruth a smile that warmed her like a hot drink on a cold day.

13

JINX CLASPED THE CHESTNUT BOX to her chest as they hurried from the cabin and rounded the house to reach the front door. She rang the bell. Through the windows, she saw Cheyenne traipsing down the staircase in an ivory silk robe and rhinestone-studded flip-flops. The peach sheen of her pajamas peeked from behind the folds of her robe. Her hair hung straight and loose around her shoulders.

Cheyenne flung open the door. "Ladies, what is all this racket? This is not a good time. I'm trying to get my beauty sleep."

"I think your beauty will survive, Cheyenne. We have something to show you," Ruth said.

"I thought you left for Minnesota."

"I almost did, but I thought better of it when I realized you need me."

"I need *you?*" Cheyenne said, incredulous.

"That's right." Ruth paused. "What's that smell?" She pushed past Cheyenne to get a look into the hallway.

Jinx followed her. The chemical stench of bug spray assaulted their senses.

Cheyenne's confident expression faltered. "It's nothing. I had a few bugs in the drawing room, okay? I sprayed them, and the exterminator is coming tomorrow."

"Trouble in paradise," Ruth said.

"Nothing I can't handle. So, what is this you're so eager to show me?" Cheyenne fixed her eyes on the intricate box Jinx was cradling. "Is something in there?"

"A diary," Jinx said. "Written by a missionary. It chronicles her experiences here during the plantation's early years. We found it buried in the mission cabin."

"Let me see that, please."

Jinx released the chestnut box into Cheyenne's hands.

Cheyenne's robe slid up her arms as she opened the lid. She peered at the top page tucked inside. "It's completely illegible," she said. "The writing's faded. What on earth does this say?"

"It's old cursive script. Jinx can make out most of it," Ruth said.

"We can't sit in the drawing room," Cheyenne said quickly. "We'll have to go to the dining room. Follow me." She slammed the front door, turned the lock, and pushed a heavy cardboard box against the lower panel.

Jinx made eye contact with Ruth, raising her eyebrows. Who, or what, was Cheyenne trying so hard to keep out?

Cheyenne led them into the dining room. The table was set just as it had been that morning—blue and white bone china on a white cloth, silver utensils, goblets. Jinx glanced up at the golden phoenix above one of the silk-draped windows, thinking of what this room had been like, what this house had been like, when Anna Rosina first visited. She imagined the press of people upstairs and down, the squeals of children and smell of pipe smoke. She imagined the warmth of the fires and light of the candles. A bustling home.

"Well?" Cheyenne said, settling in at the head of the table, where James Hold would have sat. "I'm dying to know what's in this thing." She opened the box and handed Jinx several diary pages, careful to keep the rest of them close to her.

Jinx looked at Cheyenne beside her and Ruth across the table. "Let's go in," she said.

March 15, 1815

> *The Passion Week prior to Good Friday commenced with Mr. Hold's return to his coarse estate. He brought with him a chain of wagons pulled by thick oxen and filled with an avalanche of useful and frivolous things: kettles, knives, and pottery dishes, bundles of pungent cinnamon sticks, sacks of sugar, pre-made dresses, barrels of rum, bricks of tea, leather shoes with silver buckles, fine writing papers, coats and coatees, eating utensils, reading matter, scented soaps, aprons of lace, silk scarves, hats, gloves, and a coffle of African slaves. All of these jostled one on top of the other in and behind the open topped wagons, whose creaking joints testified to their frequent use.*
>
> *Agent Meigs had informed us that the opening of the federal road adjacent to Mr. Hold's estate has played a large part in the growth of his fortune. Mr. Hold travels the road frequently to trade his field and orchard crops for manufactured wares in the finest cities of the South. Piloting each wagon home is a Negro driver with the wooden face of a painted toy soldier. Beside the first driver, the master himself sat with a grim and forceful air. Mr. Hold's skin is as*

fair as that of any white man one might encounter along the streets of Salem. He wore his wavy, pitch black hair shorn at the ears, a tailored shirt of Irish linen, and a silk cravat. His dark eyes are brooding, his jaw squarely cut, his lips the color of a bruised summer plum. When Mr. Hold swung his legs down from the seat, his body moved all of a piece, as if he were a large cat caught and corralled from the mountains behind his sprawling estate. On Mr. Hold's left hip, a dirk protruded from its sheath. Inside his right hand, he grasped a pistol. He strode about in his fine cut breeches, thick white stockings, and Hessian boots, casting his eyes over the gathered assemblage of Cherokee women and slaves. The older Mrs. Hold wore her customary simple shift with men's deerskin leggings beneath. The younger Mrs. Hold, having some sense of proper etiquette, dressed herself for reception in a garnet toned velour frock, soft wool shawl, and bonnet to secure her from the ever threatening springtime rains. Mr. Hold seemed not to notice the effort which she had made to braid and loop her long dark hair. Failing to greet her beyond a nod, he spoke a few brief words to his Negro driver, who wore a turban in the Indian style and a knife at his side like his master. Repeating the Cherokee words that his master had spoken, the driver called to the other black men who had gathered by the side of the dusty road. They then began to unload mounds of supplies, carrying items within their arms or across their backs, to the main house, the barn, and a log storehouse several paces away.

From a wheat or cotton field far off in the distance, a bulky man whom I had not met began a slow approach. His pantaloons were worn at the ankles, his straw hat stiffened with sweat, and his work boots caked with soil and loose sprouts of grass. Unlike Mr. Hold's tightly woven dress shirt, this man's shirt was homespun from coarse linsey wool, a fabric rougher even than the sunburnt skin of his taut, irregular features. I took him to be of Scotch-Irish stock, the descendant of unruly Highlanders, quite like his half breed Indian employer. Upon reaching the motley crowd assembled by the wagons—made up of Mr. Hold's family and slaves, Mr. Gamble and myself, the clerk Mr. Geiger, and a few unaccounted for white men and Cherokees—he shook Mr. Hold's hand, barked an order to the nearest Negro, and came to stand before the line of tethered slaves that stretched behind the wagons like a trail of dried blood.

They were a pitiful sight to behold, those men, two women, and a single small child, whose lives were now entwined by the thick rope that bound them. Their twelve bowed bodies were draped in rags. Their feet were bare. One man limped, his toes chewed away by the morning frosts of a long forced journey. A middle-aged woman with cracked, dry skin crawled on her hands and knees, apparently affected by the same cruel malady. The child, who seemed to belong with her, clung to her neck and sobbed. A young woman beside the pair flicked her gaze about, keenly taking in the surroundings. The smooth skin of her face glowed a buckeye brown. Her eyes flashed the color and shape of almonds. Her hair wound around itself in a series of spiral knots. Her limbs were long and lithe. She stepped slightly forward, as if to shield the weaker two with her half clothed frame. The man I took for the overseer halted before her, stretched out his arm, and pounded her chin with the force of a gale, pushing her back into line with the others. She reached out an arm behind her, fingers fanned, not to break her own fall, but to cushion the woman and child, who shrunk in the shadow of the man. But it was she who crashed back, rather than they, under the crush of the overseer's fist. "My name is Samuel Talley," he grunted to the woman and line of eleven others in a voice low and thick. "And y'all nigras are mine now."

The crowd loosened as men and women alike stumbled back from the scene unfolding, waves of anxiety fanning out like ripples in a human pond. The younger Mrs. Hold gasped but did not speak. The older Mrs. Hold mumbled something at once furious and unintelligible, beckoned to an aged black man and woman, and began a slow retreat with them across the yard and toward the dense canebrake. Mr. Geiger scribbled on his fluttering leaves, keeping a written inventory for Mr. Hold. I had never in my life seen such a display. The possession of Negroes by our church to assist with the necessary labors of life was quiet and humane. Black servants could join the church if they professed the faith, worship in Home Church sanctuary, and, until recent years when the Strangers' Cemetery became the preferred practice, be buried in God's Acre along with their white brothers and sisters. My husband watched the scene unfold, expressionless.

The stricken woman rolled on her heels, a bloom of blood trickling from the corner of her nose to merge with another sprouting from her lip. Her breasts were now exposed by the sagging neck of her ragged shift. She lifted her eyes from the ground. Talley knotted his fist. Mr. Hold raised his hand, causing Talley to pause. Mr. Hold approached the woman on the ground, rolled his gaze over her flesh—the quaking shoulders, the brilliant blood. When he bent to cup the roundness of her upper arm, the tassels on his Hessian boots hissed.

"What is your name?" he murmured, near enough to her ear to bestow a kiss.

"Patience." She was softly crying now, her brown eyes directed toward the ground.

"Give this one to my little wife," he said to his overseer, rising. "Send the men to the field cabins. And these damaged ones," he continued, gesturing toward the shuddering woman and child, "they should do for the missionaries." Mr. Hold looked directly, then, at my husband, rudely acknowledging his presence.

This exchange constituted the first English words that the master of Hold Hill had spoken in our midst, and there was in them no trace of the heathen tongue. Educated from the time of his youth by a private tutor, Mr. Hold was now a perfect chameleon, his colors shifting fluidly from white man to red Indian, leaving no trace from one form to the next. Talley flushed beneath his leathered skin, feeling, perhaps, the acid sting of open rebuke.

Mr. Hold then commenced a long legged stride toward the big brick house. The wagons had been emptied, the women and child cut from the rope line, the male slaves led away to the fields of wheat and cotton. The slave called Patience was directed to the house by an elderly, coal black woman named Grace, whose calm countenance could not obscure the sadness in her eyes. I followed my husband, who followed Mr. Hold. Behind us, the crippled woman crawled, her young son grasping the hem of her filthy dress. The smell of cinnamon, sweat, and fear clung to the air. I felt within me a stain of shame for having been present at this spectacle, the silent witness to an evil spreading its blackened wings.

March 22, 1815

Easter Sunday. The weather was stormy again. We attempted a morning service in the brick house of the Holds. The crippled woman assigned to us, who answers to the name of Faith, her little son, and the household slaves were our sole co-celebrants. The downcast Patience seemed glad of the chance to escape the bedchamber of Mr. and Mrs. Hold, where she is often retained to administer some service or other, even in the absence of her mistress. Our hope of bringing the Gospel here has yet to find fertile ground. It looks very dark in this land.

March 28, 1815

We have been one month in the home of the Holds. Faith does little more than manage my sewing and stir the coals beneath the stewing pots. Her little son, Michael, a yellow boy about the age of ten, fetches firewood from the nearby forest and tends to my husband's personal effects. Patience cooks for the Holds and their motley stream of ruffian guests, replacing the bumbling machinations of the twelve year old girl whose sour hominy greeted us upon our arrival. Unlike the girl, who was born and raised in Cherokee country and knows only the Indians' dishes and tongue, Patience came to the Holds with suitable experience as a cook for white people. Her yeast rolls we have found quite agreeable, as well as her chicken pie, which she spices with pennyroyal from the herbs I have planted in hollowed gourds. The girl, we have learned, has since been sent to Mr. Hold's older sister, where she might find an audience more eager for her savage fare. Her mother was also disposed of at that time, being sent to the wife of the Assistant Cherokee Agent William Lovely, who had put in an order for a Negress.

April 1, 1815

We now have milk. The elder Mrs. Hold brought us a cow from the cattle range at the far edge of Mr. Hold's establishment. There, I have learned from Faith, an elderly couple from Africa who speak only their native tongue, keep the cattle. As we had nowhere to pen this cow, we asked Mrs. Hold to take it back for the time being. Through the younger Mrs. Hold's translations, she entreated us to keep it, lest Mr. Hold become angry with her. Gone was the threatening Sibyl whose presence had commanded this house upon our arrival. Now that her husband had returned, the older

Mrs. Hold appeared shrunken in the doorway, her indecipherable words like a dust cloud around her, the faded calico dress hanging loose as a shroud. It was then that I began to suspect a darker side to Mr. Hold, who seems to hold his two wives in invisible chains. She turned and retreated to her peculiar dwelling in the trees, where an aged black couple that she has owned since her childhood live with her as equals. We have tied the cow behind the brick house for the moment, for there are no fences here.

April 9, 1815

All sins and scandals are going full swing and one can see clearly that the prince of this realm still keeps the Indians bound with chains of darkness. Mr. Hold's Negroes cart rum by the barrel into the dwelling house, where Mr. Hold, his Indian guests, his overseer and craftsmen, all partake together. On Tuesday last, Mr. Hold shot at the elder Mrs. Hold because she refused him some meat belonging to her aged slave couple. Her life was spared by a courageous black servant named Demas, who stood between her and the threatening specter of her husband. Demas's life was saved in turn by Mr. Hold's wavering aim, hindered, as he was, by his rum induced state. After the altercation, Mr. Hold had Demas dragged from his bed, disrobed, whipped, and chained to the hitching post for all to see.

April 10, 1815

The elder Mrs. Hold has determined to relocate to Etowah town together with her Negroes to live in the household of her brother. She *says that she cannot reside near this husband any longer. Mr. Hold's house has indeed become a Sodom during his stays between trading ventures. He lays about the place in his ruffle fronted shirts, swigging rum and dancing with his slaves to the tune of the Negro Isaac's fiddle. His constant companions are his pistol and dirk, which he hesitates not to unveil at the slightest provocation. His younger wife, appareled in long skirts of somber hues, wilts in the corners on these occasions, trying to disappear herself into the plaster walls. But having no respect for the delicacy of the female sex, Mr. Hold hikes her up, swinging her to his right side in a rough embrace whilst hoisting the slave woman, Patience, on his left. I see from the distant look in her eyes that the younger Mrs. Hold longs for an elsewhere. I speak to her at every opportunity about the salvation of the Lord and the everlasting peace of His Heavens, so that she may one day be brought to the knowledge of her one true friend, Jesus Christ our Lord.*

Beyond Mr. Hold's home and fields, his mill at the creek, and his ferry at the river, lies a wild mountain fastness. We are sequestered at a far remove from Christian civilization. And Mr. Hold behaves like a heathen lord of his manor.

April 14, 1815

In need of a proper place to begin our work in the virgin field of the Lord, my husband requested assistance in building a house of our own. Mr. Hold determined instead to remake his separate log frame kitchen into a mission station whilst building a new kitchen in the cellar of the brick house. He lent ten of his slaves, who proved to be able workmen, to accomplish the task. They added two rear rooms to the one room kitchen, complete with cut glass windows.

They whitewashed the inner rooms until our cabin glowed like a single star of civilization in the firmament of this heathen land.

I have set myself to the task of making our cabin into a house of God. Oh, how I long to bring the light into this little domicile. For surely from our hearth Good News will flow, and a light will be set upon this darkened country. Our public meeting space has been established in the front of the structure, within the former kitchen. The bedchamber that Mr. Gamble and I are to share is situated toward the back of the cabin. The second rear room will be used to house our scholars until such time as it becomes overfull, whereupon the students will be moved to board in the garret of the main house under the care of Mrs. Hold. Our wide brick oven, fashioned to my specifications by Isaac, one of Mr. Hold's most highly skilled slaves, occupies the front room sidewall, where a sleeping enclosure was also fitted for Faith, the crippled woman, and her son, our mission's servants. We procured our furnishings from Mr. Hold's storehouse, where he kept several pieces carved by his former master craftsman, a Negro lately sold for a hefty price to the Nathaniel Russell family of Charleston. The Negro Isaac, a slave of many talents, was the artisan's protégée.

I have sewn curtains of blue cotton produced by the slave women in the weaving house, arranged the woolens we brought with us inside the carved blanket chest, lined our beloved books along the poplar shelving, and hung sage and rosemary from the front room window. The young Mrs. Hold has supplied us with gourds for carrying water and serving. To these, we have added proper dishes sent to us by our dear brothers and sisters back in Salem. The mail is slow to arrive in this part of the country. Mr. Hold has the only contract with the U. States government to deliver it, which he fulfills with the labor of his slave boys, whose minds become distracted, or whose legs cannot go the distance from settlement to distant settlement. But oh, the joy of receiving packages from our old friends, with their accounts of the mission stations around the world, shoes for Mr. Gamble and our servants, fabric for my sewing, and robust coffee beans. We should want for medicines too, for my latent cough and Mr. Gamble's joints, but our crippled slave woman Faith has turned out to have a very fine working knowledge of herbal remedies. Mr. Hold may find in time that he has undervalued that one in trading her at a discount.

April 21, 1815

On this the second Sunday of the month, the sun rose high and clear above the eastern mountains. I instructed the crippled slave woman Faith on how to bake the potato buns of our traditional Home Church Lovefeasts. She kneaded the dough on her knees and worked at a bench foreshortened by Isaac to accommodate her malady. The cabin smelled of hot bread baking and the fresh butter that I have taught yellow Michael how to churn. I was sorely reminded of home and longed to look upon the faces of my dear countrywomen. Mr. Gamble need not have reminded me that we are here in this darkened land to do the work of the Lord, that our sacrifices are nothing when compared to those of our suffering Savior, who gave all for our sins.

After the praying of the Church Litany, we held our first public service in the mission cabin. Mr. Gamble presided, delivering an enlightening message on the Holy Trinity and leading the singing in German. I stood behind and held a Bible aloft to symbolize to those gathered the sacredness of the book. Sunlight glinted through our single pane windows, casting the light of a thousand angels over the modest room. Our audience consisted mainly of slaves who are not required to labor on Sundays, that being a day that Mr. Hold does not trade or manage the affairs of his plantation, so that he can drink and carouse. Old and blind, young and ignorant, women and men in the full strength of youth, all came of their own accord to hear my husband preach the Gospel. They managed, despite the limitations of their daily working attire, to piece together colorful dresses, deerskin leggings, and hair decorations fashioned, I suspect, from the grosgrain ribbon ordered for Mrs. Hold's bonnets. The eagerness in their shadow rimmed eyes quelled my disappointment at the absence of many Indians among the congregants. It has long been a mission of our fellowship to minister to the blacks as well. That work was begun seventy years before in the West Indies missions, about which I often read in the Church dispatches that arrive by post.

One of the black congregants at our mission, Samuel Cotterell, a self described free Ethiopian preacher, at times during the service translated my husband's words into an African language, which he appears to know as well as English. Mr. Cotterell can read the Bible and carries one of his own in a leather pouch at his side. He is white haired and distinctive despite his color. Patience attended along with her mistress, the young Mrs. Hold, who, I observed, listened feelingly to Mr. Gamble's words. Mrs. Hold has taken to Patience and seems to love her like a sister. For Patience is a woman just out of girlhood, close to her mistress's own young age, and possesses, like her mistress, a light behind her almond eyes that shines brightest in the absence of Mr. Hold.

After the service, I served to all of those in attendance the sweet rolls Faith had baked, together with our Moravian coffee, thick with milk and sugar. At the forbearance of her generous mistress, Patience, who possesses a deeply kind heart, stayed behind to help our crippled Faith scour the iron pots. I put the chairs in order, cleaned the floor of grit, folded and stored my husband's white shirt and kerchief. I permitted Faith to feed little Michael the last of the buns, which he ate with early season wild strawberries, having always an eager stomach. I retired to the rear bedchamber with a little book of nature poems lately sent by my former students in Bethlehem. A warm evening breeze drifted through the open window, flickering the flame of my beeswax candle and carrying into my awareness the sharp scents and muffled sounds of the nearest slave quarters. I should have wanted someone with whom to share my observations—of the steady awakening of Mrs. Hold, the rumbling voice of the itinerant preacher, the slave girls dressed in their vibrant hues, the rounded Lovefeast buns. But my husband, with a mind set toward the next day's labors and the importance of making our mission integral to this place, had gone to survey the plantation grounds alongside Mr. Hold.

"Wait," Cheyenne said, holding up a hand and breaking their concentration. Her eyes shone in the artificial light with a sheen that looked almost drug-induced. "I don't know if I can listen to any more of this."

Jinx looked up from the half-read page to find the portrait of James Hold hanging like a threat before her. His penetrating eyes bore down on the three of them from the cobalt-colored wall. His velvet riding jacket, a deep maroon, brought to mind Anna Gamble's description of slaves lined up like a trail of dried-up blood.

"You mean you don't want to hear it," Ruth said. "Wanting to and being able to are different things."

"I didn't buy this house to dig up dirt on all the shit that happened here. Do you hear who James Hold was? Abusive. A tyrant."

Ruth's head jerked up at Cheyenne's words, an involuntary action that drew Jinx's eye.

"You bought this house to chase a dream," Jinx said. "But for some of the women who lived here, that dream was a nightmare. If they could live through all that crap, don't you think the least we can do is read about it, know about it? Isn't it honoring their memory to be a witness for their lives? You can leave if you have to, but I'm going to keep reading. Mary Ann Battis is bound to show up sometime soon."

"Battis," Cheyenne repeated, her eyes sharpening again. "As in Adam Battis."

"Exactly," Jinx said.

14

April 22, 1815

The last frost has melted away, and finally I dig in the ground, setting in place the lines of my garden between our mission cabin and the big house. Each plot shall have a path leading to its center, so that I might tend the plants separately, according to kind. I have brought with me seeds and cuttings from Bethlehem and Salem. I have likewise collected seeds from the Indians who come calling at our mission in the hopes of receiving food or supplies at no expense. My garden shall soon have varieties of peas, large leafed lettuce, beans, squash (prickly cucumbers), ornamental flowers of various kinds, and a few rows of cotton. It shall also have a healthy supply of medicinal plants. For the crippled servant Faith has proven most knowledgeable in this arena and has already used her skills to treat the visiting Indians with salves and teas. Beyond my garden is the mission's large cornfield, which we will soon have sown. Mr. Hold, being generous according to the custom of his people in the use of land, apportioned to us a fifth of his cleared fields and peach orchards.

When he is not preaching, leading liturgical service, or se-cluded in Bible study, Mr. Gamble spends the hours traveling with Mr. Hold. He has become in some ways an advisor, keep-ing a record of Mr. Hold's legal affairs and accompanying him to the nearest Cherokee villages. He hopes that through such care-ful ministrations and the establishment of trust between them, he might lead Mr. Hold, along with his dependents, to an abiding belief in the Lord. As we yet have no scholars, and I am often on my own save for the crippled Faith and her son, I have taken to walking about in search of plant life, as I once used to do along the Lehigh River. Here, the Conasauga's loamy banks afford a home for a vast array of plants. Eager to set my eye upon each one, to sketch them in pencil, describe them in words, and harvest their seeds for planting, I tramp freely about the place with my white cap tied at the neck, hanging loose on my shoulders.

I have begun to assemble a list of plants in the Cherokee area and have commenced sending samples to my northerly brethren in Christ, Rev. Henry Muhlenberg, Rev. Henry Steinhauer, and Rev. Elias Cornelius, who likewise subscribe to the study of Lin-naeus's principles of botanical schema. I have found Mr. Hold's mail system so sluggish, however, that I have enlisted Mr. Hold's most trusted slave, Isaac the craftsman, to carry these samples as far as Kentucky on my behalf. In the Cherokee nation, no passes are required for Negro slaves in transit, but for his smooth passage through Tennessee I have fashioned him a letter of allowance.

April 30, 1815

Having become accustomed to this place and its natural shape, the lay and thrust of the land, I pulled on my husband's boots and set out for the woods earlier this day. Great was my anticipation. A fresh spring rain had fallen, and newborn seedlings are already sprouting. I wore a burlap seed pack on my waist looped about the ties of my skirt and petticoat and carried a wax bound sheath of papers in my hand. The spring air was warm on the bare skin of my neck. The sun shone above like a beacon. Coming over a rise in the Holds' freshly sowed cornfield one mile west of the main house, I scanned the dense wood below. Pine, hickory, oak, chestnut, walnut, mulberry, poplar, and sourwood trees thrive there, thick and inviting.

The Negress Patience was ambling along the forest's interior edge, seeming to take pleasure in the natural scene about her. She did not observe me on the hillside above as she went about her quiet task, gracefully circumventing the sassafras and sumach underbrush while pausing to touch one glossy leaf that beckoned to her. Barefoot, buckeye skin glistening in the afternoon light, Patience hiked her muddy skirt up about her hips, bending low to collect the wild potatoes and onions that are a staple of the Indians' diet. It was then with a lightning speed that Mr. Hold appeared beside her, together with a thundering herd of five other men. They were each of them members of the Lighthorse brigade lately authorized by the Cherokee Council to track and punish horse thieves. Mr. Hold is known as a passionate judge of his fellows, whipping his tribesmen with a fury that even the heathens see fit to question. I lowered myself within the field, sensing that I should not draw notice.

The contingent below became a blur of motion and sound as they dismounted and stomped their thick heeled boots. One man wore a traditional scalplock of knotted hair; another bore a strand of red turkey feathers dangling from his hat. Mr. Hold, in his cleanly knotted blue silk cravat, was the most civilized in appearance among them, and the most brutal. He knocked Patience to the ground without a word of warning, as if felling a sapling on a field he intended to clear. Her basket of gathered onions tumbled to the forest floor. She grasped for it. But the basket rolled away, and then she had nothing to reach for. When Mr. Hold defiled her, he forced her eyes open, pressing her lashes apart with his thumbs as he crushed her with the weight of his body. Sated, he threw her to her knees, sending her skirts to the treetops, cajoling the men to take her, then, but only from behind. They would not be allowed to look into her almond eyes. Only he, her master and possessor, had free reign to search her gaze, hunting incessantly for the light which must dim still more each time he looks at her. When the other men had finished with their wicked acts, they abandoned her in a pool of filth. Blood, urine, seed, saliva seeped into the blameless ground. I gathered my skirts about me, fleeing the young woman's shame, which had somehow become my own, scattering my notes and sketches, in which I had taken such delight, to the far corners of the cornfield.

May 1, 1815

Today, as I dug in my kitchen garden, tending the wild transplanted strawberries and looking up from time to time at the penetrating sunlight, Patience emerged from the rear door of the brick house. I watched her approach from the slaves' work yard, it being the only boundary between the Hold family home and our mission cabin. On legs that bowed weakly like violin strings, she passed by the slave women making soap and scalding bed linens. She wobbled

*into the little gate that marked the entrance to my garden, cut for
me from fallen timber by the itinerant preacher Mr. Sam Cotterell.
With her slender arms wrapped around a broad bottomed basket woven of river cane and dyed a deep crimson with the roots
of the* Sanguinaria canadensis *(bloodroot), she approached me.
Her countenance was withholding, her skin everywhere marred by
pulpy wounds. She reached inside the basket and drew out handfuls
of wild onions and potatoes. "My mistress wishes you to have these,
Mrs. Gamble, for next Sabbath service," she said. How, oh how,
had she managed to gather each curled onion again? How had she
stood? How had she moved? How had she commenced a new day? I
accepted the offering. The wild potatoes were small and clean, free of
the loose dirt and leaves that should have clung to their skins, given
the circumstances of their collection. But the basket Patience carried
was well constructed, made to shed grime through its fine grained
sifting seams.*

*Patience reached inside the basket a second time and withdrew
my lost papers and seed bag, placing them beside me on the garden ground, speaking not a word about where she had found them.
The papers had come loose from the thin wax mooring; nothing
held them together now. Only the dissected drawings of plant parts
showed how the pages had connected before—the stem of a* Trad-
escantia virginica *(spiderwort) on one page, its striped, oval leaf on
another, the likeness of its seedpod buried at the bottom of the loose
leaf stack. I stared at the words and shapes I had formed and began
to blindly rearrange them in my mind.*

*A Beginning List of Plants found in the Neighbourhood of the
Conasauga River, (Cherokee Country) where Hold Hill is situated;
made by Mrs. Gamble.*

Aesculus pavia—*The nuts pounded, are used in poultices.*

Asarum virginicum—*The leaves; fresh, they are applied to wounds.*

Cornus florida—*The bark of the root is used to heal wounds, and in poultices.*

Saururus cernuus—*The roots roasted and mashed, used for poultices.*

Liriodendrum tulipifera—*Of the bark of the root, a tea is made and given in fevers. It is also used in poultices.*

"Patience," I whispered, withdrawing my focus from the solace of plant life, "I am sorry."

"Yes, ma'am," was her only reply. Her eyes remained fixed on her basket until she noticed Faith, who with great effort had appeared at the cabin doorway.

Faith's frost gnawed feet still made it necessary for her to crawl to each destination, but she never complained of this difficulty. Neither did her features reveal surprise at Patience's lamentable condition. Faith hears and learns things through a network of Negroes and poor Cherokees who seem to place their trust in her maternal wisdom. From her knees, Faith extended a hand toward Patience and pressed a vial of acorn balsam into the young woman's palm. "This will ease your pain, daughter," she said. Patience nodded, bowed to hug Faith's waist, then left again with her river cane basket, into which she placed the vial. I watched her pass through the gate and move across the slaves' work yard, her lovely neck long and dark above her overburdened shoulders.

That night, with my husband sleeping beside me, I dreamt of poison hemlock.

"Shit, shit," Cheyenne said, shooting from her Chippendale chair and rubbing her upper arms. "What an asshole." Her face was a crumpled flower, all illusions shattered. "And why is it so damn cold in here?"

"I can't believe it—what he did to Patience." Ruth was shaking her head, tears wet on her cheeks.

Jinx laid the diary page upside down on top of the one before it. Her eyes fell on Ruth. "Cheyenne, do you have any tissues?"

"Oh, sorry. Of course." Cheyenne had started pacing in front of James Hold's portrait, the rhinestones on her flip-flops flashing in the chandelier's muted light. She stopped abruptly now and walked through the swinging doors into the kitchenette and butler's pantry. Then came the echo of cupboard doors opening and closing as Cheyenne looked for supplies.

The next sound they heard was a scream.

"Cheyenne!" Ruth said, jumping up.

Jinx and Ruth found Cheyenne standing on a stepstool beside the open pantry, hand clasped over her mouth. The door was thrown back beside her. Cheyenne stood frozen, gazing at an upper shelf just out of reach. Ruth peered into the storage space. It looked like a stuffed animal at first, soft and orange, glassy eyes the color of grass blades. But the cat was real. Real and dead, its neck twisted unnaturally to one side. There was no smell. Death had been recent—while Cheyenne was resting in bed, or when they had found the ground safe.

"It's Sorbet. That's Sorbet," Cheyenne said, shoulders trembling beneath the ivory robe. "He killed her."

"What?" Ruth said. "Who killed her?" She hadn't even known Cheyenne had a pet, and couldn't have imagined her deigning to deal with a litter box and cat hair.

"Let's sort this out," Jinx said, holding a hand up to Cheyenne. "You should come down from there first."

Cheyenne stepped to the floor, her face drained of emotion. "When

I bought this house at the auction," she said, "there was one big contender. His name is Mason Allen."

"Right. I've heard of him," Jinx said. "He ran into me, literally, at the Marathon station. Not so nice a guy."

"He wanted this place as much as I did. I could see it in his eyes. He stared daggers at me the entire auction. But afterward, he shook my hand and even made a little joke. 'Sleep tight,' he said. 'Don't let the bedbugs bite.' And then strange things started to happen."

"What kind of things?" Ruth said. She had dried her face with the backs of her hands and was focused now on Cheyenne.

"Someone cut the blossoms off my azalea bushes. A little thing. Then I found a bunch of filthy cockroaches in the drawing-room fireplace. This house was not infested before I bought it, I'm fairly sure of that. I went out for a few hours. You-all came over. And now the cat is dead. She was a stray, a smart, pretty thing."

"You think Mason Allen is doing this?" Ruth said.

Cheyenne's voice shot up. "Who else could it be? Unless I'm imaging all of this. Maybe the blossoms blew off. Maybe the roaches were in the walls. Maybe Sorbet was already sick and climbed up there to die."

"I don't think much that goes on at this place is random," Jinx said. "We'll get the exterminator to remove the dead cat tomorrow. Let's just close that door and figure out what to do next."

Ruth rummaged in the kitchenette drawers, then made tea in the microwave. She returned to the dining room with a tray of full Styrofoam cups.

Cheyenne wrinkled her nose. "Next time, use the good china," she said. And then, quietly, "Thank you, Ruth."

Ruth sat at the table and wrapped the cashmere throw from the upstairs bedroom around Cheyenne's shoulders. "You're welcome." She looked briefly into Cheyenne's eyes and gave her a swift hug. "Have some tea. They say it cures all ills."

"I'm pretty sure they didn't mean Lipton," Cheyenne said, but she reached for a cup anyway, taking a cautious sip of the steaming liquid.

"You should call the police and report this," Ruth said.

"What would I report?"

"Vandalism. Breaking and entering. There must be some legal term for what's going on around here."

"But I don't really know that anyone did this purposely. I can't prove a thing about Mason Allen."

"Cheyenne, that man is threatening you," Ruth said. "That's what this is all about. Intimidation. Causing you fear. Don't let him get away with it."

"Don't let him get away with it?" Cheyenne shrugged the throw off her shoulders. "Are *you* really lecturing *me* on the finer points of disclosure, Ruthie? Open your own closet and see how your skeleton's doing lately. I will not put my reputation at risk in this town by accusing their golden boy of infantile pranks. I'd be the one to suffer for it, not him. I have a business to launch, and it *will* be successful."

"We can decide this in the morning," Jinx said. "We're all tired. It's been a day. One thing's for sure, Cheyenne. We're not leaving you alone here tonight."

"Fine," Cheyenne said, relief in her voice beneath the bluster. "You two can sleep in the guest room."

"And you're coming with us," Ruth said, "whether you want to or not."

Cheyenne left all the lights on and mounted the grand staircase. Jinx and Ruth went outside to collect a few things from Ruth's Beetle. In the small first-floor bathroom, Jinx unwound her braid, brushed her teeth, and changed into a heather tank top and boxer shorts. Ruth emerged from the bathroom next, smelling like cherries and wearing a *Muppet Movie* nightshirt that clung to her curves. The headband was gone. Loose curls tumbled over her forehead, threatening to overtake her eyes. Jinx held out a hand to Ruth, who hesitated only a moment before taking it.

The old home settled in sighs while each of them found a spot in the guest room. Cheyenne took the queen-sized bed, propping the embroidered pillows behind her. Ruth sat on the end of the mahogany sleigh bed—carved, by the look of it, from a single piece of wood. Jinx joined Ruth, gently draping a lace coverlet over both of their knees.

Cheyenne noticed the gesture, her eyes taking on a speculative cast as she met Ruth's defiant dark brown gaze. "Well, well. It looks like this old house is full of surprises," she said.

15

THE DEEP DARKNESS OF MIDNIGHT had gathered outside the windows. Jinx adjusted a pillow behind her back and smoothed the loose strands of hair that shadowed her now-straining eyes. She sipped the tepid tea from her cup and tugged the chain of the tulip-shaped Tiffany lamp. She could hear the breathing of the other two women as they waited for her to begin. She reached for the chestnut box nestled between her leg and Ruth's and picked up where they had stopped.

May 7, 1815

All is calm about the place since Mr. Hold has been away at the government trading post in Tellico, Tennessee. In his absence, the house Negroes do what they please, and Mrs. Hold declines to exert authority over them. The field slaves too take their liberties, refusing to work at night, and the overseer, a vile, lazy man, slips in his vigilance. Mr. Gamble complains that our mission slave Faith has been infected by this wanton attitude of the Hold slaves, and as a result has slowed down the housework that she can accomplish even on crippled feet.

But to my understanding, she has been occupied with far more worthy endeavors. Our thriving garden now includes 32 medicinal plants, of which Faith is the chief alchemist. Faith receives many visits from the Negroes as well as the Indians, who seek her healing salves. She confirms that among the Negroes, Isaac is suspected of taking his leave, and among the common Cherokees, whose language Isaac speaks, having been born in this country and raised among the Indians, he is much missed. Tongues wag about where Isaac has gone, how long he will stay there, and by what means he made his escape. I dare not speak a word to another soul on this subject. I pray fervently on my knees each day that the Lord may forgive my poor judgment in sending Isaac on so foolish a journey. I pray too that my husband does not discover my indiscretion. For even in our Church, where women's talents are valued, men stand at the helm. As Head Missionary to the Cherokees, my husband could send me away from this place and these people, around whose hearts I have begun to twine my own.

May 14, 1815

Mr. Hold is still away on his trading venture. And so the loveliest month of the year has brought with it a welcome warmth and seven new scholars for our fledgling boarding school. Three of the children, Joseph, Mary, and Jesse, are Mr. Hold's own, sent to us by their various mothers. Three come from prominent Cherokee families of Coosawattee and Coosa towns, whose parents entrust to us their instruction in reading, writing, arithmetic, and moral reasoning. One is an older girl called Mary Ann Battis, sent to us from a Methodist mission school in Creek country. Mulatto in color with pensive dark eyes and bean like limbs, she is said to be the unfortunate child of a poor Creek woman and a Negro. Her father having run away, and her mother unable to feed all of her children begotten by him, Mary Ann was sent to the Creek mission by the Indian Agent from the U. States, to be housed and educated there. By native right, she was born free and eligible for full support at the school, where she distinguished herself among the Indian pupils. Quick of mind, she is also quick of hand, for Agent Meigs related that the girl is suspected of having set fire to the place. Even now, she has been sent to us while her old mission schoolhouse lies in ashes on the ground of the Alabama-Georgia border. The Creek Agent has begun an investigation, and the head Missionary, accused of improper management and other improprieties beside, has been sent back to his home in South Carolina.

I wonder at the wisdom of this troubled girl of questionable parentage having been sent here to us, and can only surmise that my husband's reputation for sound judgment and a firm hand has traveled as far as the Creek territory to the west. The girl reads and writes well, and keeps to herself in the main, often burying her face in the pages of her spelling book. She refuses to let Mr. Gamble meet her eyes. When he gestures to her in simple greeting, she jerks her hand away as if his touch might sear her flesh. She seems not to have faith in the majority of humanity, suspecting every action of secret motivations. Even my own gentle direction she tolerates with suspicious looks. She seems to have taken only to the Negro preacher, Sam Cotterell, who remains in the vicinity. Perhaps Mr. Cotterell reminds the girl of her own lost father.

Isaac has not yet returned. He has been absent nearly three weeks, and even the lazy overseer has begun to ask questions.

May 18, 1815

I am in receipt of a letter from Rev. Muhlenberg in Philadelphia. He has received the plant samples and predicts this Cherokee collection that I am amassing to be the only one of its kind. Meanwhile, the Negro Isaac who delivered the samples has not come back. I grow anxious by the day that Mr. Hold will miss him upon his return.

May 22, 1815

One day this month, I awoke and departed my bedroom to find a strange thing had occurred. The Negroes who are often about pleading for food or Faith's medicine had come this day bearing plants of all description. They crowded into our mission hearth room, having with them cuttings and seedpods gathered from the far corners of Mr. Hold's acreage. I hesitated at this curious outpouring and reached for my white cap, which, having just awakened, I had not yet placed on my head. Across the cabin, Faith sat on her low wood bench, wearing an indigo head wrap and kneading dough. She watched me while appearing not to. Our new and promising student of the Creek nation, Mary Ann, also watched from the side of the room, where she sat with a book in Faith's sleeping enclosure. Her pensive eyes fixed on my face, awaiting my response with greater anxiety, perhaps, than the crowd of suffering humanity

*before me. Little Michael had pulled the Sunday meeting chairs
into a haphazard row for the older members of the visiting party.
I paused by Faith's side and bent to her ear, smelling the St. John's
wort and sage that she had been crushing the evening last. "Faith,
what is this? Do you know?" I whispered.*

*"No, ma'am, I surely don't," she answered, then paused. "Un-
less it has to do with Isaac."*

*"Isaac?" I repeated, my heart lunging into a race with my
tongue.*

*The itinerant Negro preacher, Mr. Sam Cotterell, then made
himself visible at the end of the line, his white hair a thundercloud
atop his head and his Bible in its leather pouch at his side.*

*"I understand that you are a student of plants," he said, his
voice a rumble, his eyes steadily searching mine, "that you collect 'em
and send 'em beyond the Cherokee lands to your associates in the
North. Gander, Caty, Bob, Peter, Sam, Big Jenny, and Hannah,
here, have gone to great lengths to bring these cuttings to you. May
be that you see fit to send one among 'em on an errand someday."*

*I was beyond shock at his boldness. My knees buckled beneath
my petticoat. I had not time to ascertain how he surmised my role
in Isaac's journey. I looked at the assemblage gathered before me,
at the plant stems tucked into baskets, wrapped in squares of woven cloth, gathered with twine, dried between bark, and grasped in
worn, callused hands. "Mr. Cotterell," I said firmly, my eyes fixed
on his Bible pouch, "I fear to what misunderstandings I owe these
gifts."*

*"You might see that you find a use for 'em, sometime or other."
He nodded to the gathered Negroes, who heaped their supply of
dazzling plant life upon the center table as if it were a beloved's
grave. Mr. Cotterell departed from the cabin. The line of slaves
trickled out behind him.*

Faith has indeed made good use of these cuttings, isolating some of the seeds to enhance our medicinal garden and learning of their applications from an old Cherokee man named Earbob, who comes from time to time to talk with her. These include the use of Acer rubrum—*the inner bark boiled to a syrup, made into pills, and these dissolved in water for cases of unseeing eyes, the eyes washed therewith, and of* Podophyllum peltatum—*a drop of the juice of the fresh root in the ear, is a cure for deafness. Earbob is held up by the Cherokees as a healer, though his methods are far from scientific. Besides his use of herbs, which is at least within reason, he places red and white corals afloat in vessels of water for divination purposes. If the corals rise in the water, this is taken as a sign that the patient will recover from his, or her, malady.*

May 27, 1815

Mr. Cotterell has seen fit to continue his sojourn here to urge the bondsmen of Mr. Hold to the light of salvation. It is said that Mr. Cotterell was once a slave of the Indians himself before purchasing his freedom, converting to Methodism, and taking to the road. He has collected on his journeys a working knowledge of many languages, not only the Cherokee and English spoken here, and an unnamed African tongue, but also the Creek tongue. He visits our mission often to soothe the children who cry in the night, longing for their mothers' cooking fires. Mary Ann especially takes his words to heart, as he can converse with her in her native language. In the heat of the afternoon beneath the peach trees that line the boundary of our mission, he takes off his hat, abandons his walking stick, and lowers himself to the ground, regaling the children with stories of wily rabbits and dancing billy goats. He has asked me to teach

*him the German word for this or that and at times punctuates his
stories with the gems of his new vocabulary. On these occasions,
we are quite alone—the children, Mr. Cotterell, and I, except for
a visit from Mr. Hold's slaves, who drift over from their work yard
to hear about the goings on of Brer Rabbit the story character, and
the younger Mrs. Hold, who seems drawn to the sound of children's
laughter floating freely across the garden.*

June 1, 1815

*The meadows are alive with green grass and clover. Summer
has come. I have taken chief charge of our little school, guiding the
pupils in reading and script. All whom we accept are the children
of heathen Indians. We make no distinction here between Indians
and half castes, as the Cherokees themselves do not. For several
hours in the morning and afternoon, the students are in classes.
Otherwise, they are kept busy in the field, garden, or yard.*

*Mary Ann is so talented as to serve as my teaching assistant.
She works in the main with the youngest scholars. Her eagerness
to absorb new knowledge has gotten the better of her resentment at
having been sent here among us, when she had hoped to be returned
to her mother after the fire. On Saturdays while the Indian pupils
run about the woods in the company of the Negro children, a habit
which they cannot be broken of, I devote my time to instructing
Mary Ann in my own beloved subjects of botany and the poetic
arts. Even the work of Linnaeus and Bartram is not beyond her
grasp. Mary Ann in turn has taken to tutoring Mrs. Hold, who is
determined to learn how to read and write the English language, so
that she might decipher the Holy Book for herself.*

Mr. Gamble leaves the schooling to me and spends his days all about the place, making rounds on behalf of Mr. Hold in his absence and planning for the Sunday message, which he now preaches to a room crowded with Indians and slaves, so that Faith and I can hardly keep abreast of the baking.

June 15, 1815

Our house overflows with scholars. Three more have joined our sundry flock, nieces and cousins of Mrs. Hold, whose parents have become convinced of the good purpose of our enterprise. They squeeze in, head to toe, on cots in the rear sleeping room, while my own little Mary Ann has forfeited her cot to share my chamber, where ample room is to be found, due to my husband's frequent absences. Faith complains of the washing for all our scholars, so much so that I must aid her over the boiling pots. Little Michael assists by hanging the clothing out to dry in the sunlight.

My work in the garden suffers for want of time. It has been weeks since I last gathered wildflowers, which show off their spectrum of color now in the fullness of their beauty. I am kept busy here, so that I have not the time to collect the plants that tempted me to the woods last spring.

July 1, 1815

Patience is with child. The younger Mrs. Hold is in a state of near despair, fearing not that the child is her husband's, which everyone has suspected, given the occurrences that transpire here, but that her husband might sell Patience away, along with the unborn babe. I have taken the opportunity to have a heart to heart talk with

Mrs. Hold, our dear burdened Peggy, for her to know the Savior and find comfort in His Word. She shows great change. She seeks the Savior and is not without the feeling of His love in her heart. She continues to study writing with Mary Ann on Saturdays and to come to service on Sundays, accompanied by Patience, so that we almost have a little church family here in the Indian wilderness.

On Sunday evenings, after Mr. Gamble has gone to walk about the grounds or consult with the visiting chiefs who often stop by the plantation, I find myself settled before the hearth with a small circle of unexpected but beloved companions: Mrs. Hold and Patience, whose belly grows by the day, the crippled Faith and little Michael, my protégée Mary Ann, and Mr. Sam Cotterell, who has become like a father to the latter. I read to them aloud from the dispatched diaries of our brethren and sisters in the West Indies mission field. It seems that Patience, Faith, and likewise Mary Ann, are most feelingly moved by the stories of people of their own race seeking the truth of the crucified Savior in far away lands. Mr. Cotterell, who possesses a deep, melodic voice, shares in the reading when I become tired, stokes my tea with freshly crushed leaves, and opens the door to let in the breezes in the warm summer nights. Except for a stubborn one or two who strain to stay awake, our little red scholars sleep through these evenings, rolled onto their mats and cots in the rear bedroom, bare limbs stretched wide in the heat.

July 3, 1815

Mr. Hold has lately returned from an extended sojourn northward, where he traded slaves for cattle with his business partner, a fellow Scot to whom Hold is linked through his late father's connections. He called for Isaac to play the fiddle, and hence has dis-

covered Isaac's absence. Mr. Hold presumes him to have run away. Enraged, he acts as if he has lost his mind. The suffocating summer heat only drives him on. Last night, he was in his house shooting, burning, and ravaging, such that no one's life was safe. I dare not speak a word about my part in this to anyone but the Lord.

July 4, 1815

We heard horrible things about what Mr. Hold had done overnight, especially that he mistreated his wife so badly that it cannot be repeated. When the opportunity presented itself, Mrs. Hold escaped to our cabin. Her tender face was a sea of blue where her husband had struck her. The Cherokee scholars were fast asleep on their mats in the rear of the building, but Mary Ann was alert and stiff in the hemp gown I had sewn for her, attuned like a fawn to the scent of men with muskets. I inquired after Patience. Mrs. Hold shook her head, closing her eyes against a blinding thought. I persisted with my questioning until she reported that Mr. Hold has shut Patience up in the garret, binding her with the steadfast rope of the Annona bark.

I pulled Mary Ann to my chest and covered her ears with my hands. I did not wish her to know the cruelty and tyranny which is practiced in that house. Her small body trembled against mine, damp with sweat. Her long braids fell like open wings around me.

July 6, 1815

We missed Patience for three days and two nights. When we saw her again, she could not stand and support the weight of *her protruding belly. It is rumored that Mr. Hold is not beyond torture. He has been known to hang his slaves by fingers or toes from log beams in his garret. Patience's offense, we learned through Faith, was alleged relations with the absent Isaac. Faith tended the wounds. Mrs. Hold stayed with us until Patience regained strength. And then she returned, God help her, to the prison house of her husband.*

It is further revealed with each passing day that Mr. Hold brought us here solely for the betterment of his own position—to educate his children in the English language, strengthen his trading outlets, and increase his status with the government Agent who oversees the tribe. Mr. Hold does not care anything about our religion, or about our warnings of hellfire and the vengeance of the Lord. Oh, if the Savior would only have mercy on him and free him from the hands of the evil enemy who has him completely under his power!

July 9, 1815

Mr. Hold was drunk again last night. He lit a torch and rampaged through the slave quarters, burning down three cabins of his Negro men, whom he accused of aiding in Isaac's escape. He would have burned more if his clerk Mr. Geiger had not stopped him with his pistol. We had to listen to the noise of shooting and shouting all through the night. I prayed in the dark on my knees, asking the Lord to show Mr. Hold that the Savior died for him as well. My dear Mary Ann prayed beside me, gripping the bed quilt in her hands. Might God free our evil host from Satan's chains which bind him. Might God free us all.

July 10, 1815

On the breaking of dawn, I sought out my husband to impress upon him the need of our mission for a second Negro woman. A servant is indispensable for milking, laundering, cooking, baking, and the like, and one cannot deny that this work, which is no small matter in our establishment, has hitherto been done incompletely by Faith. An additional servant would aid in getting the necessary work done, which has been much increased by boarding and washing for our eleven Indian scholars. Mr. Gamble sought to persuade me that the Church could not consent to such luxury, but on this notion I would not be moved. We might forgo our monthly supply of coffee, I told him, for I could roast our own from the seeds of the wild Cassia occidentalis *(coffee senna) weed. "It is for the benefit of the students. Our crippled Negro woman cannot keep pace with the labor of the mission. We must have Patience," I said.*

Assessing my request with the calm calculation that is his chief strength, my husband narrowed his eyes. "Yes, I see," he said, observing my ardent state. "You desire a second Negro woman from among Mr. Hold's stock. But Patience will not do, for her master will never part with her."

I looked into my husband's eyes, wondering what dark knowledge he held secret there. Had he witnessed scenes such as that which I endured in the cornfield, during his frequent visits to the Hold house? Had he been cajoled, like the men of the Lighthorse brigade, to take part in awful acts? I saw in his eyes that he had shed the mantle of God and now shared one mind with those thieves of spirits and bodies that polite society refers to as "planters."

"Patience must do," I boldly persisted. "She must." I knew that my eyes were as fierce now as those of the wild cats that live in the corners of the barns here, jumping and biting people at the

least provocation. I could feel the sweat damped strands of my hair sticking to my cheeks and tongue. I grasped for my Bible, which is never far from my side. "Our crucified Christ loves all," I said. "He watches over all, and gave all for all. The Holy Spirit is no respecter of persons."

My husband glanced at the Holy Book and, I thought, relented. "Yes, I see. I will speak with Mr. Hold," he said, striding from the room. He turned at the doorway to look at me. "Provided that Isaac can be convinced to return," he added, and was gone.

His words stopped my heart. I lost my bearings in the swirling space of the hearth room and grabbed at the table for support. The edge was firm in my hands, solid as the pine tree that a slave had carved to shape it. I have never felt the natural love of a wife for her husband. In pursuit of the higher aim of spreading the light of the Gospel, I have endured my husband's disdain for my feelings and grasping hands in the night. And all the while, he had corrupted his calling, becoming nothing more than a purveyor of flesh, worse, as he is a man of God, than a common Georgia slave trader.

Jinx placed the manuscript pages back in the box, enraged and incredulous. She glanced at her companions. Cheyenne had drifted off to sleep on the antique queen bed. Ruth had taken off her glasses, watching the pictures in her mind as Jinx read the words. Jinx sat up, wondering if the sleigh bed that held her had been crafted by a slave, by the missing Isaac, wondering what would happen—what had happened—to Patience, Isaac, and Mary Ann.

"What's that?" Ruth whispered, her voice husky from the nearness of sleep. Her face took on a waxen cast as she stared out the window. She leaned into the glass, elbow pressed against the frame, feeling for her glasses on the end table.

Jinx circled to Ruth's side of the bed, handed the glasses to her, and peered over her shoulder. She saw nothing but shape and shadow in the light of the full moon. "What are you looking at?"

"The girl who called me. I think she's back." Ruth flung off the coverlet and slid from the bed. "Cheyenne, wake up."

Cheyenne lifted her eye mask and snapped open her lids, registering Jinx's bare feet, Ruth's crooked glasses, the unkempt hair flying around each of their heads. "What's wrong? What time is it?"

"Four," Ruth said. "We need to go out to the gardens, to the cane field."

"Why? What's happened now?" Cheyenne's voice rose with alarm.

"Yesterday in the mission cabin, I thought I saw a girl in the doorway, but then she disappeared. I didn't know what she was at the time. Now I think she was Mary Ann Battis, showing me where to find the diary. I think I see her again now, but I'm too far away to be sure."

"So you're telling us you saw a girl in the garden? A ghost girl?" Cheyenne said.

"I didn't say she was a ghost."

"But that's what you meant."

"This place was never destined to be a show house bed-and-breakfast, Cheyenne. It's a two-hundred-year-old plantation from the slaveholding South," Ruth said.

"So I should have expected it to be haunted? Is that what you mean?"

"I feel like she wants me to come to her. I feel like she's calling me."

Jinx was at the door before Ruth, grabbing and flinging on an oversized Old Navy hoodie. Ruth slapped on her clogs, taking the steps two by two.

"Jinx," Ruth said, "can you go back and bring the diary?"

"Great," Cheyenne said. "Now we're ghost hunting." She cinched the robe around her waist and pushed on her rhinestone flip-flops.

16

Ruth's glasses steamed in the humid morning air. She wiped them, leaving behind blurry streaks. Followed by Jinx and Cheyenne, she crept through the back door, breathing in the fragrance of rose petals. Ruth had heard the shakiness in Cheyenne's voice, felt anxiety rising from Jinx, could smell the pungent perspiration clinging to her own flushed skin. They plunged into the garden. Rambling wildflowers gave way to river cane stalks tipped with open tufts. Ruth wrapped her arms across her chest, wishing she were wearing something more substantial than the flimsy *Muppet Movie* nightshirt, which she now thought seemed absurd for a woman her age. She felt exposed out in the elements, as vulnerable as she had been the day her father told her that her mother had drowned.

Exactly how it happened, her father never said; he kept the truth buttoned down like the broadcloth dress shirts he wore each day to his accounting firm. A drowning accident—that was all Ruth knew, all she had managed to extract from him. Her mother was taken by a wave on her parents' second honeymoon, the Caribbean escape they had planned to save their rocky marriage. Her father shielded her from the garish local news coverage. He couldn't protect her, though, from the lurid whispers that trailed her at school like clouds of gnats—the rumors that her father had her mother's blood on his hands, that he had snapped from envy of her mother's success. In the twenty-two years since, Ruth had never searched for answers to the questions of why, how, or who was responsible. Her father's cloak of silence had been complete—and somehow a comfort. She had willed herself into forgetfulness, until she met the rose garden.

Out in the canebrake, someone stood beckoning to Ruth from the shadowed opening of the round earth house: a girl on the cusp of womanhood, ribbons dangling from her hair, a floral print skirt banding her legs. The girl seemed to stand within a spidery light. Her ribbons of black, red, and white danced in that light, as though filtered through a kaleidoscope held in the hands of a child. Ruth could not deny her a second time. Mary Ann Battis was really there, leaning against the doorframe, staring at her.

"You see her, don't you?" Jinx said.

"She's standing in the doorway of the round house."

Cheyenne squinted at the shadows. "There's nothing out there."

Ruth moved forward. Her stomach was a knot. She rushed across the garden, reached the phosphorescent light, could almost stretch out a hand to touch the apparition. And then the girl was gone. Ruth plunged into the gap where the figure had been, feeling a cool mist like the dissipation of mountain clouds.

She heard the uneven rush of Jinx's breathing behind her.

"Did you feel that?" Ruth said. Inside the dark enclosure, she breathed in the rich smell of silt. "Why did she call us here? What did she want us to find?" Ruth paced the tight, dark space—once, again, three times, a fourth, pressing her fingers to the walls of mud, squatting beside the fire pit and examining the ground. "I don't feel anything hidden."

"What about the diary?" Jinx said. "Maybe that's how she's talking to you. And it *is* you she's communicating with. Something links you together."

"Okay, ladies," Cheyenne said. "We followed the ghost and came up empty. I have to tell you, I find all of this fairly hard to believe."

"Like a strangled cat in a cupboard is hard to believe," Jinx said quietly.

"Let's not mix the natural with the supernatural, Jennifer. A country bully is one thing. A ghost is another. Can we go back inside now? We only got four hours of sleep."

"You want to go back to your beauty sleep when Patience and Isaac are in danger?" Ruth said. "And what about the black preacher, Samuel Cotterell? You have to be curious about why you have his last name."

Cheyenne's face grew serious. The vein at her temple pulsed. Jinx could see that the story wasn't quite what Cheyenne had expected. Her ancestor, by the sound of things, was somehow a homeless man who had lived a simple life of faith. Cheyenne slowly lowered herself to the dirt floor, sacrificing her ivory robe. She took the flashlight Jinx held out and shone it on the page.

July 11, 1815

    There was but one man I could turn to with my confidence. I sought out Samuel Cotterell and told him all. If he knew where Isaac was, a message must be sent to him. Mr. Hold would continue to torture Patience and terrorize the slave quarters until the day of

Isaac's return. Though Mr. Cotterell consented to help me, his eyes held the sorrow of a million men. I pressed my hand to the jagged white hairs that rose from his face. He leaned his bearded jaw into my palm before quickly, self consciously, withdrawing. He turned on the heel of his travel boots. I touched the offending hand to my forehead. It was hot, as if with fever.

August 27, 1815

Isaac has returned of his own accord. The first few nights after his arrival, he has slept, under cover of secrecy, on the floor of the mission barn. He applied his last free hours to his craft. And before submitting himself to the authority of his master, Isaac presented us with gifts: a chair fashioned of river cane reeds affixed to wheelbarrow casters for Faith to move about in, and an image of the Holy Cross formed in the likeness of sweetgum leaves carved upon the mantel of our hearth.

The Head Missionary to the Cherokees was true to his sordid word. Upon Isaac's appearance at Hold's rear doorstep, Patience was released for purchase by the mission. I have this evening penned a letter of explanation of this expenditure to our elders in the Church, of which follows a true copy.

To Our Brethren of the General Helpers Conference, Salem:

This letter confirms that a week ago today Mr. James Hold, master of Hold Hill, transferred to us a Negress who is to be under my direction to help with the housekeeping for the Cherokee mission and school. Head Missionary Gamble has lately received power of attorney over her. Mr. Hold sold this Negress, called by the name of Patience, for only 130 dollars cash, though she is with child and therefore hampered in her work for a time. Once the child is born, however, the mission will acquire another little Negro or Mulatto servant to be added to the credit side of our ledger. Patience, a strong, black one of nearly twenty years, can now be counted among the assets of the Church. With gratitude for your unceasing support of this mission, we continue our efforts in the salvation of the heathen.

Yours in the Wounds of Christ,

Anna Rosina Kliest Gamble

My head grew dizzy as I placed my pen beside the pot of ink and cast my eyes about the rooms of our cabin. In the crevice by the stove, Mary Ann dozed in Faith's loft enclosure, her spelling book and a pair of my spectacles grasped loosely in her hand. The younger Cherokee pupils, together with Michael, slept on cots in the rear bedroom. Before the hearth, a bean soup simmered in readiness for the next day's afternoon meal. Patience, who was now, praise be to God, out of the reach of her former master, tended the soup with a steady hand on the ladle. And good Faith, my steady companion, rested on her knees at her kitchen workbench, mixing a salve for a Cherokee pupil stung by a honeybee from our hive that day. Beside her was a vessel of water left behind by the healer Earbob for a patient undisclosed. Crystalline corals floated across the surface, having risen to the top.

I found that I could not breathe as I took in this peaceable scene. These women could be bought, sold, traded, and used for a spiteful man's spittoon; even Mary Ann might be snatched away by illegal traders due to her Negro patriliny. I felt my chest constrict. I needed God's air. I plunged through the fog of stewing soup, baking bread, and sweat-soaked children that filled the mission cabin with the scents of life. I escaped into my garden that night to find my equilibrium, but utterly failed even there.

August 28, 1815

Mr. Sam Cotterell appeared at the garden gate past evenfall bearing a seed specimen. Speaking in a muted voice so as not to awake Faith and the children, I bid him remain outside. I joined him beneath the white peach tree, under whose canopy we had sat many times as he conversed with Mary Ann in her language and regaled our students with fanciful stories. We spoke in low tones of Isaac's bravery, of Patience's improved fate, of Mary Ann's progress. The night air felt balmy on my cheeks, intoxicating with the scent of evening primrose which shone, ever so softly, in the darkness. I held my hand out to Sam Cotterell and accepted his gift. He took my hand in his, wrapping his warmth around me. In more than forty years of life, I had never experienced a touch so sincere. I vowed that I would plant in my garden the seeds that he so tenderly gave me and tend whatsoever should grow there.

When I awoke later in a blanket of dew and wildflowers, I felt first the sensation of a new day's sun on my uncovered head. My hair had come loose from its braid in the night, and it fell to the ground around me, tangling with the switchgrass and plant stems. I realized then where I was and what nature of thing I had done. I cast my eyes about with a start, searching first for Sam Cotterell, and then for any other soul who might have witnessed my transgression. Sam Cotterell had left his linsey shirt drawn about me and disappeared into the early morning light, latching behind him the garden gate that he had carved as a gift for me. I pressed my eyes closed, ashamed at my instinct toward self protection. It mattered not what man had seen. I could not hide from the face of the Lord. I rose from a supine position to my hands and knees, digging my palms in the dirt, praying to He who forgives all to have mercy on his straying daughter.

I felt a touch on my shoulder and started, thinking that Sam Cotterell might have returned, wishing that God might make possible a new life for us on this earth. But Peggy Hold knelt beside me, dampening her dress in the dew, worrying her silver buttons. She brushed her fingers to my hair and gently gathered it back, but did not at first attempt to meet my eyes. She smelled of the lavender oil and sage that she daily smoothed through her long, black tresses. "I had only one husband," she whispered, "whom I no longer love. You had only one husband, whom you never loved. Surely the spirit above understands these things better than you and I. The dance of the Green Corn comes very soon. We will go there and be cleansed. All will be forgiven. A new fire will be lit."

I looked at her through tears, this young Indian woman whom I had sought to bring to God, and before whom I was now lowered in a base state of sinful humanity. I had no doubt that her ardent faith sprang from a lingering heathen superstition. And yet, in a single aspect, her people were correct. The one God, the true God, does forgive all—in exchange for the dearest sacrifice. "Thank you, Peggy, thank you."

I rose then, straightened the length of my skirts, and returned to the mission cabin. I refused to let little Michael collect the water for my bath, and instead purged myself in the muddy waters of the Conasauga.

August 29, 1815

Mr. Hold has made an example of Isaac and hanged him from the oak tree beside the stone wall. I am beyond sorrow.

August 31, 1815

On the night of the day that Mr. Hold took Isaac's life, he sent to the mission for Patience. Mr. Gamble came to deliver the message, giving consent for Mr. Hold's Negro driver to rip her from my grasping arms. Then, his face a shadow beneath the brim of his hat, Mr. Gamble left our cabin for the comfort of Mr. Geiger's house, where all manner of evil is witnessed.

I cannot say how horribly Mr. Hold treated his good wife and her servant in his drunkenness. Peggy stumbled into the mission after the ordeal, unable to speak a word to us, silenced by the cruelty she had endured as both victim and audience of her husband's aggressions. Patience accompanied her former mistress to the shelter of our cabin, her flax gown torn, her black face a stone, her belly suspended before her like a melon on the vine. The blood on her thighs made me fear that she might lose her child.

I could not hold back my tears at the sight of them. Mary Ann clung to the wall, her eyes wide and fearful. In a flurry of words and signals, Faith sent our Cherokee scholars along with her son Michael out to the mission barn. She instructed us to lay the two women on rolls of soft bedding. Faith was the doctor, Mary Ann and I her assistants. The voiceless Peggy Hold was ensconced on one of our scholars' cots before an open window, through which a relieving breeze flowed. Faith sent Mary Ann to glean from my red apothecary rose, then concocted a most unusual conserve, which *she said was a curative for hoarseness. Throughout the long night, Peggy took a teaspoonful of the brew at regular intervals from Mary Ann, while I assisted Faith with the birth of Patience's child back in my sleeping chamber. For Patience's baby was indeed born that night, too early and deathly weak, its face punctuated with the plum colored lips and brooding eyes of Mr. James Hold.*

Patience would not look at the babe, and gave Faith leave to name him. "Adam," Faith said. She dropped her eyes, and for an instant I glimpsed the pain in them. How many infants had she seen die from ill health of the mother? How many children had she seen sold away in her forty some years? She treated Patience with mother wort to calm convulsions of the womb and gently kneaded the younger woman's slack skinned belly.

September 2, 1815

Today, under the untiring ministrations of Faith, Peggy recovered her speaking voice. She spoke her first words to Patience in the Cherokee language, which Patience, having become her former mistress's most intimate companion, readily understood. The eyes of the two women communicated much more. No translation was given me, but Mary Ann seemed to comprehend some part of what was spoken. She rose and began to make preparations, setting aside changes of clothing, dried meat and apples, and a walking stick that Sam Cotterell has taken to leaving in the corner of the hearth room. Then she sat at the center table to write in the elegant, sweeping cursive that I was so proud to see her master. I watched her while a dawning awareness and trepidation came over me. Her purpose was a counterfeit letter of manumission.

September 3, 1815

This country affords several species of Rosa. The climbing, moon flowered Cherokee rose seems to be used purely as ornament, admired as it is for its tenacious beauty. The Indians boil the roots of the wild ground rose as a treatment for dysentery. Only the slaves seem to know the foreign red rose as a cure for lost voice. I have given a detailed description of Cherokee country roses—their cups, flowers, chives, pestles, seedboxes, stalks, leaves, and uses, together with drawings, in my botanic papers. The recipe for making a conserve of red roses in the manner of the slaves follows herein: Take rose buds, and pick them; cut off the white part from the red, and sift the red part of the flower through a sieve to take out the seeds; then weigh them, and to every pound of flowers take two pounds and a half of loaf sugar; beat the flowers pretty fine in a stone mortar, then by degrees put sugar to them, and beat it 'til it is well incorporated; then put it into gallipots, tie it over with paper, over that a leather, and it will keep seven years.

September 5, 1815

Peggy and Patience walked into the outside air for the first time since the ordeal. Arms interlinked like ivy, they made their way to the bubbling waters of a spring on the property, called sacred by the Indians. There, with Peggy holding each of Patience's hands to guide her into the deep sand creek, together they bathed.

September 6, 1815

We could not risk the observation of the Cherokee scholars, for three of them are the offspring of Mr. Hold himself, and most of the children are the progeny of other slaveholders. Neither could we risk the witness of Faith's Michael, who has already seen and heard more than his young soul should have to bear. The mission is also often full of the many Indian visitors who crowd in to seek Faith's medicines, beg for food, or ask for aid in translating some exchange with the white people. Most of these common Cherokees appear sympathetic with the plight of the Negroes, but nevertheless caution must be taken with the future of one so dear to us.

It was at Peggy's urging, therefore, that we moved our talks to the old mud hut at the edge of the settlement. The clay and mica house, half hidden in a field of cane reeds, was built by ancient Indians. The older Mrs. Hold, Peggy's sister, had made this hut her home during her time as Mr. Hold's wife. It was a round dwelling with a small aperture at the apex for the escape of smoke from the old time cooking fires. Late in the night, a week before the Green Corn festival, the four of us met in this place. Faith stayed behind to manage the mission kitchen, mind the scholars, and deflect any queries regarding our whereabouts.

Inside the mud hut, Peggy held the infant Adam to her bosom while I outfitted Patience with sturdy clothing and the pass that she will surely need once she makes it to the U. States. Adam was born too small to suckle from his mother's breast, which I bound with layered gauze to blot the flowing milk. Faith has been feeding him the boiled down juices of collards and cabbage by way of a hollow river cane rod, and he is growing by the day on this concoction. His eyes shine like onyx from beneath the swaddle of Peggy's scarlet scarf.

The fact of his son's birth would be impossible to hide from the master of Hold Hill, who, given his impetuous nature, might seize the babe or sell him down the river for a good price. But Mr. Hold took leave on the day following the ordeal, and Mr. Gamble departed with him, covered, it must be said, with shame. Peggy has resided at the mission cabin since that time, helping to care for Patience and nurse the child whom Patience has not the heart left to notice. The babe's eyes follow Peggy now as if she is his natural mother. But to protect him from the ravings of his capricious father, he will be raised under the cover of anonymity as a sickly black child, born in the slave quarters and taken in by the mission for medicinal care. By the time Mr. Hold returns with the Head Missionary to the Cherokees, Patience will be gone from this place and the child she birthed vanished into the slave population.

Mary Ann changed into young men's pantaloons, stockings, and boots that I procured from the clothing sent by our brothers and sisters in Christ for the use of the Cherokee scholars. I unbraided and combed her thick, dark hair and watched in silence while Peggy cut it in the Indian style. Like a torn swath of midnight, her hair fell to the floor. Without it, Mary Ann looks small, fragile, and more like a girl of fourteen years than she ever has before.

Mary Ann and Patience will travel together to the boundary of Cherokee territory, posing as a young Indian master and his slave. I have instructed Mary Ann to go no farther than the border of Kentucky and Tennessee. I think of wolves, poisonous snakes, and land hungry squatters' camps. My heart shuddered as I watched them step into the iron darkness.

September 13, 1815

My Mary Ann has returned, lovely to behold. She reports that

*along their journey, she and our fugitive sister followed in the foot-
steps of a dearly departed friend, for along the route north, a growth
of wild strawberries stretched through the woods in the likeness of a
trail. Mary Ann, having studied with me in the psychic garden behind the mission, recognized the star-like flowers of the plant which
Isaac had carried along with 150 other specimens. Knowingly or
unknowingly, he had dispersed the strawberry seeds all along his
way. In the heavy rains of April, they had taken root.*

September 20, 1815

*Patience has been gone two weeks, and Mr. Hold, now re-
turned, knows not where to direct his rage. Peggy spends her days
in the mission cabin, and because she has lately accepted Jesus as
her Lord and Savior, the Head Missionary to the Cherokees dares
not insist upon her removal. Mr. Gamble now chooses to reside all
of the time in the home of our un-Christian host.*

September 22, 1815

*In his quest for self indulgence, Mr. Hold attended our last
Sunday's church meeting. The Head Missionary to the Cherokees
continues to preach on the Sabbath and gave Mr. Hold the choicest
seat at the forefront of the hearth room. I could not bear the sight
of his cruel lips and smoldering eyes. I busied myself with cooking,
serving, and whispering encouragements to our newest Cherokee
scholars. Peggy kept company with Faith in the kitchen, the joy of
our faith communion having been pierced by her husband's presence. When I turned away briefly from the boy over whose hair I*

bent, pointing out the English words in his hymnal, I saw it like the gust of air that blows the candle out: Mr. Hold's wolfish eyes falling on Mary Ann as she stood in her pure white blouse and cap. With Patience as good as gone, he had now fixed his desire on Mary Ann, and whether for a slave or a wife, it matters not to her future. My thoughts raced. What means have I to protect her? My breath flew from my body and out the window of the stifling room. My heart and strength went with it. I was left a bag of bones. Not Mary Ann. Not my daughter. No.

September 23, 1815

These are words that should never be written. With the aid of the Head Missionary to the Cherokees and a hired slave tracker from the Georgia settlements, Mr. Hold retook Patience beyond the border of Kentucky. Upon her return, he had her dumped in ropes at the doorstep of his overseer, who used and beat her beyond this life within the space of an hour.

We were in the mission garden when we heard the news, brought to us by Sam Cotterell, whose hat was in his hands. Mary Ann's eyes widened in terror at her future, for Mr. Hold's admiration has been nakedly apparent in the passing weeks. Peggy could not be consoled. Her grief was consuming at the loss of this sister. With baby Adam strapped to her back amidst a tangle of loosened hair, she fell to her knees and wailed to the Heavens, as is the custom in this country.

Faith and I knew without speaking what must be done.

September 24, 1815

Peggy has not yet returned to the home of her husband. She says she will never do so again. Mr. Hold has sent a message, by way of the Head Missionary to the Cherokees, that he wishes our Mary Ann to move into the brick house and assist in the care of the Cherokee scholars who will soon board there.

Faith has begun the preparations in her kitchen. I have begun to write my letters with the aid of Mary Ann, who duplicates my work with the grace and skill of a classically trained scribe. We put the letters into the hands of little Michael and bid him rush to the closest mail station beyond the range of Mr. Hold's estate. Michael took off like buckshot through the trees, having some inchoate knowledge of the import of his mission.

I pray to the Lord for forgiveness and guidance, bowing my head. Mary Ann joins me on her knees, fervently adding the sweet tones of her innocent voice to my own.

September 26, 1815

Patience was buried yesterday at evenfall on the edge of our mission garden. The ceremony was beautifully conducted by our dear Sam Cotterell. The Negro people sang a hymn soothing to the gathered mourners, who represented every shade of humanity. Our Cherokee pupils read a series of poems that they had themselves written about the mercy of God and the peace of His Heavens. There was not one among the Negro population upon whom Patience had not smiled with her shining almond eyes. We have, the women of this mission, planted a variety of roses around and about her grave in remembrance. The Cherokee rose (Rosa laegivata) predominates, as it is native here, and will grow in time to crown this spot in pure white blooms. Besides these wild creeping ones, which Peggy adores, there are roses here that have never been grown together in one spot of earth.

A lifetime ago, before I set out for the Cherokees' wilderness, before I saw all manner of evil that goes on here, a wagonload arrived in Salem from Cape Fear, N.C. with numerous special goods, among them white and red rosebushes (Rosa alba, R. Gallica officinalis). I brought samples of them with me hither, harvested the seeds, and planted them in my botanic garden beside the mission. These are the same roses that revived Peggy's will to speak after the ordeal. Among an assortment of wild plants, they have fared well in this foreign soil—better, perhaps, than they would have done in the orderly gardens of Salem.

The night of Patience's burial, a lunar eclipse cloaked the sky in a darkness deep as winter. We were prepared for this, having heard tell of its coming by the Cherokee healer Earbob. Under this cover, Peggy, Mary Ann, and I led those Negroes who wished to come to the old hut built of mud and mica. Inside, we lit a candle to cast a circle of light. We girdled the gathered men, women, and children, altogether a party of twenty-eight, with clothing, provisions, letters of purpose, maps, and knives. We have divided them into groups for greater efficiency of movement. They will follow routes north, seeking out the trail of the strawberry plant, the leaves of which they carry in their sacks for point of reference. I have enlisted them for the express purpose of carrying seeds to my botanical colleagues in Philadelphia, who await their packages, and are of like mind. It is in Patience's honor, for her stolen life, that I violate the legal principles of property. Christ's love, not man's law, reigns supreme.

September 27, 1815

    The eclipse of last night was followed by a swell of storms that felled three oak trees and studded the mission buildings with hailstones. Mr. Hold was away doing business in the city of Augusta. The Head Missionary to the Cherokees, true to his demonstrated character, cowered within the walls of the brick plantation house. We women kept about our work. Faith ran the operations of the mission while secretly making her preparations. I monitored arrivals to and departures from the Hold house. At the urging of an elderly woman who speaks her native African tongue, Mary Ann has memorialized the ones who have left, casting the shape of their names in shells on the inside walls of the hut. It is tradition in the old woman's country that those now departed who once brought wealth to the master's house must never be forgotten. Together, they represent nearly a quarter of Mr. Hold's human property. Haste is required by the pilgrims before the Godless Talley makes a full accounting of the Negroes lost during the hailstorms. One thought alone brings me comfort. Should Mr. Hold learn of their absence and seek to recapture them, due solely to his rampant greed, he could not, would not, kill them all.

A low rustling sound penetrated the silence of their enclosure, yoked to the smell of acrid smoke. A burst of molten light curled in the darkness.

Jinx halted her recitation. Ruth straightened, alert.

Cheyenne jumped to her feet. "Fire," she whispered.

As she watched it all burn through the slim poplar door of the round mud house, Cheyenne felt she should have known. She should have remembered this was a place where Cherokee homes had been stolen by law, where black people had swung from trees to cheering crowds. Mason Allen was responsible. Who else would set her land on fire, far enough from the house to ultimately protect it? Waves of grass and tall weeds glowed hot before her eyes, turning her yard into a wasteland. She watched the flames gnaw away at her acreage, overtaken by the fear that she would lose it all. The roots of a cane stalk caught just yards in front of them. The fire was spreading.

"There's cogon grass in your yard," Ruth said. "It's highly flammable, and with this hot summer weather continuing into the fall . . ."

"This is no grass fire," Cheyenne interrupted. "It was him. Mason Allen. We have to get out of here, get back to the house and call for help."

"I don't see anybody," Jinx said, clasping the chestnut box to her chest.

"He was here," Cheyenne insisted. "He had to be."

The scene in the yard seemed to unfurl in slow motion—the fire, the smoke, the stench. Cheyenne pushed through the doorway, cursing as flames approached the mud walls, scorching the very cane stalks she had planned to upend.

Ruth knew Cheyenne was right, that they should leave immediately. But she couldn't help holding back, turning around to look. She had to see if the girl was there, if the commotion had summoned her again. "Oh, my," she breathed aloud when she saw it.

The earth house was set aglow by the light of the fire outside it, revealing a now-visible sheen to the mica-strewn mud. Tiny alabaster bits of precious stone, crushed into the plaster mix, glittered in the darkness. White seashells were interspersed among the stone flecks, pressed into familiar linguistic patterns.

Jinx and Cheyenne turned when they heard her exclaim. A constellation of floating symbols shaped in shells spiraled around them on the walls.

"Is that writing?" Cheyenne said.

"It is," Ruth whispered. "Who would have done this?" She seized a breath, knowing at once it was Mary Ann.

"These are the names," Jinx said, tracing her fingers across the shells. "The names Mary Ann fixed to the wall, the people who ran away from Hold in the hailstorm."

"A list of names," Cheyenne repeated, her voice going flat. "Runaway slaves."

Ruth watched emotions shift across Cheyenne's face, her cheeks streaked with trails of sweat. Cheyenne had wanted to find the secret list her grandmother spoke of—a list she thought would name her black Indian family and prove she belonged to the tribe. Maybe this was the reason Cheyenne had been drawn to Ruth when they were young, a reason beyond the obvious self-aggrandizing pity. Cheyenne had seen in Ruth someone like herself—a girl hungry for close connection, for kindred who had been snatched away. Ruth reached out to touch Cheyenne's arm. Cheyenne's eyes locked on hers.

Through the doorway, Ruth saw cane stalks tipping over like dominoes. The closer the fire inched, the brighter the shells and mica shone, flashing like gemstones deep in the core of the earth.

"These names matter, Cheyenne. We can remember them if we try." Ruth began a frantic reading of the names, raising her voice above the roar of fire. "Isaac the First, Patience, Gander, Bob, Peter, Sam, Caty, Renee, Old Ned, Big Jenny, Little Isaac, Hannah, Will, Candace, Peter, Magdalena, Matthew, Butler, Mila, Infant Rose, Grace with her Jacob, Aged Betty, Aged July, April, May, Hagar." The names filled her mouth, filled the old clay dwelling, until the smoky air hummed.

They grasped for each other's hands in the darkness, crawling low as the smoke pushed in, then rising and running as they pressed outside. Ruth thought of those runaway slaves whose names she had spoken. They had found the courage to leave their tormenter. The women, the network of caring, had made the impossible possible. But Ruthie's own mother had been alone—alone when her husband abused her. Alone except for the little girl, a witness of it all.

Cheyenne yanked open the door at the back of the house. They stumbled inside, searching for breath while Cheyenne slammed the lock into place. They stood there in an uncertain clump, like tulip bulbs planted too close in a soft heap of upturned ground. Cheyenne blinked, then lunged toward the hallway, where the coal-black telephone sat on the secretary. Ruthie saw her dial the old rotary numbers through a haze, vaguely heard her speak to someone on the line at the fire department. But Ruthie didn't wait while Cheyenne described the scene outside to the dispatcher. She snuck away like she always had, needing to hide, to find a shell, to get far away from the sight and sounds of primitive struggle. She climbed the stairs to the second floor and tried to go farther. The attic stairway stood in waiting beyond the arabesque of the bridge.

"Ruth?" Jinx called after her.

"I just want to be alone!" Ruthie caught the heel of a clog in the wooden bridge. She fell to the floor and shut her eyes, remembering the sight of blood. "Oh, no," she said. "No." The pictures were upon her. She saw her father slam her mother against an unmoving flank of wall, saw herself crouched in a closet, silently begging him to stop. Ruth was drowning now in a wave of images crashing through open floodgates. She hated him and blamed herself for letting the memory of her mother go. How could she exorcise so much pain? She felt the vomit welling up as her throat constricted.

"Ruth?" Jinx wrapped an arm around her, sitting with her on the floor of the bridge. "Breathe. You need to breathe. It's okay. We're here with you." Jinx held Ruth against her, trying to take all of her weight. Ruth ripped her glasses off, wiping at her tear-blurred eyes.

"She needs air," Cheyenne said tightly, moving toward the massive window on the hallway landing. She lifted the latch and opened the glass. A firm, wet, driven breeze swept up the scrim of smoke outside and carried it into the waiting house as the rain began to fall. The sweet scent of soaking grass mixed with the curling smoke.

Jinx urged Ruth up, walked her toward the open window.

"The fire truck is on its way," Cheyenne said quietly to Jinx.

Ruth squinted into the early-morning darkness. There she was. Mary Ann. Floating in the old rose garden, a fan of incandescent pages dangling from her fingers. Ruth watched as Mary Ann raised her arms, wrapping the smoke around her like a spirit gown, then lifted her arms a second time and gave wing to the pages. They seemed to fly from her hand into the churning, rain-washed air. She was releasing it all to them, all of the pages, all of the pain. She had trust in their care. She was letting it go.

"Do you see her?" Ruth whispered to her companions. "Do you see her now?"

Their silence was Ruth's answer. Only she saw.

"We need to know what happened," she said. "What happened to the women."

Flashing lights penetrated the darkness as a fire truck careened up the avenue of oaks.

"You'll stay with her?" Cheyenne asked. Jinx nodded. And Cheyenne pounded down the steps to meet the firefighters and defend her home.

17

September 28, 1815

Our plan continues its forward motion. Within one week's time will commence the major festival of the Cherokees, the ritual of the new green corn, through which transgressions are atoned and crossed relations mended. Peggy is adamant that all must be completed before this ritual begins. The long absent Mr. Hold paid an overnight visit home with plans to set out again next day for this annual ceremony. He attends yearly, I have learned, more for the purpose of intermingling with other powerful chiefs than for observing the sacred aspects of this communal ritual. A chance has been presented to us. I pray that he will not have time to walk through the slave quarters and look upon the faces of his now depleted property.

Against my best judgment, but with the wise counsel of Faith, I determined to send my beloved daughter to Mr. Hold. My heart was in my mouth as I watched them follow the stone path that the now deceased Isaac had laid across my garden floor. Peggy, with Mary Ann at her side, approached the house, bearing gifts for Mr. Hold in river cane baskets: honey laced corn cakes prepared by Faith, and freshly picked cherries gathered by the Cherokee scholars. Desiring reconciliation with his estranged wife and currying the favor of young Mary Ann, Mr. Hold readily admitted them. Peggy held her husband at length with fervent promises that all should soon be reconciled. After the sacred festival of renewal, she told him, she would return to his home.

By design, Faith's preparation will be slow acting. Into the golden corn cakes she has baked the seeds of Calycanthus floridus (sweetshrub). These are used by the Cherokees for poisoning wolves, among which Mr. Hold can be counted as kin.

September 30, 1815

Mr. Hold set out at dawn for the appointed town where the Green Corn ritual will be held. A turbaned Negro driver saddled the finest horses and mounted a steed beside his master. The Head Missionary to the Cherokees, having long disavowed such ceremonies as nothing more than heathen superstition, remained behind in the brick house, as did Mary Ann, the baby Adam, and I, in the mission cabin. I did not know that Peggy would follow behind her husband's party on her own stout bay horse, cloaked in a woven hood that covered her hair, and carrying one of her husband's rifles. I should never have known, had Michael not glimpsed her from the loft of the mission barn, where he often plays with the Cherokee pupils.

Hours before Peggy returned covered in road dust, her hair a storm cloud, we learned of the shocking occurrence from Indian passersby who often visit the mission. Mr. Hold is dead, shot by a *rifle as he sat sipping his whiskey. The shooting occurred at the tavern of Mr. Buffington, where Mr. Hold had stopped to rest en route to the festival. The perpetrator is as yet undiscovered.*

I spoke of Peggy's absence to Faith, and of the deadly seeds to Peggy. It is best left unknown if Faith's method of destruction would have better accomplished the deed, or would have been more fully justified. Mr. Hold was buried in an unmarked grave near where he fell. All was done quickly and without fanfare by those who had been his companions in drink and vice. Patience, the object of his torture, had garnered more mourners than this famed captain of enterprise, a prominent chief of the Cherokee tribe. Due to Mr. Hold's great number of enemies, it is said his assailant will not be searched for and may never be found.

At Peggy's insistence, we put out our fires and rode all evening to watch the Green Corn dances, the Indians' festival of thanksgiving. The night sky was a whorl of ethereal light above us. Faith and I were seated in the front of a wagon driven by Sam Cotterell. I felt every dip and rise of the rough road and thought that I might be sickened, as I have been often of late. Faith unwrapped a square of cloth and handed me a slice of flat bread. Mary Ann sat behind us in the bed of the wagon humming in a low voice to baby Adam, who slept fitfully in her lap. Michael and our Cherokee scholars were tucked in snugly beside her. Peggy led the way on the back of her bay horse, hair loose and flying wild into the air behind her.

Once we arrived at the encampment, Earbob the healer, with the assistance of Peggy, Sam, and the older boys, built temporary structures for our party beyond the square ground. We feasted on the first day, during which Earbob came to speak with Faith and made her a comfortable place to sit. As we camped there, a new fire was made by a conjurer and his assistants. The green corn was sanctified, after which the women and men danced, tortoise shell rattles shaking like seed packs about the women's legs. All who were

gathered feasted again on new corn, dried meat, fish, beans, pumpkins, and fruits.

After the ceremony, each family came forward to collect a spark
from the fire to carry back to their homes. Peggy's face glowed in
the reflection of the virgin flames. Mary Ann seemed to likewise
glimpse a renewed path before her. I touched my hand to my belly
on the bed of straw that Sam Cotterell had prepared for me, certain
of the new life growing within. No dance, no fire, can ever restore
me to my former self.

October 1, 1815

The seeds of the new fire have been planted in the hearths of every dwelling on the plantation—Cherokee, Negro, and white alike.
The houses of Hold Hill have been cleansed.

October 5, 1815

The weather is russet in its warmth; the leaves have begun their
turning. With Mr. Hold now gone and his enterprises shut down,
the white traders rarely come to our isolated mountain location.
Even the Agent for the U. States has turned his attention elsewhere,
devoting his time to meetings with the other big men in the tribe:
Chief Doublehead, Mr. Ross, Mr. Ridge, and Mr. Watie, the father
of our former students Buck and Stand. Peggy thrives in the midst
of this neglect, trying an experiment that has perhaps never been
ventured before in slavery's territory. Peggy has set the slaves at liberty to work for themselves, and they have run off the Godless Talley, threatening him with knives and sickles. The Head Missionary
to the Cherokees, in fear or in shame, has departed for our Home

Church and left me as sole proprietress of this mission until such time as the Church appoints his replacement, which I suspect they will be reluctant to pursue now that Mr. Hold, our sponsor, is dead.

October 10, 1815

Peggy has sent to Charleston, repurchased Mr. Hold's master craftsman Butler, and reunited him with his family. Like the other slaves on this estate, he now has the liberty to come and go as a free man. She has, besides, enlisted Butler to recast the character of her home to dispel the memory of her dead husband's presence. She has selected a palette of earthly hues and has envisioned a beautiful floral design. The likeness of the Cherokee rose, being her favorite flower and its seeds having been planted at the grave of Patience, shall be made in repetition and set in place throughout the house.

Peggy has renamed her home the Cherokee Rose in sympathy with her affections for the sister she has lost, who lies on the hillside even now, covered by a blanket of roses. Hold Hill remains the name written upon the maps and records drawn by the Cherokee Agent of the U. States. But to Peggy, it is Cherokee Rose, and to the slaves as well, who respect her now as a friend.

November 1, 1815

Fall is waning with the sun, and winter waits with bated breath. The Cherokee and Negro women rush to dry their peaches. I have word that my seed packets have been delivered to the North. And trails of strawberry plants stretch in four directions spreading out from the Conasauga River valley.

December 10, 1815

All things must begin and end, and so it is with Mr. Hold's grand plantation enterprise. Mr. Hold entrusted his legal affairs to the Head Missionary to the Cherokees, who ensured the protection of Mr. Hold's property in the Georgia courts. The appointed administrators of the estate have seen to it that while Peggy can retain the house, mission complex, outbuildings, and furnishings at the insistence of the Cherokee Council, she has no jurisdiction over the slaves, save for the ones that she brought with her from her father's house at the time of her marriage. The others must be sold at auction to satisfy Mr. Hold's contracts and debts. Peggy has seen to it that baby Adam be known hereafter as the child of Mary Ann Battis, so that he might never be counted among Mr. Hold's enslaved population.

December 25, 1815

We gathered this holy day with Peggy, our Cherokee pupils, and a large number of the neighboring Negroes, for the celebration of Christmas. For this purpose, the floor of the hearth room was scattered with green spruce branches, and a window was decorated with a wreath of the same. At the top of the window, beautifully lit by burning candles, were the words "Christ Is Born!" written in gold letters by my dear Mary Ann. After singing a few stanzas, Sam Cotterell spoke on the meaning of this celebration. Then he read the story about the birth of our dear Lord, and, along with all those present, fell to his knees. We finished with a splendid repast prepared by Faith and a number of the Negro women, who had been laboring over their festive dishes for the better part of a week.

There was sadness, together with joy, in the demeanor of those in at-tendance. Accompanied by the evident presence of God Incarnate, the service was closed, and all bid their farewells.

January 1, 1816

A new year has commenced. Faith tells me that the adminis-trators of the estate have finally arrived from Charleston to find the plantation empty of slaves, save for those belonging on paper to Peggy Hold or the Cherokee mission. The others have gone the way of seeds in the wind, and Peggy could not give a clear account of them to the administrators. Women, they presumed, have no heads for the careful management of property, and thus the widow will not be held liable. They will now begin the sale of Mr. Hold's trading post, ferry, cattle, horses, and gristmill to raise the proceeds needed to settle his debts. And so this once thriving plantation has become a spirit town, and we few who remain are left to ourselves.

February 2, 1816

My pregnancy is far advanced, and the pains in my chest are such that it is evident the child and I cannot both survive. I have requested that all my earthly possessions here, in Salem, and in Bethlehem be sold. As much as I detest the act itself, I have used the collected sum to purchase Faith as well as Michael and set them at their liberty. Faith holds their free papers, and Mary Ann possesses a copy.

February 17, 1816

Cold shakes the windows of our cabin. I keep to my bed day and night, waiting for the change. I continue to read with my dear Mary Ann in the subjects of botany and poetry. In the main, she reads to me now, her eyes clouding when she looks upon me. Sam Cotterell is often about the place, doing whatsoever chores Faith has for him and sitting long hours by my bedside, telling stories about magic grapevines and reading from his Bible. He has given up the road and is no longer an itinerant preacher. He will make his home here, he promises me.

March 12, 1816

My body can no longer bear the strain of the child who curls beneath my heart. I feel time growing short. I have instructed my dear Mary Ann, who tends to me with tearful eyes, not to speak a word of my eventful life. She and Sam Cotterell will adopt my unborn child as if it is their own. Peggy has bestowed on them the mission cabin, where they will make their home as adopted father and daughter, and continue the teachings of the Lord in this land. Patience's son Baby Adam is quite a handsome child with a serious disposition and precocious mind. Now that the administrators have left, Peggy prepares to bring him into the brick house, where she intends to raise him with Mary Ann's steady help. After convincing the parents of our pupils to entrust their children to her care even in the wake of Mr. Hold's violent demise, she has likewise made her home a lodging for those students. I have no doubt that the work of the mission school will go on in my absence.

April 5, 1816

Easter draws near. My Mary Ann has traversed the fields and riverbank as I once loved to do. She has collected a bouquet of wild-flowers in wanton bloom and placed them atop my writing desk. Sun glints through the windows, touching the verdant leaves.

April 18, 1816

Though I am weak with the effort, I must write of joyous news. On this day I gave birth to my own precious babe, Isaac Samuel Cotterell, on the Cherokee Rose Plantation. He bears the name of Isaac, a noble soul, and of his father, a true man of God. I pushed Isaac out into Faith's hands amidst the piercing pains of my heart. My body could hardly bear up to it. My breaths came as mere flutters and will soon not come at all. The good Faith bid me drink a cup of tansy tea, which will soon soothe me into forever sleep.

I trust my dear Mary Ann to destroy this diary as I have requested. The work of the mission that brought me here is not yet complete, and would forever be tainted by the truth of my rare story. Little Mary Ann, do not cry as the baby does, flailing in our dear Faith's able arms. For surely our reunion will occur in Heaven a mere lifetime from now. Merciful God, your forgiveness is perfect. Your vengeance is true. May this place live on to prove the truly miraculous works which only a just God can authorize. I remain in death as in life a servant of our loving Christ, whose sufferings were not in vain.

Jinx turned over the final page of Anna Gamble's diary. The three of them sprawled shoulder to shoulder on the staircase landing. They looked at each other through a silence that seemed to cast the Hold House—the home Peggy had redesigned in honor of her adopted sister, Patience—in an otherworldly stillness. Jinx turned to look at Ruth, whose dark chocolate eyes were clearer than they had been before, free of the cloud of separation holding her troubled spirit back. Ruth had seen terrible things as a child, that much was evident, but now she knew intimately the tale of a circle of women who proved that love could triumph over pain.

Jinx felt in that moment that she had found what she came here for. She hadn't searched for Mary Ann Battis. Mary Ann had called her. She now knew her better than anyone living could, anyone except for Ruth. Mary Ann seemed to have a special feeling for Ruth that went beyond obvious links of race and culture, a connection that made new bonds, sacred ties, out of the thickness of common experience. That was why, Jinx theorized, Mary Ann appeared to Ruth, a kindred spirit, a motherless child.

Ruth had been the only one to see the ghost, but it was Cheyenne's mascara-smudged eyes that seemed the most haunted. Cheyenne knew now that she descended from Anna Rosina Gamble and Samuel Cotterell; these were not the Cherokee roots she had longed for. What would she do when she next saw Adam Battis, on moral grounds the rightful heir to this property?

Ruth was the first to voice the thoughts tumbling inside. "They got him," she said. "They won."

Part III
The Three Sisters

"In late spring, we plant the corn and beans and squash. They're not just plants—we call them the three sisters. We plant them together, three kinds of seeds in one hole."

Chief Louis Farmer (Onondaga),
Michael J. Caduto, and Joseph Bruchac,
*Native American Gardening: Stories,
Projects, and Recipes for Families*

18

"Hello? Hello? Where are y'all?" A bright voice lilted through the lower corners of the house. "Are y'all all right? Hello?"

Jinx felt the stair-rail balustrades pressing against her spine like bone spurs. She pulled herself to a sitting position, feeling the strain in her lower back. Light shone high and thin through the landing's leaded-glass windows. It was still morning. She breathed in through her nose. The smoke had cleared, leaving behind a scent like tanned deer hide. The smell reminded her of home, of smoked meat, fry bread, and dried fruit packed together inside Aunt Angie's stomp-dance tent. She felt like Dorothy from *The Wizard of Oz*, as if she had been hurtling through disparate worlds, all the while desperately hoping that home was still possible.

She turned toward Ruth, whose hip angled up toward the plaster of

Paris ceiling, her full legs tapering like candlesticks. Jinx indulged in a long look at the smooth skin of Ruth's face, the rounded shoulder bared by her gown, an ocean of dark caramel.

"Anybody home? It's me. Sally Perdue from the gas station?"

"Hello?" A deep drawl echoed Sally's from the lower floor. "Jennifer? Ruth? Cheyenne?"

Footsteps sounded on the stairs. The solid figures of Sally Perdue, a wriggling baby, and Adam Battis materialized.

"There y'all are." Sally's cornflower-blue eyes, framed by a tumble of short red curls, peeked above the steps. She was as charged as the day Jinx had met her, those same faint lines of exhaustion beneath her inquisitive eyes. The infant on her hip sucked intently on a pacifier and stared at them with his mother's bright baby blues. He wore a white onesie with *Thursday* emblazoned on the chest. He kicked his chubby bare feet. "I was worried sick when I saw the smoke from the station lot this morning. I called Adam, and we got here as fast as we could. But it looks like y'all are all right and the Hold House is still standing." She switched the baby to her other hip.

Jinx pushed back a swath of hair. "Sally, hi. Thanks for coming to check on us. Sally Perdue, these are my friends Ruth Mayes and Cheyenne Cotterell. Cheyenne owns the house."

"Oh, I know that." Sally swatted the air with her hand. "Word travels fast around here. And besides, we met before when she stopped by for gas on Saturday. I wouldn't expect you to remember me, Miss Cotterell. I hope you liked the muffins and jam Adam left for you. I didn't have time to make the muffins from scratch, but the Jiffy folks do a pretty good job in a pinch. The jam, now, that I always make myself. My grandfolks used to own the Ball Fruit Stand before it went belly up, so I know a thing or two about jams and pie fillings."

Cheyenne's eyes widened at the onslaught of enthusiasm. "Thank you," she said. Cheyenne glanced at Sally's worn Lee jeans and Murray

County Cook-off T-shirt, but Jinx could see her thoughts were focused on Adam, who held a door key in his hand.

"So what the heck happened here?" Sally asked with a familiarity that made it seem as if she had known them all their lives. She settled in next to them on the landing, baby on her lap. "You three look like you lost your mama."

"I think it's more like we found her . . . or found them," Ruth said.

Adam mounted the stairs and halted near the landing, one knee jack-knifed up to a higher step. He wore loose jeans and a wash-softened T-shirt the color of summer plums. He turned his pensive gaze to where they sat, a tangle of wild, dark hair, wrinkled pajamas, and sweat-streaked faces. "I'm sorry to barge in like this, Cheyenne," he said. "I thought we should stop by to make sure everything was all right. Sally told me she saw smoke. She was worried. I was worried."

Jinx looked at Cheyenne, who stared without speaking at Adam's brass key. "We had what you could call a misadventure early this morning," Jinx offered. "There was a grass fire in the yard. It was fairly contained. By the time the firefighters arrived, the rain had nearly put it out. Cheyenne thinks Mason Allen may have set it."

"Shit," Sally said. "I never could stand that Mase. He's nothing but a burner set on low, waiting to explode. Are y'all okay? Is anybody hurt?"

"We were scared," Ruth said. "But we made it. We'll be okay."

"You should press charges against that jackass. And if you don't, I will. A fire like that could have spread for miles, and our fire department's all-volunteer," Sally said.

Adam listened, a quiet storm gathering on his face. "It would be hard proving he started a grass fire, but that doesn't bar me from having a talk with him."

Cheyenne stared through Adam, eyes fixed on a distant scene. Jinx imagined what she was seeing, the silent film scrolling in her mind: a premature, sickly infant born in the missionaries' cabin to a slave named

Patience and Chief James Hold. That child was the first Adam Battis, whose name would never appear on any Cherokee census roll, even though he was the son of a powerful tribal leader. The man standing before them now was that boy's descendant and the holder of his name. Jinx wondered if Adam knew his family members in Oklahoma, if his family knew about him. She hoped the descendants of James Hold's wives and siblings would listen to Adam's side of the family story, that they would see the past as a stage of possibility and unexpected occurrences.

Cheyenne wrapped the ivory robe, dingy with dust and ash, around her delicate waist. She descended the stairs, meeting Adam where he stood, aligning her eyes with his. "You have a key to this house," she said. "An original key. Where did you get it?"

"I've always had a key, even before I took the job here. It's been in my family for generations. My grandfolks said it was given to Mary Ann Battis by Peggy Hold herself. I shouldn't have used it, though, now that you own the house. You're right about that. No one answered when we knocked. We wanted—I wanted—to be sure you were okay."

"Do you know who you are?" Cheyenne demanded.

Adam froze, startled.

"Do you know who you really are? Your tie to this plantation?"

Adam shifted his gaze from Cheyenne's searching eyes to the faces of the women beside her. "Yeah," he nodded after a beat. "I know where I come from. I know my family's history, if that's what you mean. What about you? Do you know who you are, Cheyenne?"

"I thought I did when I bought this place," Cheyenne said quietly. "But now I think I have to figure that out all over again. I must look like a fool to you. Buying this plantation, treating it like a dollhouse, acting like it was my personal inheritance."

"It doesn't matter, Cheyenne." Adam lifted his hand and touched a palm to her temple, where perspiration was spiraling her dark, straightened hair. "You had a right to bid on the Hold House. You did nothing wrong."

But Cheyenne's crushed expression said she knew differently. Her hunger for this land had been as selfish and blind as Mason Allen's. Cheyenne's eyes were wet, her mouth set in a colorless line. Jinx had seen that crestfallen look on someone's face before, back when she was doing dissertation research deep in the basement of the Oklahoma Historical Society. A starry-eyed genealogist questing for Indian roots had emerged from the microfilm machines disillusioned, coming up empty-handed—and worse, in his mind, finding an ancestor on the Dawes Rolls recorded as "Freedman" instead of "Indian by Blood." Cheyenne's forbears had been teachers, preachers, and brave freedom fighters, but they had not been Indian. Could she accept that? Could she turn the page?

"This property, this land, should never have been put up at auction," Cheyenne said. "This is not my house. And as long as I can fight it, it will never be Mason Allen's either. Peggy, her family, the Cherokee people—it still belongs to them." Her voice dragged as she pushed against the catch in her throat. "It still belongs to you."

Adam hesitated a moment, his eyes going dark with unspoken feeling. "Maybe this isn't your house in the way you mean. But that doesn't mean it couldn't become your home."

Cheyenne's shoulders quaked as she stood on the stairs of her manor house, dirty, sweaty, makeup washed away. Ruth descended the steps to wrap her in a hug. Turning into the sooty cotton of Ruth's nightshirt, Cheyenne leaned on the strength of her childhood friend.

"No offense, but y'all are a mess," Sally said, breaking the silence. "Let's get y'all dressed and out of here and find some breakfast. And you," she added, looking pointedly at Cheyenne, "are in need of a slice of this county's best strawberry pie."

Jinx smiled, thinking of Deb's pie back home, and of Mary Ann's second family on the Cherokee Rose Plantation. Ruth, Cheyenne, Adam, Sally, and the little baby with a word on his chest: these were her people.

When dusk fell, Ruth lay on the thinning rug in the rear parlor of the plantation house. The hand-woven Persian textile swirled with color, its rich shades forming the intricate pattern of a hunt. Turbaned men rode astride long-necked steeds, chasing their antlered prey in an endless, searching circle. Ruth had showered, changed into a faded Purple Rain concert T-shirt and Lucky Brand jeans, and pulled her hair back with an orange bandanna. She lay on her back beside the fire Adam had built from kindling and logs cut and stacked back when he was employed at the place. The fire did its humanizing work, flickering before the four of them like a miniature dance of the sun, making them feel safe, alive, linked to each other.

Ruth looked from the fire to Jinx, who sat with her back pressed against Ruth's knees, her braided hair, wet from a shower, dampening Ruth's faded blue jeans. Jinx had fashioned a makeshift library carrel on the carpet before the hearth, using a fringed pillow for a lap desk. She sat within a nest of books and loose legal-pad pages, intent on putting the fragments together, connecting the dots of the story. Over fried eggs and grits at Adam's cabin that morning, she had quizzed Ruth and Cheyenne about what they remembered from the diary. Then she had put Adam through a battery of questions about the oral history of the Battises and the Holds. Now that Sally had gone home with Junior, leaving behind a fresh strawberry pie, she wanted to get all of their versions down on paper. The scratching of her pen and popping of the fire echoed in the room.

Cheyenne lounged on a silk settee, legs neatly folded beneath the pressed lime skirt of her poplin dress. Adam sat nearby, grinning at her as she took experimental bites of gooey strawberry pie.

"Are you still going to write that column, Jinx, about Mary Ann Battis?" Cheyenne asked after swallowing a mouthful as delicately as possible and taking a sip from her crystal water glass.

Jinx pulled her eyes from her notepad and straightened away from Ruth's knees. "Some people in my community, owing in part to me, think Mary Ann abandoned her family when she converted to Christianity, that she chose to stay behind in the South and turn her back on her Indian kin because she was a traitor. But it turns out she was a child taken from her family, like so many others since colonization began. She wanted to stay here, where her beloved women, her adopted mothers, were buried. Mary Ann was a witness for all of them: Anna Rosina, Patience, Peggy, Faith, even the slaves whose names she inscribed on the mud house walls. And now I'm a witness for her. I have to pass the story on."

Ruth rubbed Jinx's back, which loosened under the gentle pressure.

"I'm going to write a history of this plantation," Jinx said, "finish my dissertation, and get my Ph.D."

"I'm all for anybody pursuing their education," Adam said. "But is it what Anna Gamble would have wanted? You-all said she told Mary Ann to burn that diary." He gestured toward the chestnut box beside Jinx.

Jinx tucked damp strands of hair behind an ear, gathering her answer. "Mary Ann buried it for someone to find, led Ruth to the pit and the names. She wanted us to know what happened here; she made sure we knew. All stories have their time, and I think this one's time has come. The only evidence that something extraordinary took place here exists in that diary."

"Not the only evidence," Adam said. "After all, we're still here. Descendants of the Cherokee Rose."

"What should we do with it?" Ruth said, gently touching her finger to the floral pattern carved in the box.

"Donate it to a research library?" Jinx said. "The Moravian Archives would be perfect, or the Southern Historical Collection at the University of North Carolina. What do you think, Cheyenne? The diary was written by your ancestor."

"Well," Cheyenne said, glancing in Adam's direction, "I guess I'd like to keep it. For a while, at least. If I ever have children, I'd want to hand it down."

"And what about Mary Ann?" Ruth said. "Shouldn't we find a way to say goodbye?"

The moon was high overhead when they waded into the garden. They left the rear doors of the house open behind them, allowing the late-September breeze to flow in at will. They each held a beeswax candle Adam had produced from the bottom of a Chippendale credenza. The lights of their candles burned over the tangle of garden flowers as the wide sea of river cane swayed at a distance before them. Some of the reedy stalks—the ones nearest the mud house—had lost their fullness in the fire, but most retained their feathery heads, forming a loose, fibrous net between earth and sky.

A heap of clay was all that remained of the earth house. *Ashes to ashes, dust to dust*, Ruth thought. She slowed as they neared the center of the flower garden, letting Adam lead. He knew this place better than any of them. He could find where the bodies were buried.

Adam stopped beside the place where the hill dipped, where Ruth had first noticed the roses. The cluster of mounds he pointed out appeared at first as natural features on the landscape. But the rise in the center was covered with roses of every description, some in bloom, some at rest after a full summer's show. Three slight mounds surrounded that middle plot, complemented by rosebushes less thickly planted.

Jinx grasped the braid of sweetgrass Aunt Angie had made for her, which she had once sworn never to burn. She held the tip of the braid out to Adam. He lit it with his candle, releasing smoke and a rich aroma to float around them. Jinx fanned the smoke toward her face and torso. She turned to the others, inviting them to mirror her.

Adam was the first to speak: "Lord, help us remember this woman and all of those who dwelled here."

"Mary Ann," Ruth said, "it's time for you to go back. Sister Maker, Keeper of the Treasure. Come. Go back."

"Thank you. Rest in peace," Cheyenne whispered.

Sweetgrass smoke rose above the burial mounds and hillside. Jinx took Ruth's hand, and also reached out for Cheyenne, who extended her left hand to Adam. The four of them stood before the graves, thinking of the ones below and also the ones above, the ones who had come before and the ones who would come after, hoping that Mary Ann Battis, a woman-child no longer alone, would find her rightful place among them.

19

RUTH TRIED TO RISE from the pencil-post bed she had shared with Jinx that night, their bodies curved together like question marks at the end of a wandering sentence.

"Where do you think you're going?" Jinx reached out, pressing her face into the coils of Ruth's hair. They had slept late. The house was quiet around them.

Ruth had to make herself pause, had to give herself permission to lean into the comfort of Jinx's arms. "Outside. There's something I want to do." Ruth wrapped herself around Jinx in a shy hug, then slid out of bed before the slow melting could begin again. "Come with me if you want."

"Try and stop me."

Jinx gave her a quiet smile while Ruth ducked her head, pulling on clothes from the day before. Jinx dressed quickly in cutoff jeans, a library book-sale T-shirt, and unlaced cherry-red high tops. Ruth led the way into the stillness of the hall.

"Upstairs?" Jinx said when Ruth turned toward the attic.

"We need to get a basket."

Ruth cracked the attic door, breathing the smell of hidden decay, feeling the steady warmth of Jinx close behind her. She pushed aside the discolored mops, nearly tripping over a fallen broom handle. Jinx grabbed Ruth's hand, helped her step over the handle, then righted the broom against the wall. Ruth paused, looking fully into Jinx's face.

"I've got you," Jinx said. "Go on."

Ruth lifted the sifting basket off its hook and slid it to the crook of her elbow.

"Ready?" Jinx said.

Ruth stared into the closet's depths, toward the narrow staircase.

"You want to see what's up there? Let's go." Jinx nudged her.

At the top of the steps, Ruth scanned the attic. It was a long coffin-like room, capped on opposite ends by semicircular eyebrow-shaped windows. Save for an antique wheelchair woven from river cane, a torn hoop skirt, and an infant's iron crib, the floor was bare. The residue of human suffering clung to the air. But other than that cloying stench, James Hold's torture chamber appeared almost mundane—just another attic in an old plantation house down a winding Southern road.

Ruth arched her neck to look up. The ceiling was formed of hand-hewn beams held together by thick wooden pegs. Her eye caught high in the tented rafters, where some kind of bird had made a nest and the gossamer webs of spiders draped like nets.

"Look," Ruth whispered, pointing toward the apex.

The rough-plank trusses were embellished with delicate floral carvings. Alabaster Cherokee roses, too many to count, clustered around the joining places of the beams. The petals were formed of mica stone, pearly and brilliant. And at the center of each decorative flower, shining in the late-morning light, was a circle of pure, bright gold.

"Peggy's tribute to Patience," Ruth said. "Even here."

"Especially here," Jinx said, looking in awe at the detailed craftsmanship. "A golden rose garden. I wonder how she did it."

"Maybe there really was gold buried here, like the legend says. Maybe James Hold had it stashed away somewhere. Peggy could have chosen to use it in the redesign of the house. She may have thought it was the best way to protect two valuable things: the memory of Patience and the gold. I've seen it done before, a floral motif made of gold, on the dome of the Library of Congress. Isaac's mentor, Butler, was a talented artisan to pull this off."

"It must be worth a fortune," Jinx said. "Do you think Cheyenne knows it's here?"

"Not yet."

Ruth cast her eyes around the barren room, finding the oddly shaped window facing east. For a reason she could not pinpoint, her gaze settled there. She imagined a female figure brooding at that window, fingertips softly disturbing gray dust on the sill.

The house seemed to inhale and exhale in the still moment that followed. This was what Mary Ann was guarding, what she had wanted Ruth to see—in the diary, in the mud house, in the attic. This is what Mary Ann had returned to enlist them all to protect: the memories of the Cherokee Rose built into the bones of the house, planted in the soil of the garden, safeguarding generations to come.

Ruth and Jinx walked downstairs, passed through the long hallway, and exited the rear doors of the house. The garden was bathed in satin light, the misted air fragrant with roses. Ruth halted close to the mission cabin. Some of the plants she recognized. Some she didn't. She knelt beside those that caught her eye or sense of smell and dug at their roots with the curved edge of a spade. She closed her eyes, picturing her mother tending this garden, coaxing it to grow and bloom even beneath a threatening sky. She knew now that it was shame that had kept her mother away from Georgia. Shame at the bruises and shattered bones she had tried to hide from Ruth, that Ruth had tried to erase from her own memory over the years. And shame at having married a man— stayed with him, made a child with him—who turned out to be just the type her family had feared. But even if her mother had chosen the isolation of exile, Ruth could go back. She could pick up the pieces and find the seeds.

"Are you going to transplant those?" Jinx dropped to kneel beside her.

"I think it's worth a try." Ruth looked up to meet Jinx's eyes. "It's a long trip, but maybe they'll take."

"I know just the place in Oklahoma. A cottage garden in need of some life."

"Yours?" Ruth said.

"My inheritance. Aunt Angie left it to me. It's about time I make it my own."

Ruth gave the garden a long last look as they made their way back toward the house. She would return here, she knew, but never again in this season of life. The wild Cherokee roses flashed in resplendent second bloom now, an autumn showing that could occur only when weather conditions were right. They were a creeping species of plant with thick roots and sharp thorns, partial to barren, long-forgotten, and obscure places. Soon they would spread to cloak the mound of the departed round house, cross the river, and retake the Strangers' Graveyard.

Cheyenne watched the incredulous faces of the state attorneys as she sat next to Adam in a paneled anteroom of the courthouse. She had dressed in an Eileen Fischer pantsuit, loose and flowing like the spun silk of a cottonwood tree. Instead of straightening her hair with her blow-dryer and flatiron, she had decided to let it find its natural wave.

The rectangular conference-room table was overpopulated with representatives from almost every conceivable constituency. Her father's lawyer had driven up from Atlanta for the last-minute meeting in a rush that had left him on edge. After trying to dissuade her from her decision, Dan Shapiro had given in to Cheyenne's will. His pinstriped suit contrasted with Adam's dark blue jeans and plaid button-down shirt. The broker, Lanie Brevard, was there, too, wearing a black pencil skirt and a frown. She sat next to the title-company representative, who was struggling to facilitate the unwieldy deal.

Adam handed over the cashier's check for twenty-five thousand dollars, prepared for him in a rush by the local bank that morning. It was only at his insistence that Cheyenne had agreed to accept any down payment at all. She had been prepared to carry the mortgage for as long as it took. She still had her job at Swag. She still had her family's money. She could even sell her condo in Candler Park, if it came to that.

Cheyenne fingered the glossy pearls around her neck. With a deep breath that was as much release as resignation, she started to sign the mountain of documents before her. Adam signed his corresponding stack, followed by their witness, Sally Perdue.

"I know what I'm doing, Danny," Cheyenne whispered to the balding man who had represented her father for as long as she could remember. His hazel eyes showed concern behind the wire-rimmed glasses. She touched a hand to his arm as he shook his head with combined affection and disbelief. "Or at least I have a pretty good idea. Do you think you can make one more stop with me before you head back to the city? I'll fill you in on the drive."

"Of course I can," he said, beckoning Cheyenne into the passenger seat of his BMW.

"Follow him," Cheyenne said to the lawyer, smiling through the open window at Adam, who had climbed into the driver's seat of his Bronco. Sally sat beside him, her red curls catching the September sunlight, her baby strapped into a car seat in the rear.

They followed Adam through the town center, past the hill where the Hold place held its quiet ground. They turned away from the road leading to the mountain and snaked down behind the Hold property line to cross a one-lane bridge. As the poplars and chestnuts parted beyond the riverbank, Cheyenne saw the construction site like an open wound. Burly men were shouting in English and Spanish, lifting and hauling materials. The land had been cleared for two hundred feet. A cement foundation had been poured inside the square indenture. Bright machines with sharp teeth and elongated necks stood at the ready. A black Grand Cherokee squatted on the edge of a road that was dirt now but that Cheyenne guessed would soon be paved.

Adam parked next to the SUV. Dan Shapiro followed. The four of them stepped out of their vehicles to see Mason Allen, wearing a yellow hard hat, break away from a huddle and stride forcefully toward them.

"Sally, Adam," he said, nodding his head in a clipped greeting. "Hello again, Miss Cotterell. Mason Allen," he said to the lawyer, holding out a hand. "And you are?"

"Daniel Shapiro, Mr. Allen. I represent Cheyenne Cotterell in the matter of the Hold House property sale."

Mason Allen's eyebrows arched over his slate-gray eyes, his jowls turning pinkish as he looked from the attorney to Cheyenne to Adam. "So it's true"—he addressed his words to Adam—"what I've been hearing around town this morning. You went and bought the Hold place from her behind my back. We've lived in this town a long time together, Adam. Our families have ties. And you're going to throw it all away. For what? A chance to fail at something too big for you to handle?"

Cheyenne doubted his meaning was lost on anyone in that tense circle. He was telling Adam to know his place.

"I won't fail, Mason, because I'm not alone in this. And I want you to know right here and now, in front of these good people, that if you come near the Hold House, or anybody living there, with ill intentions, we'll take it to the law and slap you with a restraining order."

"Adam, calm down now. You're getting your back up without good cause. If you own the place, well, that's that. I'm sure you and I can get along. It's not as if we're strangers. A property like that is expensive to maintain unless you make it work for you. I can help you do that. We'll talk over a couple of beers. The two of us, at my club next week."

"That would be the three of us," Cheyenne said. "Adam is my business partner. We own the property jointly. If you plan to deal with him, you're going to have to deal with me, and I can tell you right now I'm not available next week." Cheyenne watched Mason Allen's head spin from her face to Adam's before Dan Shapiro cut in.

"Mr. Allen, I have to inform you that we have reason to believe you're building on a burial ground of historical significance. The National Historic Preservation Act and the Native American Graves Protection and Repatriation Act say you can't do that without going through federal channels. We'll be requesting a cease-and-desist order from your county court by the end of the business day."

"And another thing, Mason," Sally piped up with Junior wiggling on her hip. "I quit."

Mason Allen stood there, absorbing the assault. The men working at the site slowed their movements, listening.

Weebles wobble, Cheyenne thought as she watched Mason Allen flounder in his hard hat, *and sometimes they fall down.*

On Saturday morning, Ruth and Jinx packed Jinx's truck with lug-
gage, laptops, books, papers, and a case of Sally's fruit preserves. Ruth
tucked the seedlings of her new plant collection into a bed of earth inside the heirloom sifting basket. The basket, a gift from Adam, balanced
on top of the jumble of things. Jinx's sweetgrass braid, the tip now black,
reposed once again on the dashboard.

Ruth turned to wave at Cheyenne, who posed beside Adam on the
veranda, wearing a belted trench dress, matching Ferragamo flats, and
perfectly applied French makeup. Cheyenne waved back like a princess
on a parade float, hair drifting down in loose waves around her face. She
and Adam had both been stunned when they returned from the graveyard to find raw gold hidden in their attic. Cheyenne had managed once
again to maintain her glass-slipper footing in a world that had rapidly
turned under her feet—but not, Ruth knew, without first wrestling her
secret insecurities and losses to the ground.

Ruth climbed into the passenger seat. She was leaving her Volkswagen Beetle in the Hold House lot. Cheyenne had promised to drive
it out on a road trip to Oklahoma that Christmas, exacting a pledge
from Adam that he would come along, given that she was forgoing both
the comfort of flying first-class and the dream of a holiday opening for
her B&B. Maybe Ruth would still be there in the cottage Jinx had described, with flower beds that hadn't been planted in years. Maybe she
would quit her job, write a field guide to Southern flowers, or take a
position in her mother's company. Ruth didn't know exactly what the
future held, only that she would not be alone in it. She sighed, breathing the scents of Twizzlers and Coca-Cola and Jinx. She felt Jinx's eyes
on her, the expectation, the waiting. And because she still didn't quite
know how to react when Jinx looked at her that way, Ruth handed her
the case of her Tribe Called Quest CD.

Jinx smiled when she saw it—the classic disk by a hip-hop group
from the nineties. That was exactly the kind of music Ruth would have

picked. But Ruth had a tribe now. And Jinx's quest was at an end, or at least a satisfying pause. Next came making a life that could bridge their separate pasts and entwine their futures. Jinx had dialed her cousin Victor from the black rotary telephone last night to tell him she wouldn't be coming back alone. "It's about time," he had said, dropping his usual teasing tone. "It's about time."

"Nice," Jinx said to Ruth, "but how about a little Poetic Justice first?"

Jinx waited for Ruth's reaction and saw that she was curious. *Good,* Jinx thought. She reached back into the pile of their things, feeling for the pocket of her messenger bag. She slid the disk by Poetic Justice, a tribal jazz ensemble, into the dashboard stereo.

The fusion of sax, flute, and drum filled the cab of the Chevy as they blazed down the winding road, the Hold House behind them, a study in handmade brick and homespun brutality, forever haloed by rose gardens.

Jinx saw Ruth recline and close her eyes, trusting that, together, they would find their way home.

Epilogue
The Song of the House

JUNIOR WAS THE FIRST TO GREET THEM, toddling down the winding gravel path. At twelve months, he was brave and boundless, happy enough to stay on his feet or tumble to the ground. He was dressed in designer baby blue jeans and a top featuring the Hungry Caterpillar in hand-stitched appliqué. *Cheyenne's doing*, Ruth thought, shaking her head.

Beside Junior, the elegant bank of azalea bushes had just begun its spring showing. The bushes blazed hot pink in the cool April air, bringing out the color in the bricks of the home behind them. Cheyenne and Adam had put their gold to immediate use, paying off the loan on the house, making the old structure shine again. An ornate wooden sign beneath the azaleas announced *The Cherokee Rose Bed-and-Breakfast*.

In the side yard, the weaving house, corncrib, and smokehouse had been refurbished with clean white paint and glistening windows. Matching signs in the same Victorian cursive style introduced *Sally's Whole Fruit, Jams & Pies*. The old, battered wooden sign picturing a flushed summer peach had been rescued from the Ball Fruit Stand and hung now as an artifact on the outside wall of the weaving house.

"Hey, y'all," Sally said, bounding three steps behind Junior, her short hair pinned back in butterfly-shaped barrettes. She raced forward to throw her arms around Jinx and Ruth. "What did you do? Speed the whole way? We weren't expecting to see you 'til suppertime."

"Not exactly," Ruth said. "We flew into Atlanta and rented a car. Turns out to be even quicker than speeding."

"I'll say. Adam's out in the orchards now, tending to his new lemon trees. Cheyenne's in the cabin, probably trying to do some last-minute planning. The inn opens the first of May, and she's been in more than a tizzy this month."

"The cabin?" Ruth said, glancing at Jinx.

"There's been quite a few changes around here," Sally said. "You two are in for a treat."

They stepped onto the wide veranda filled with white wicker rockers, potted pink geraniums, and pale, delicate ferns. A bronze National Register of Historic Places plaque had been affixed to the brick beside the antique doorbell.

Jinx took in the scene as Sally led them inside, Junior hitching a ride on her hip. The preternatural chill she had felt when first crossing this threshold was gone. She reached for Ruth's hand and squeezed, feeling her touch returned.

A reception table had been placed in the foyer. Printed brochures described the history of the plantation, listed times for historic tours, and outlined hiking trails on Fort Mountain. Gleaming oak barrister bookcases housed Adam's collection. A gourmet kitchen with granite counters and industrial-quality appliances had been built into the east side of the house, swallowing the pantry and a fair amount of hallway space. Over the carved fireplace mantel, the chestnut box had been sealed into a custom glass case.

"The drawing room will be a common area for B&B guests," Sally explained. "The bedrooms upstairs are named for the women who lived here back when. Junior and I have the room in the back on this floor—the rear parlor with the fireplace. It's the Anna Gamble Room."

Jinx smiled to herself, remembering the thoughts Anna Rosina Gamble had expressed about that parlor in her diary. The Hold House, the missionary had thought upon her arrival, was too bustling, too foreign, and too full for her delicate senses. By the looks of things, it would soon be full again.

"Cheyenne giving up her master suite and mountain view?" Ruth said. "Has that girl lost her mind?"

"You might think so," Sally said. "But I know a thing or two about losing your mind, after living seven years with Eddie Senior. So I'd say she's just changed a bit, like all the rest of us." Sally wore a smile as she took in the way Ruth and Jinx walked together without an inch of distance between them. "After you get settled, come on down. I know Cheyenne will want to show you the gardens."

Jinx and Ruth took a turn around the master bedroom, named for Patience, which looked nearly the same as it had when they were in the house last fall. The linens had been replaced with high-thread-count cotton that smelled faintly of rose petals, and Cheyenne had added the promised master bath.

They headed down the staircase and through a narrow hallway that closed off Sally's room from the back exterior doors.

The flowers and grasses were dressed in shades of tender green. The space still held its wild character. Cheyenne had not torn down the cane that dipped to the river below or built her glass breezeway to frame a water view. She had left the yard as she found it, as Anna Rosina would have remembered it. Newly planted vegetable and herb gardens fanned out from the old mission cabin, punctuated by raised soil lines and markers in the ground. The building was designated the *Mary Ann Battis House* on a sign beside the front step.

"The prodigal sisters return," Cheyenne said, sashaying out of the mission cabin with a ponytail rolling down her back and an orange kitten twining around her legs. She reached out to hug Ruth and then Jinx. "Long time since December," she said. "I missed you ladies." She ushered them inside.

Ruth took a moment to absorb it all. The raw space where she and Jinx had dug out the diary was now a shabby-chic country cabin fit for a magazine spread. The walls were a soothing eggshell white from milk paint common to the structure's original era. The front room was filled with overstuffed white linen furnishings, Ralph Lauren floral throw pillows, and a sisal rug. A painted iron chandelier hung from the cabin's rafters. A half-wall had been built around the original brick oven, which had been coaxed back to life and was emitting the heavenly smell of cornbread.

"Cheyenne," Ruth said, her mouth open in shock. "You live here? And you . . . cook?"

"Of course I live here, Ruthie." Cheyenne flashed her irresistible smile. "And Adam cooks."

The round antique table Cheyenne had placed in the center of the room overflowed with blossoms. A Simon Pearce glass vase was filled to cascading with every species of plant life then in bloom on the Hold estate.

Ruth looked at Jinx in her cargo pants and Cheyenne in her ocean pearls. Three women so different, enlisted to carry on the same story. As she breathed in the fragrance of fresh spring flowers and watched the clear sunlight glinting on their leaves, Ruth thought that Mary Ann would have approved.

Author's Note

The circumstances and characters described in this novel are drawn from my research on African American and Native American relationships, conducted over more than fifteen years. The predominant historical context for the story is Cherokee slaveholding—the practice of owning people of African descent adopted by some Cherokees (mostly, but not solely, individuals of dual Cherokee and European heritage) with the formal support, and indeed, participation of the Cherokee national government. A minority of Native Americans in the Southeast (of the Cherokee, Creek, Choctaw, Chickasaw, and Seminole nations, the so-called Five Civilized Tribes) owned black slaves in the eighteenth and nineteenth centuries for the purpose of increasing their agricultural productivity and demonstrating their level of "civilization" to American officials. A handful of Native American families became wealthy through their use of slave labor and developed plantations that rivaled those of the white South. The Cherokee Nation of the Georgia and Carolina region, and later of the Indian Territory, was the largest of these slaveholding tribes; its citizens held just over twenty-five hundred black slaves on the eve of the Civil War. The Cherokee government allied with the Confederacy during the war in large part to protect the right to own slaves. After the Civil War, the Treaty of 1866 enacted between the United States and Cherokee governments required the Cherokees to adopt former slaves as members of the nation.

Just over twenty years later, in 1887, Congress passed the Dawes Act, or General Allotment Act, which called for the dissolution of tribal governments and the division of communal tribal landholdings. Each Native American family would be assigned 160 acres within Cherokee territory and each individual over the age of eighteen 80 acres. The General Allotment Act was a policy meant to detribalize and assimilate

246

American Indians by weakening community ties through the notion of amassing private property, which a minority of tribal members had already embraced in the first half of the century in the form of slave ownership.

In order to carry out the allotment process, the United States government organized a massive census of Native Americans who qualified for tribal membership, and hence allotments of land. In the Cherokee Nation (and other nations in the Indian Territory, where the Dawes Act was implemented through the Curtis Act of 1898), this census (called the Dawes Rolls) was segmented into racial categories: "Indians by Blood," "Freedmen," and "Intermarried Whites." "Indians by Blood" were considered biologically or genetically determined Cherokees for the purposes of the census, and blood-quantum ratios were recorded for people on this list. "Intermarried Whites" were Euro-Americans who had married into the tribe, and "Freedmen" were former slaves of both sexes, and their descendants. No blood quanta were recorded for "Freedmen," which meant that no historical record was kept of the Cherokee Indian ancestry of former slaves, some of whom were in fact descended from Cherokees and would have qualified as Cherokees by blood. The structure of the Dawes Rolls codified tribal membership in racial terms that disregarded evidence of mixed Afro-Cherokee heritage.

The Cherokee Nation of Oklahoma traces membership through documented lineal descent from an individual on the established Dawes Rolls. Through the late nineteenth century and most of the twentieth, former slaves and their descendants with an ancestor on the Dawes "Freedmen" roll were considered tribal members. At various points in the twentieth and twenty-first centuries, the Cherokee Nation of Oklahoma's elected officials and citizens have argued that citizenship should belong only to those who can trace their ancestry to the "Indians by Blood" category of the Dawes Rolls. They have further argued that, as a consequence, descendants of "Freedmen" are not rightful citizens eligible for tribal government services and voting rights. The Cherokee district and supreme courts have sometimes disagreed and sometimes agreed with this argument, while the United States Department of the Interior holds that the Treaty of 1866 guarantees citizenship. Thus, the place of "Freedmen" descendants in the Cherokee Nation has been and continues to be a longstanding source of internal and public controversy. The conflict is a painful, ongoing legacy of Cherokee slaveholding.

    This novel, *The Cherokee Rose*, is set on a fictionalized plantation similar to that of a historical figure, the wealthy Cherokee entrepreneur and planter James Vann. In the early 1800s, Vann was one of the richest members of the Cherokee tribe. He was also an influential political leader who held the title of a chief on the Cherokee Tribal Council. Vann owned a plantation called Diamond Hill near the Conasauga River and the western edge of the Blue Ridge Mountains of what is now Georgia, where he held 115 slaves at the time of his death in 1809. Vann had at least two Cherokee wives on the premises, a handful of former wives and consorts in the vicinity, and several children. James Vann (of Cherokee and Scottish parentage) and his young wife, Peggy (or Margaret Ann) Scott Vann (of Cherokee and English parentage), were firmly ensconced in Cherokee cultural practices and community circles and spoke Cherokee as their primary language.

    In 1801, with Vann's assistance, the Moravian Church of North Carolina established a Protestant mission in the Cherokee Nation. In 1805, head missionary John Gambold and his wife, Anna Rosina Gambold, took charge of the Moravian mission and school on land adjacent to Vann's plantation. (In the novel, I have changed their last name to Gamble, in an effort to respect the feelings of some religious readers, who would not wish to see the historical Anna Rosina Gambold engaging in fictional acts that take place in the book. I also hoped the altered name would signal something of the psychological and physical risk Anna Rosina the character undertook when moving to Cherokee territory.) Anna Rosina Gambold was a German-American botanist (the first published woman botanist in Georgia) who meticulously recorded her observations about native plants in Cherokee country. Her vegetable and medicinal garden at the mission was widely respected, and she sent plant specimens to colleagues in North Carolina and Pennsylvania for further study.

For more on Anna Rosina Gambold, see: Daniel McKinley, "Anna Rosina (Kliest) Gambold, 1762-1821, Moravian Missionary to the Cherokees," *Transactions of the Moravian Historical Society*, vol. 28 (1994); *Records of the Moravians in North Carolina*, vol. 6, ed. Adelaide L. Fries (North Carolina Historical Commission, 1943). My rendering of Anna Rosina's interests, skills, and turns of phrase were inspired by and derived from her actual diaries and letters. My description of Anna Rosina's writing and labors in Jinx's history book comes from Anna Rosina's fellow missionary, Heinrich Gottlieb Clauder, 1836, in the John Howard Payne Papers, Newberry Library, Chicago. My description of Anna Rosina's garden in Jinx's book comes from McKinley, as well as: Anna Smith, "Unlikely Sisters: Cherokee and Moravian Women in the Early Nineteenth Century, *"Pious Pursuits"*: *German Moravians in the Atlantic World*, eds. Michelle Gillespie and Robert Beachy (Berghahn Books, 2007); Henry Steinhauer, "Extract of a Letter from Anna Rosina Gambold," Periodical Accounts Related to the Missions of the Church of the United Brethren, vol. 7 (1818).

Within the documented historical story of the Vann Plantation, several remarkable figures have emerged. A woman named Pleasant and her son, Michael, were the missionaries' slaves, owned by the Moravian Church. (In the novel, I have changed Pleasant's name to Faith to avoid confusion with the character Patience.) Among James and Peggy Vann's slaves were individuals named Patience and Isaac. Patience was beaten by Vann's overseer, Samuel Tally, after which she falls out of the historical record. It is possible and even likely that Patience died from that beating. Isaac was burned alive by James Vann as punishment for participating in a conspiracy to steal from Vann and then running away. Samuel Kerr was a free black itinerant preacher who spent time at the Moravian mission with the pupils enrolled there. (I have changed his last name to Cotterell in the novel.) Earbob was a Cherokee spiritual leader who visited the plantation for long spells and administered a cure to Pleasant on at least one occasion. Like Anna Rosina, Pleasant was greatly admired for her garden.

Peggy Vann inherited the original Diamond Hill plantation house after James's unsolved murder in 1809, but she chose instead to live in a small cabin on the grounds. James Vann's favored son, Joseph Vann, known as "Rich Joe," inherited the plantation as a whole and commissioned builders to construct the formal brick manor house that has become an icon in Cherokee history.

After newly elected president Andrew Jackson championed Indian removal in his 1829 State of the Union address, Congress passed the Indian Removal Act. This legislation led to the relocation of numerous tribes east of the Mississippi and the forced expulsion of Cherokees from the South to Indian Territory (what is now eastern Oklahoma) during the historical event known as the Trail of Tears. Concurrently, the Georgia legislature passed laws to repress Cherokee autonomy after gold mines were discovered on Cherokee lands. One of these laws expelled Cherokee owners from their property and redistributed it to Georgia residents through a lottery system. Joseph Vann lost the plantation to white residents during the repressive period of the Georgia gold rush and federal Indian removal, and the Vanns moved west to Indian Territory with their slaves to begin new lives.

Mary Ann Battis, another historical figure on whom parts of the novel are based, was a young woman of Creek, black, and white ancestry. In the 1820s, Mary Ann attended the Asbury Manual Labor School for Creek children, run by Methodist missionaries near Fort Mitchell, Alabama. A star pupil whose special accomplishments were noted by visitors, Mary Ann lived at the school between the ages of twelve and eighteen and was in residence at the time of Creek removal. Mary Ann's mother and uncle begged for her to accompany them west to Indian Territory, but the missionaries protested. An unusual conflict developed over Mary Ann's future, as her Creek family, missionary teachers, the United States Indian agent to the Creeks, and the secretary of war argued about whether she should stay in the Southeast or move with her family and tribe. In the end, Mary Ann remained in Alabama with her missionary teacher, Jane Hill. By 1832, she married (becoming Mary Ann Rogers) and was living in Georgia. Historians know little more than this outline of Mary Ann's life, and her presence on the Cherokee plantation at the center of the novel is imagined.

While I have altered or imagined details of their lives, the historical characters in the novel are based on people who lived on James Vann's plantation, at the Moravian Springplace Mission, and at the Methodist Asbury Mission school. The first names of many of those characters have been retained as an act of remembrance.

In contrast, all the present-day characters are fictional, though they, too, draw on the experience of real life. My description of the role, methods, and means of inspiration of a tribal historian was inspired by a presentation given by the late Cheyenne tribal historian John Sipes to the Native American Studies Program at the University of Michigan. Snipes described a method that combined oral and written sources and was responsive to community needs, and said he knew he needed to pursue a topic when he kept feeling prodded toward it in intangible ways.

Most of the events in the historical section of the narrative did, in fact, take place on or around Diamond Hill in the early 1800s, including the arrival of a missionary couple and the establishment of a mission school, the bravery and punishment of Demas, the departure of James's elder wife, the slave order by Agent Lovely, the presence of Earbob the healer, the arrival of Sam the black preacher, the dispatch of plants to Pennsylvania by Anna Rosina, the Christian conversion of Peggy, the treatment of Patience and Isaac, the lunar eclipse and hailstorms, and the murder and burial of James. However, I have added fictional elements including the relationship between Anna Rosina and Sam, Peggy's adoption of a slave child, and Mary Ann's experience at the Methodist mission school. Peggy's friendship with Patience is an elaboration of a reportedly close relationship that the actual Peggy Vann had with a slave named Caty. In two important instances—the murder of James Vann and the fire that destroys the Methodist mission in Alabama—events are historically accurate, but their attribution to the actions of certain characters is purely imagined. Although all of the actual events took place in the early nineteenth century, I have modified precise dates throughout the narrative in order to accommodate the alignment of Cherokee and Creek story lines and an expanded scope of action for the characters.

For a nonfiction account of the historic site and the Vann family, I invite you to see my previous work of history, *The House on Diamond Hill: A Cherokee Plantation Story* (University of North Carolina Press, 2010), For a modern translation of Anna Rosina Gambold's original mission diary that deeply influenced the novel, see: *The Moravian Spring Place Mission to the Cherokees*, ed. Rowena McClinton (University of Nebraska Press, 2007). For published translations of Cherokee Mission letters that also informed the novel, see: *Records of the Moravians among the Cherokees*, vols. 1 & 2, eds. Daniel Crews and Richard W. Starbuck (Cherokee National Press, 2010). For my scholarly take on the young adulthood of Mary Ann Battis, I invite you to see my article "Notes from the Field. The Lost Letter of Mary Ann Battis: A Troubling Case of Gender and Race in Creek Country," published in the *Journal of the Native American and Indigenous Studies Association* (Spring 2014).

The garden theme of the novel was inspired by the historical realities of Anna Rosina's passionate study of plants, Pleasant's coveted garden, and the rose carvings preserved throughout the Vann family's brick plantation house. In addition to its cultural meaning for Cherokees as a symbol of hope during the hardships of the Trail of Tears, the Cherokee rose is the state flower of Georgia. The memory-garden concept described in the narrative is derived from an African American cultural tradition of growing a plant cherished by a loved one who has left, often attached to a story about that person. Memory gardens were especially meaningful in the Northern cities to which many African Americans moved during the Great Migration of the late nineteenth and early twentieth centuries.

I drew information about Cherokee and native Georgia plants and their uses from the following sources: Anna Rosina Gambold, "A List of Plants found in the neighbourhood of the Connasarga [*sic*] River," in *Plants of the Cherokee Country* (*American Journal of Science*, 1818–19), which is noted in Anna Rosina Gamble's fictional diary; William H. Banks Jr., *Plants of the Cherokee* (Great Smoky Mountains Association, 2004); Paul B. Hamel and Mary U. Chiltoskey, *Cherokee Plants, their uses—a 400 year history* (1975); Flora Ann L. Bynum, *Cultivated Plants of the Wachovia Tract in North Carolina, 1759–1764* (Old Salem, Inc.); Kay Moss, *A Backcountry Herbal, 18th Century Backcountry Lifeways Program* (Schiele Museum, 1993), which contains the rose remedy for hoarseness; Daniel E. Moerman, *Native American Medicinal Plants: An Ethnobotanical Dictionary* (Timber Press, 2009); the Georgia Native Plant Society's website (http://www.gnps.org/indexes/Plant_Gallery_

Index.php); *Rivercane* website, Department of Plant and Soil Sciences, Mississippi State University (www.rivercane.msstate.edu/about/); and Amy Stewart, *Wicked Plants* (Algonquin, 2009). For an enlightening study of the life and work of a formerly enslaved gardener, see Myra B. Young Armstead, *Freedom's Gardener: James F. Brown, Horticulture, and the Hudson Valley in Antebellum America* (New York University Press, 2012).

The Chief Hold House Museum, central to the contemporary portion of the novel, is based on the Chief Vann House State Historic Site, located in Chatsworth, Georgia. The site is owned by the state and operated by the Georgia Department of Natural Resources. Unlike the house museum in the novel, the real Vann House has not been closed or sold. However, staffing has been drastically cut and hours reduced. In recent years, the Georgia State Archives narrowly avoided being closed due to budget cuts. It was saved for public use thanks to mass organized protest and the intervention of the governor. I cannot help noting the irony that this novel portrays a present time—our time—in which stories of the past are meaningful and necessary, at a moment when access to historical sites and sources seems to be under threat in Georgia.

I will leave you, though, with a symbol of hope and a treasure hunt. If you ever pay a visit to the Chief Vann House (and I hope you will), look for the many carved flowers on the walls and porches of the building. It seems that each time I tour that grand, old, storied home, I notice a small, white rose where I had not seen one before.

I'd like to express a depth of gratitude to the many people who, knowingly or unknowingly, helped this book along its way over the course of many years. I am grateful, as always, to my loving parents, Patricia King, Benny Miles, Montroue Miles, and Jim King; my wise husband, Joe Gone; my incredibly patient children, Nali, Noa, and Sylvan Gone (who are here with me reading their bedtime books as I write this); my sister and brother, Erin and Erik Miles; my in-laws, Stephanie Iron Shooter, Sharon Juelfs, Roxanne Gone, Bertha Snow, Rena Gone, and Alicia Werk; and my uncles and aunts, Steve McCullom, Deborah Banks, and the Walker family. I have fond memories of, and owe a warm thanks to, my past creative-writing companions, Sunita Dhurandhar and Josie Fowler. I am blessed to have had brilliant writing-group members, writing confidants, and dear friends in Ann Arbor: Martha Jones, Kristin Hass, Liz Cole, Angela Dillard, Kelly Cunningham, Meg Sweeney, and Magda Zaborowska.

I am thankful to many colleagues and friends for being sources of information, inspiration, and aid: Julia Autry, Rowena McClinton, Sian Hunter, Celia Naylor, Stephanie Morgan, Rebecca Walkowitz, Barbara Spindel, Barbara Krauthamer, Sharon Holland, Barbara Savage, Darlene Clark Hine, Beth James, Mary Kelley, Phil Deloria, Greg Dowd, Emily Macgillivray Angela Walton-Raji, Angie Parker, Richard Starbuck, Chase Parker, Dave Roediger, David Chang, Craig Womack, Jennifer Brody, Claudio Saunt, Michael Witgen, Penny Von Eschen, Eisa Ulen, Alexandria Cadotte, Soraya Binetti, Andy Smith, Meg Noodin, Audra Simpson, Dale Turner, Robert Warrior, Dennis Tibbetts, Scott Lyons, Derek Collins, and Wayne High.

I am grateful to the organizers of the Bear River Writers' Conference, to my wonderful teachers there (Elizabeth Kostova, James Hynes, Michael Byers, and Valerie Laken), and to my fellow workshop participants; to the organizers of the Scribblers' Retreat Writers' Conference on St. Simons Island, where I always felt revived by the sea; and to the Loft Literary Center's Mentor Program and its speakers and teachers, particularly Jewelle Gomez, Ellen Hart, and Lee Young Lee, whose personal words inscribed in my book of his poems ("Sister maker, keeper of the treasure") have always stayed with me. I am likewise grateful to

Debby Keller-Cohen and the Institute for Research on Women and Gender at the University of Michigan, which funded me to begin a serious draft of this work (the funding included child care, a godsend to mother-writers), and to Kevin Gaines and the Department of Afroamerican and African Studies at Michigan, for funding that allowed me to attend writing conferences. I have drawn more satisfaction and inspiration than I can measure from students in my women of color courses at Michigan, Chicago, and Berkeley; I thank those students, as well as my fellow young women writers of *The Rag* feminist collective at Radcliffe when I was a student there.

Finally, I am deeply grateful to my agent, Deirdre Mullane, the president of John F. Blair, Publisher, Carolyn Sakowski, and my dedicated editor there, Steve Kirk, for taking a chance on a first novel by an academic writer of hidden histories. If I have forgotten to name you, I am nevertheless thankful to you; please forgive the omission.